FINN'S FATE

FINN'S FATE

A Viking Odyssey

Michael Wills

Book Guild Publishing
Sussex, England

First published in Great Britain in 2011 by
The Book Guild Ltd
Pavilion View
19 New Road
Brighton, BN1 1UF

Although real historical figures feature in this book,
this is a work of fiction.

Typesetting in Baskerville by
Norman Tilley Graphics Ltd, Northampton

Printed in Great Britain by
CPI Group (UK) Ltd, Croydon, CR0 4YY

A catalogue record for this book is available from
The British Library

ISBN 978 1 84624 666 1

Contents

List of Characters

Agna	The grandmother in the settlement at Floga.
Ahl	A crew member of the trading ship.
Aneka	A Danish slave girl.
Arvid	Finn's father, an iron worker and blacksmith.
Axeln	A senior Danish longship captain.
Birgir	A longship crew member with a knowledge of Anglo-Saxon.
Birna	Finn's twin sister.
Botvid	A crew member of the trading ship.
Dagr	An old comrade of Hacun's.
Einar	The captain of the trading ship.
Erke	Birna's suitor.
Finn	The youngest of three sons at Floga.
Gudmar	A crew member of the trading ship.
Gunnar	The oldest of the three brothers at Floga.
Hacun	A warrior and member of King Erik's body-guard.
Hilda	An Anglo-Saxon girl.
Ingir	The mother of the three brothers and Birna.
Ingolf	Captain of the longship *Orme*.
Ivar	A crew member of the trading ship.
Jan	A settler in the northern trading hamlet.
Jarl	Jarl of the two shores – Aneka's father.

King Erik   c. 945–995. Later known as 'Erik the Victori-
              ous' after his defeat of Styrbjorn the Strong's
              army at the Battle of Fyrisvellir, near Uppsala,
              in 985.

King Harald   935–986. Mistakenly known as 'Harald Blue-
              tooth'. His name was actually Harald Ble Tan,
              (Old Danish for 'swarthy, great man'). A
              Christian convert warrior king who at the
              height of his powers ruled Denmark and
              Norway. Eventually killed by his son, Sweyn
              Forkbeard or his supporters.

King Sweyn   c. 960–1014. An aggressive Danish king who
Forkbeard   expanded his kingdom by force. At the end of
              his reign he was king of Denmark, Norway and
              England.

Leif   Captain of the trading ship.

Olof   A settler in the northern trading hamlet.

Ottarr   Captain of the longship *Wolf.*

Pasha   A slave from the eastlands.

Ragnar   A crew member of the trading ship.

Sif   The daughter of one of the settlers in the
              trading hamlet.

Siward   A Frisian slave.

Styrbjorn   The violent nephew of King Erik. He was
              bribed by Erik, with a gift of sixty longships to
              forgo his claim to the throne.

Sverker   A settler in the northern trading hamlet.

Torsten   The second oldest of the three brothers at
              Floga.

Vanja   A slave from the eastlands.

Acknowledgements

I am indebted to several people who helped me in the writing of this book. To John Farthing for his diligent scholarship, to Dr Jan Persson for his carefully researched answers to my curious questions, and to my daughters: Sarah Ewen for her enthusiasm when acting as a sounding board for the story, and Emma Wills-Davies for the assiduity with which she checked my first draft of the book. Thanks are also due to Philip Ewen for help with graphics.

Most of all I am grateful to my wife, Barbro, for her encouragement, but also for her tolerance and forbearance when I turned every holiday into a research field trip and spent innumerable hours in windy, cold and wet places looking at sites, ships and seas.

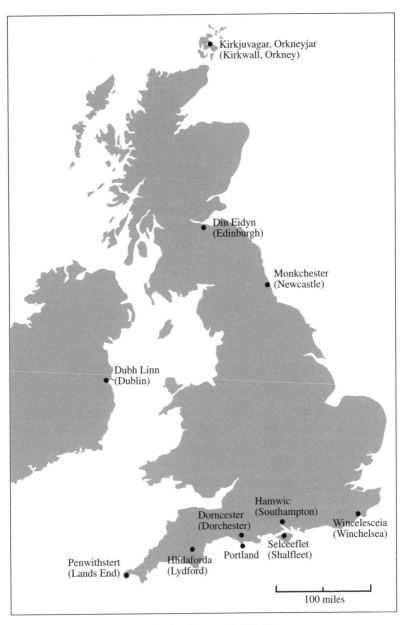

Britain in the year 1000 AD

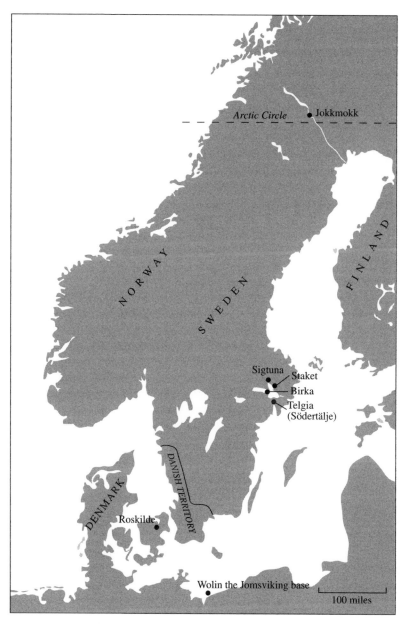

The Nordic countries in the year 1000 AD

Part 1
The Northlands

Chapter 1
Floga

The pack of wolves huddling together for protection from the blizzard were at first puzzled by the sounds carried on the wind, but soon they caught the scent of smoke. The pack, a family of eleven, was near their den, which was on a steep rocky mountainside overlooking the frozen lake. There were three generations of the same family in the pack and as winter loomed the parents had been teaching the youngest pups to hunt. Soon, even though visibility was restricted by the snow, their yellow eyes could detect a flickering red glow from the direction of the lake. They were instinctively afraid of anything unusual, but when the first goats appeared, struggling through the snow below the den, they quickly overcame their fear and the pups got their first chance of a kill. Before long their hunt was a massacre.

While the pack's territory was over 150 square kilometres, they tended to spend most of their time in the core of their territory to avoid disputes with neighbouring packs. They frequently roamed near to the small settlement by the lake in the hope of finding a stray goat kid or perhaps a chicken. But the settlers had surrounded their living compound with a tall fence made of sharpened poles placed vertically next to each other, to lessen the chance of this happening.

As the first millennium neared its end, the small

settlement, in a fertile area of flat lakeside land protected by the high mountain behind and situated just inside the Polar Circle, had been lived in by four generations of the same family. The settlement had originally been started by a merchant from Birka, the main Scandinavian trading centre which was on an island in the lake west of what is now Stockholm. He had decided that instead of transporting iron goods a vast distance to trade with the nomadic inhabitants of Lapland, the Sami, for furs and reindeer antlers, he would produce the goods himself using the plentiful bog iron in the far north. Once a year he had made the long trek south-east with his goods to a small port where the trading ships from Birka gathered in the spring to trade for Sami produce.

He had learnt the specialised skills of iron production and the working of iron from his father in the south, before becoming a travelling merchant. In his new home, besides producing iron, he and his Sami wife had had to learn to be farmers as they lived in a harsh, unforgiving climate and had to be almost self-sufficient in food and clothing.

The current occupants of the simple wooden settlement buildings were the merchant's daughter Agna, now a widow, her son Arvid and his Sami wife Ingir, and their four children. Gunnar, at twenty, was the eldest. Torsten was nineteen and his twin brother and sister, Finn and Birna, were seventeen. Birna's name in Old Norse meant 'she bear'. At birth she was weaker than Finn, but showed great determination to survive. According to Sami tradition she was honoured by being given the name of a dead relative of great character in recognition of her fortitude. Her ability to assert herself in competition with her three brothers confirmed that the name had been a good choice.

Ingir had all the typical Sami physical characteristics. She was fairly short, but sturdy. Her wide face, which was framed by long black hair, had high cheekbones and her eyes were slightly narrowed. These characteristics were to an extent carried by her children, though most noticeably by Birna. Her husband, though mostly of southern blood, was shorter than what might be called medium height, though his red hair and blue eyes marked him as the son and grandson of southerners. He was powerfully built and quietly content that though his sons had darker hair and high cheekbones, they had inherited his physique.

At this time of year it was hard to distinguish any physical characteristics, as even when they were indoors the family were wrapped in layers of clothes which made them all roughly the same shape. However, when they gathered round the fire in the middle of the main house and could take off their fur waistcoats it was clear that Gunnar was the bigger of the three brothers and not just because he was older than them and had been doing heavy work for that much longer. Torsten was just as tall as him, but not as broad and never would be. Finn was slightly shorter than Gunnar, but though very similar to his eldest brother in shape, he did not have the muscle build. Perhaps, one day, he might develop the enviable broad forearms and heavy biceps which marked Gunnar as a man of considerable strength. However, Finn's most notable features, often joked about by his brothers, who had brownish-black hair and brown eyes, were his reddish hair and blue eyes.

Arvid had met Ingir when her family had come to the settlement to trade for iron. Her father approved of the match, partly because she had two sisters and so he would still be well looked after and would have one less mouth to feed, but also because he could see that he might have a trading advantage in the future. There was little alternative for Arvid to find a wife, as southern women did not travel this far north. In Ingir he had a partner who had the incredible, innate, ability to survive and prosper in this most inhospitable climate. She knew every food source, every natural remedy, and had learnt the practical skills to run a household and provide a home. Although the predominant culture of the family was that of the southerners, Ingir still wore the traditional dress of the Sami, the *gakti*, when it was practical to do so. This tunic with a high collar was made from reindeer skin, which after having been dyed green was embroidered with contrasting colours. She wore a long skirt and reindeer-skin trousers. Like the rest of her family she wore reindeer-skin shoes, though in the winter these were lined with the fur of a wolverine because of its outstanding heat retaining properties. Her tunic was gathered at the waist by a belt with a square buckle. The shape of the buckle and the square buttons indicated that she was married. She encouraged Birna to wear a *gakti* which she had made for her with round buttons to indicate that she was unmarried, but Birna was more inclined to wear a heavy *colt*, a cloak with a hood, over her shift. Both women wore their hair in a pigtail and the only jewellery they wore were leather neck-laces, each with three bear's claws. In Sami lore the bear was the father of the forest, possessing mystical power. Killing a bear gave the hunter the bear's power, and its claws were said to ward off evil and to protect the wearer.

The men wore reindeer-skin tunics, but without the high collar. These were gathered at the waist by a leather belt. Their trousers were made of cloth woven by the women folk and were worn tucked in to the top of their boots. Both men and women carried a knife in a scabbard on their belts as well as a leather pouch in which, besides a wooden spoon to use at mealtimes, they carried small items needed for their everyday work.

Agna was now in her late fifties, though by dint of the considerable physical hardships of living and bringing up a family in harsh circumstances she was an old woman, racked with arthritis and other ailments caused by exertion and poor diet. Her father had met her mother while trading near the coast, and while she was still a baby they had brought her to the edge of the Polar Circle in search of suitable land, near to the traditional Sami nomadic paths, on which they could make a home. They needed to be close to a lake or a river so that they could be guaranteed good fishing, and they must have a flat area on which they could build. They also had to have a plentiful supply of timber for producing charcoal to smelt the iron and to heat their forge.

After a long trek north from the coast, late one early autumn evening they first saw the lake by which the family now lived. It was bathed in and reflecting the dazzling colours of the aurora borealis, the Northern Lights. Her father called the place Floga, or sea fire, after the mythical legend where a dragon was said to breathe flames onto a lake. The site was perfect for them. There was a narrow peninsula of flat land pointing out into the lake with a marsh on one side which would provide wild grass for winter fodder for their animals. The mountain behind the lake was perilously steep and rocky on the side nearest to them, but the other sides were covered with fir and pine, the latter being the preferred wood for charcoal making. And, importantly, there were two mountain streams which emptied into a peat bog. The pools of water in the bog showed streaks of oily film, a sure sign that there was bog iron buried near the surface of the peat. There was even a sandy beach which would provide the sand needed to mix with clay for building a kiln. It was on this peninsula that they made their home.

Their first priority was to build a hut to live in before the onset of winter, a winter which they barely survived. They lost the two ponies which they had used as pack animals on the journey. These had been tethered outside the hut and had been easy prey for wolves and wolverines. In the spring, as soon as the hard earth yielded enough to allow digging, they traded some axe heads with a group of Sami in return for which they got help to put up a palisade around their home. By summer they had built their first charcoal oven and had started the exhausting job of collecting bog iron from under the muddy peat at the bottom of the mountain. They needed a quantity nearly half a man's weight to be able to start smelting. By the autumn they had produced a small quantity of iron and in the winter they forged their first arrow heads and axes. Iron was a very valuable commodity and nowhere more so than in the Polar Regions which, paradoxically, one day long in the future would yield iron in immense quantities.

But much of their time was spent in finding food and ensuring a supply of dried meat and fish for the winter. They traded their iron goods with the Sami for reindeer meat, but also for furs which in turn the settlers could trade on the coast. In the winter they added to their tradable supplies by trapping polar foxes for their fur. These hardy animals, which could survive on almost any food from berries to fish and carrion, bred widely in the mountains nearby and with their litters of up to ten cubs, were plentiful, though a wily quarry. Their furs were especially sought after in the south. Their winter coats which had turned from brown and white in the summer to the much sought after pure white in the winter gave status to the wearer. As, indeed, did the ermine pelts which they were occasionally able to barter from the Sami.

Two generations later the palisade had grown in size, but the living was just as precarious. The winters were long and savage, and as there were more mouths to feed it had become necessary for them to become farmers in addition to producing iron. As well as having to be almost self-sufficient in food they had to produce most of their own clothing. To this end they had a small flock of sheep and goats which provided wool for the women to weave cloth.

They kept two cows for their milk and had a few chickens and geese. Grandmother Agna kept a small cottage garden during the summer to provide vegetables and fruit, some of which they preserved for the winter. But most of their food was provided by fishing and hunting reindeer and elk.

The elements were not the only challenge for the family. Outside the settlement in the forest clearings, where they had felled trees, the sheep grazed in the daytime, always watched over by one of the family. But they were also watched by covert predators. In summer the wolves were able to find other quarry, though they would take a chance at a kill of a stray sheep. But other eyes greedily watched the settlers' stock. While a cunning lynx on the prowl could be very difficult for the shepherd to spot, a bear had no inhibitions and only a lucky arrow could stop an attack. The most cunning of the predators was the bear-like wolverine which in fact was neither wolf nor bear, but the largest of the weasel family. Although no larger than a medium-sized dog this animal was a ferocious and clever hunter, killing prey many times its size. At night all the stock had to be kept inside the settlement, and in winter they stayed in all the time and were fed on hay harvested from the marsh.

The settlement was roughly circular with two gates, one to the east next to the lake to allow easy access to water, and one, the main entrance, to the south. There were three wooden buildings, the largest of which on the western side was the lodging house. The family lived, ate and slept in this one-roomed building. They depended on the fire in the centre of the house for heat, for comfort and for cooking. Next to and east of this building was the fodder and wood store. On the far side of the compound was a storehouse where they kept animal skins stretched on frames for drying and cleaning. In part of this building they kept their stock of cured pelts and fresh furs which they would trade with merchants from the coast who came to visit in the early summer each year, for by this time they were well known as fur traders and they no longer had to make the trek to the coast themselves. In the centre of the palisade, well away from the other buildings, was a shelter with the forging kiln where they worked in the winter. The larger iron smelting kiln was outside the stockade on the land to the south.

It was when Agna went out in the dark to collect firewood that it happened. Carrying a tallow candle in a horn lantern to light her way, she limped out to the store. The men had just returned from a long, unsuccessful hunt and were resting in the house. Inside the store she stepped over some loose hay on the ground and lifted the lantern to locate the easiest logs for her to reach. At least she tried to. An arthritic pain shot up her arm and she dropped the lantern on to the hay. The candle fell out of the lantern and immediately ignited the dry hay. She knew that the most effective way of stopping the fire would be to smother it. She tore at her shawl with her painful fingers and threw it onto the spreading fire. The effect was dramatic. Through the weeks and months she had been wearing the shawl it had soaked up fat from animal skin scrapings, cooking and candle-making. The blaze soared and spread with terrifying speed in the fodder and wood pile. She screamed as much as her croaky voice would let her. It was not this that brought the family out of the house, however, but the noise of the panic which was breaking out among the livestock which had previously settled for the night, but could now see the fire through the open door.

The heavy snow was being driven by a strong easterly wind. The same wind made the wood store into a blast furnace. Ingir, Birna and the men raced to open the gate to fill their buckets with water. The ice had laid early on the lake that year, but there was a recently made hole where the ice had been broken in the afternoon to collect water and where the ice had not yet reformed very thickly. Gunnar worked feverishly, smashing a pole into the ice to reopen the hole, and then started to fill buckets and pass them back to the others.

Agna, with the foolishness of one distraught with guilt, was risking her life weakly and uselessly beating the flames with a broom. The flames scorched her long woollen shift and the heat seared her face. All too late she realised that rather than stopping the fire she had become part of it. She stumbled out into the mêlée outside with her clothes on fire. Through the snow by the ghastly light from the fire she could see the terrified sheep and goats actually climbing over one another to form a seething mass of wool and legs on the far side of the compound, on the same side as the family were trying to collect water to quench the flames. Their fearful bleating, the bellowing of the cows and the twin roars of the wind and the flames formed a dreadful cacophonous symphony. The two cows were tied up, covered with their reindeer-skin blankets. They were straining at their tethers with a force which looked as if they might decapitate themselves.

As Agna frantically tried to put out the flames on her clothing she saw the gate to the lake open as the others sought to bring the buckets of water in. The sheep and goats saw the same thing and with a furious unscrambling of bodies, first one, then all of them charged towards the gate which by now was wide open. The bucket bearers leapt aside to escape the tumultuous exit of the animals, dropping buckets and sprawling in the snow. Once outside, after initially heading off in different directions, the sheep and goats all turned and started plodding through the snow, keeping the wind on their backs.

Arvid ran in through the gate only to be met by the two cows running towards him with their head collars still attached to their tethers and these in turn dragging the stakes which had previously been deep in the soil. He caught sight of Agna in flames and ran to throw her, face first, into the snow. She lay there moaning as the heat of the fire gave way to the cold of the snow. But she did not feel it. She would not feel anything again.

The rest of the family came through the gates again with a new supply of water, but quickly realised the futility of their task. The flames from the store had carried to the roof of the main house. They could not reach up high enough with the water to halt the inevitable.

'Get into the house and save everything you can!' the father ordered. 'First food, then clothes and tools.'

As ever, there was no dissent when Arvid issued orders. They ran in and out of the house several times, bringing out goods and piling them at a safe distance from the flames. Meanwhile, Arvid ran back out through the gate to see if he could recover any of the animals. When he returned, having realised that it was a hopeless endeavour, he was in time to see the roof of the main house collapse and Gunnar leap out of the door and throw himself into the snow to douse a shower of sparks which were covering his clothes.

They stood and looked for a while as the remains of their home were slowly, but inexorably, consumed by the flames. Arvid was silent, shocked by the triple loss; his home, his livelihood and his mother.

Ingir spoke. 'Fire is a good servant, but a bad master.'

The boys looked shiftily at each other to see if anyone was going to dare to suggest a course of action to Arvid. Gunnar plucked up the courage.

'Let's get what we can into the fur store and see what we have saved.'

Arvid grunted in agreement and they started to clear some space in the store and move their goods in. Meanwhile, on what used to be the floor of the wood store, where the permafrost had not yet penetrated, Arvid was using a wooden spade which had been hanging near the gate to dig a hole long enough for his mother and deep enough so that, when covered, the wolves would not disturb her.

They assembled in the fur store. It reeked of the scrapings from the furs, but it was the only shelter they had. When Arvid came in Ingir put into words what they all knew. 'We cannot stay here. Death will come by starvation or from the cold.'

'Shut up woman,' growled Arvid. 'I will decide in the morning.'

The boys knew better than to comment. They should wait for his proclamation in the morning. They fashioned some sleeping arrangements and used the plentiful supply of reindeer skins to ward off the cold.

Each of the three young men knew what they wanted to do. They had never been to the trading post on the coast, but their imaginations were fired by the stories they had heard from the merchants, who visited them once every year, about the towns in the south. Stories of wealth, comfort and, of course, women. But the distance to the coast was fifteen or sixteen days' walk in summer, though it was quicker to take a boat down the great river as far as the massive rapids over which no boat could travel. But in winter, could it be possible to reach the trading post?

Gunnar whispered to his brothers, 'Wait until father is asleep and then come outside to talk.'

By the early hours the snow had abated, but the cold was bitter in the fresh wind. The three of them huddled outside in the shelter of the fur store. Gunnar assumed his usual dominant role, taking it for granted that as the elder brother he was senior.

'I know what mother will want. She will want us to travel to Jokkmokk and spend the winter with her relatives. We will be reduced to being beggars in the Sami village. We can't speak their language and we're not used to their ways.

Then in the spring we will have to start rebuilding this place. I have had enough of spending my days up to my knees in mud looking for iron, being eaten alive by mosquitoes. And when we are not doing that we are slaving over a charcoal oven. No, I have had enough.'

Jokkmokk – quite literally meaning in Sami 'river bend' – was the site of traditional winter quarters for some wandering Sami. It was on the bank of the great river and just two days' walk from Floga in summer. The Sami were known for their courtesy and hospitality to outsiders: even though they were not full-blooded Sami, the family could be certain that they would be accepted and supported in the settlement.

'We must persuade father that we can travel to the coast on *skio*. It will be possible if we take enough provisions with us and make a tent with the reindeer hides. The three of us can pull a sled loaded with the tent and our food.'

The use of skis had been known for almost 5,000 years, but the style and shape of them varied through time and place. The settlers' skis, or in Old Norse, *skio* – meaning 'split piece of wood' – were similar to those used by the Sami. The settlers were proficient skiers as during the seven months of winter there was no other means of transport apart from sledges.

'But father will be furious if we argue with him,' said Finn.

Torsten mumbled agreement, though half afraid of invoking his elder brother's fury. Both younger brothers had experienced Gunnar's violent nature and his ready use of his fists. But Torsten recognised the merit of Gunnar's proposal. He too wanted to get to the coast and find another occupation, and maybe, who knows, become wealthy.

'I will deal with father and you will support me,' said Gunnar. 'Now go to bed.' The other two knew that the discussion was over and they should do as they were told.

What they did not realise was that Arvid was very much awake, wrapped in furs, sitting in the far corner of the store. He had heard the boys go out and though he could not hear what they were saying, he had some idea of what might be going on. When the boys came back in and he was sure that they were asleep he crept to the door and slipped out into the yard. There he groped around in the dark and eventually found the spade he had used to bury Agna. He went over to her grave and started digging. He was careful not to disturb the body, leaving a thin layer of earth over the corpse. He undid his coat and the belt round his tunic. With fingers which were by now really suffering from the cold he slipped his leather purse off of his belt. Fumbling with the contents he took several small pieces of silver and put them into the pouch on his belt and put the belt back on. He placed the leather purse on the soil which still covered Agna and then heaped the rest of the pile of soil over her grave.

He was well content that he had hidden most of his silver in a place where no one would ever dare to look. He knew it would be safe from robbers, and indeed from his sons, until he could recover it next spring. He quietly went back inside and slept.

Chapter 2
A Family Feud

Finn was woken by the sound of scratching near his make-shift bed. It was dark and would be until mid-morning, but from the smell he knew that it must be a rat trying to get into one of the bags of provisions they had saved from the fire and which he was using as a pillow. It was not only the humans who had lost their home and sought refuge in the fur store.

Finn considered his options. He did not want to wake the others; he wanted to delay the inevitable row as long as possible. The thought of it filled him with dread. He was equally terrified by the prospect of his father's rage as he was of Gunnar's. He would have to take the side of one of them – not to do so would mean that both of them would bully him for support and their persuasion tactics were unlikely to remain verbal. Taking someone's side would at least mean that he would have a protector.

He had lain awake considering the two options open to them. He sympathised with his mother. This land was the home of her ancestors. She had given up the nomadic existence of the Sami following the reindeer herds, and had lived with Arvid for over twenty years. She had suffered the privations of a farmer's life, bad seasons, illness, hunger, worry and heavy work. She had family who would be wintering in Jokkmokk who would provide for them until the spring. She would never be happy living in a southerner's village on the coast.

And what of Gunnar? As eldest son, by tradition, he would one day own the settlement. Or, rather, what was left of it until it was rebuilt. If he went to the coast he would have nothing more than he could carry, but he was prepared to risk all, intoxicated as he was by the merchants' stories of silver and adventure. And there was reason for Torsten, who was two years older than Finn, to support him. When Gunnar inherited, the two younger men would be in thrall to him. They would have no possessions, no rights and only the prospect of working for their keep for the rest of their lives. Good reason for Finn too to look for a new life and take Gunnar's side.

The rat scratched again. Finn got out of his bed quietly enough not to disturb the others, but noisily enough to make the rat scurry off. He crept to the door and went outside. In the dim light he could see that fresh snowfall had disguised some of the disaster of the night before. But low black piles of wreckage indicated where the two buildings had once stood, the new snow having melted on the still warm cinders. There was no wind now and the smell of burnt wood hung in the air. He decided to light a fire so that they could cook some breakfast and warm themselves. Perhaps a warm fire might make the antagonists more good humoured.

Just like his father and brothers, he kept an oval-shaped striking flint hanging from his belt. Hunting around in the half light he found some dry wood shavings under the fur store. The building was raised on supports in the style of the Sami storehouses to help protect against vermin, though as Finn had heard, not totally efficiently.

After several unsuccessful attempts at getting a good spark from grazing the flint across the blunt edge of his knife, he gently blew on a red dot on the linen. When the dot got big enough he placed the flax on top. The oily flax quickly caught fire and then he placed the shavings on the flames. The fragile fire grew until he could place a pine-wood root, in which there was naturally occurring tar, onto the flames. This caused the fire to blaze brightly and he heaped on logs from a wood pile under the storehouse.

The door of the store crashed open and his father greeted him grumpily. He shuffled across to the palisade to relieve himself. Finn felt a turmoil of emotions, among which was sympathy, even pity, for his father who had lost his business and his mother in the space of a few hours. But he knew that in the harsh world of Arctic farming, where life was on the edge of survival and their occupation on the cusp of viability, there was little room for sentiment.

Finn went into the store to find a cooking pot and packed it with snow before placing it on the fire. The process had to be repeated many times because even packed tightly in the pot, melted snow did not produce much water. Eventually, the pot of water was boiling on the fire, by which time all the family, wrapped in reindeer coats, were stand-ing in the dancing light of the flames, warming their hands. After taking turns at scooping a drink of hot water with a large wooden ladle, Ingir passed round dried deer meat and rye bread which had been recovered from the house. The sun was rising in the east and for the first time they could see clearly the partly snow-covered remains of their home as the low sun shone through the breaks in the badly burned palisade wall.

A cackling sound at the side of the store caught their attention. Arvid took a brand from the fire and in the combined light of the early dawn and the flames found that two geese had found their way back to the security of the farm. Doubtless the predators outside had had their fill and had not prowled around the broken palisade last night.

'We have no food for them,' said Arvid. 'So we will slaughter them before the journey; we need food for four days.'

'The journey where?' said Gunnar.

'To Jokkmokk of course, where else do you think we can find shelter and food until the spring? Or do you want to stay here?' his father added sarcastically.

'We are not going to spend a winter in Jokkmokk, we have decided to go to the coast.'

'Are you mad! It would take you weeks to get there. I think your brain has been affected by the smoke. Get the sled. We must fashion a harness so that we can pull it ourselves, two at a time. Don't stand there looking stupid, get on with it!'

'I said, we are not going. We have had enough of this filthy life. You and the women can take the sled. We can make one for ourselves.'

Arvid was in his early forties, but could still move very quickly. Both of the other boys had been momentarily eyeing the snow at their feet rather than catch their father's eye and so did not see him leap forward and slash the back of his hand across Gunnar's face. Gunnar took a step back and then sprang forward and grabbed his father by the throat. The action was so violent that Arvid fell backwards and Gunnar crashed down on top of him, still gripping his father's throat.

Ingir screamed and covered her face with her hands, peeping through her fingers at the terrible scene on the ground. The two boys looked on paralysed with shock, hoping that Gunnar would release his grip so they did not have to intervene. Suddenly, there was a loud thump as Birna, who had seized the wooden spade which her father had left propped up against the store, crashed the flat surface of the heavy tool against Gunnar's back. The result was dramatic. Gunnar collapsed on top of his father, totally winded by the blow despite the thick fur coat he was wearing, and released his grip. Arvid gave Gunnar a mighty heave and the younger man rolled over, face up in the snow. Birna leapt forward, dagger in hand and knelt next to Gunnar, pushing the dagger against his throat as he recovered.

'Move and I kill you!' shouted the girl. Addressing the other two boys, who she had seen edging towards her, she screamed, 'And if you move another step this knife goes in his throat!'

Gunnar was by now aware of his situation and started to raise his right arm towards Birna.

'I warned you!' she said quietly, and slowly pushed the blade so that blood began to flow from a skin wound. Gunnar felt the sting of the cut and realised that he would not be able to move fast enough to avoid what she had threatened. He dropped his arm and lay rigid.

By this time Arvid had recovered sufficiently to pick up the spade and hold it over Gunnar.

'Now you will do what I say,' he said triumphantly.

'No father,' said Birna. 'You cannot force the boys to stay here if they do not want to. Listen, I will stay with you and mother. We can spend the winter in Jokkmokk and then in the spring I will help you rebuild the homestead. If your grandfather and grandmother could do it alone with a baby to look after, the three of us will manage.'

At this point Ingir intervened. 'Birna is right Arvid. Let the boys make the journey if they feel so strongly about it. But the sensible thing to do would be for all of us to travel to the Sami encampment. It is by the great river and in a few weeks the river will be frozen, even the rapids. The boys could follow it all the way to the coast. If we take our axe heads with us we can trade them with the Sami for food for the boys to take on their journey. We can also take our best furs for them to take with them to the coast to trade with the merchants. We can leave all the tools and things we don't need in the store over the winter.'

Gunnar was bemused. His sister, holding a knife to his throat, had actually been arguing his case and his mother was agreeing. Arvid put the spade down silently and looked round at his wife who had been addressing him from behind. The two boys standing on the other side of Gunnar's prostrate body looked on anxiously, fearing that they would now have to intervene in a fight between husband and wife.

'My grandfather and my father built this place. They made a home out of this wilderness. I am now asked to accept that my sons, for whom we have laboured for years to bring up, will abandon Floga and Gunnar will give up his birthright.'

'But Arvid, the boys themselves must decide their own futures. Gunnar is not giving up his birthright, I am sure he and the others will one day return.'

There was a long silence, broken only by the crackling of the fire.

Arvid looked at Gunnar, then at the other two boys. 'All right. But Gunnar, I charge you with the responsibility to look after your brothers and if you don't then a pox on you.'

As he spoke he leant over Gunnar and offered him his right hand. He nodded to Birna and she lifted the knife from her brother's throat. She moved smartly aside in case Gunnar retaliated. Father and son grasped each other's right wrists and Arvid pulled Gunnar up. 'Come on, let's start preparing for the journey while we have enough light. Ingir, prepare food for four days' journey. Birna, I want you to sew together six or seven reindeer skins so that we can use them as a tent cover. Finn, go out to the forest and cut down eight sapling firs, about twice the height of a man, and branches of a birch tree, the straightest you can find.

Torsten, slaughter the two geese, bleed them and give your mother the blood for cooking before you pluck them so that the blood is warm. Gunnar, come with me to sort the store and help me to make the harness. We sleep here tonight and leave at first light tomorrow.' There were no dissenters and each of them set about their allotted tasks.

The atmosphere was lightened when they watched Torsten trying to catch the geese. He had to corner them where the palisade had no holes in it or he might lose them for good. After watching him dive into the snow a few times trying to catch them, it was impossible for the those watching not to laugh at his futile attempts. Eventually, Ingir intervened and lured the hungry geese into a corner behind the store with some heads of corn. Soon the birds were tied by the feet.

Torsten stunned the geese with a wooden stave before dispatching them with his knife. Having removed their heads he hung them upside down so that their blood ran into two wooden bowls beneath them. While this was happening Ingir had fed the fire and was boiling a pan of water.

Gunnar and Arvid were sorting out the tools and equipment from the forge, cleaning them and putting them into the storehouse. Then they set about the task of adapting the leather harness, which previously had been used by a reindeer, so that two of the family at a time could draw the sledge. It was going to be heavy work as they would have to pull their furs, ironware and food for the journey.

Meanwhile, when the water was boiling, Ingir mixed the goose blood with the precious flour which they had saved from the blaze, added some herbs and then, a little later, used a large wooden spoon to put lumps of the mix into the boiling water. She rolled the mix on the edge of the saucepan to make it roughly into the shape of a ball and then let the heat of the water loosen the lump from the spoon.

She continued making blood bread until all the mix was finished and then let the lumps cook in the boiling water, now and again making sure they did not stick together, until they came floating to the top. When she had finished the bread it was time to roast the two geese. Torsten had lit the fire in the forge and was using the bellows to heat up the oven so that they could put dismembered parts of the geese in to be roasted. Ingir supervised this and sent Torsten off to get more wood. By this time there was little wood left under the storehouse and, since their main store had been burnt the night before, Torsten had to take an axe and start chopping up some of the remaining stakes in the palisade.

The sun set in the middle of the afternoon, shortly after Finn arrived, struggling through the snow and dragging the poles and the birch branches requested by Arvid for their tent. Birna had finished her work on the reindeer skins and so they set about trimming the poles and tying lines to the base of each one. Birna split the birch branches into thin pieces and put them end to end, overlapping, so that Finn could tie the pieces together with twine. She gradually bent the length of wood into a circle. They tied further pieces on to strengthen the construction until it was to their satisfaction. They then tied each pole, a short distance from the top, at equal distances around the circle. Next they stood the poles up and spread the base of each one out on the ground so that the whole frame stood up rigidly. Finally, they used string made from the sinews of deer to tie the base of each pole to the next one to stop them slipping outwards. At head height they tied a horizontal pole on which they would hang their cooking pot so that it was just above the fire. This was to be the tent which would be the key to their survival for the next few days.

Working on the inside and the outside they pulled the reindeer pelts over the frame and secured them with string.

The store was now full so the tent would be their home tonight. Torsten took some round stones from under the store and put them in a small circle in the middle of the tent. Inside these he built and lit a fire. The smoke rose and escaped through the hole provided by the circle at the top.

Ingir had packed the blood bread, dried fish and other bits and pieces of food they had saved from the fire into a wooden box, which had been Arvid's tool box, and they carried this into the tent where it would be as safe as possible from vermin. They decided to have one of the geese for supper and kept the other for the journey. Soon the family were sitting around the fire in the tent, eating what was to be their last supper together at Floga.

Before first light they were woken by the sound of thumping. Opening the flap of the tent they could see in the moonlight that there had been no new snow. They quickly realised that Arvid was out on the ice trying to make a hole to collect water. He was using an iron-tipped pole to break the ice. Gunnar got up and went to help him. He took with him a fishing line in the hope that they might get a fish for breakfast.

Torsten and Finn busied about relighting the fire in the tent to give light so that the two women could start to pack things in preparation for the journey. Finn pulled the sled up outside and they loaded first the ironware at the bottom, leaving room to place the lighter items on top.

As the dawn light increased and enough light filtered through the ice to illuminate the lure on Gunnar's line, a hungry lavaret made the mistake of confusing it with real food. Gunnar whooped with delight and hauled the fish up through the hole in the ice. It was big enough to provide some breakfast for the whole family. He quickly gutted it before it froze and went back to the tent to present it to Ingir.

They breakfasted and then continued to load the sled.

After putting their provisions on top of the ironware it was obvious that they would have too many goods, once they had packed the tent frame and covering. 'We will have to make up backpacks to carry the furs,' said Arvid. 'Ingir, select the best furs, and Finn, you help her to make rolls of furs for each of us to carry.'

By the time they had packed the tent and put the fur rolls on their backs the sun had already risen above the tree tops; it would not get much higher all day. The family tied on their skis and Torsten and Finn were strapped into the harness. The weight of the sled had made it sink into the snow and those not pulling had to push to get it moving. Arvid went ahead and opened the gate which was still intact in the undamaged part of the palisade. They guided the sled through the opening and onto the ice. Ingir and Arvid turned to look at their ruined home. The smoke was still rising from the fire on which they had cooked their breakfast. The curling black smudge against the blue sky seemed symbolic of the disaster of the night before last. They looked at each other, a look which betrayed defiance of the circumstances which had led them to this situation. They noticed that Birna too was standing looking at the homestead, and they were pleased. The young men however indulged in no such dalliance. With Gunnar in the lead the other two were pulling the sled quickly in the direction of the mid-morning sun. Their long, long journey had begun.

Part of the detail on an ancient Sami Holy Man's (Shaman) drum.
The three main gods of the Sami, Thor with two hammers, Frey
and the Wind God.

Chapter 3
The Sami

Although their mother was Sami and their father had Sami blood, the three boys and Birna had been brought up in the culture and traditions of the south. They had been taught some woodcraft and a little about Sami traditions by their mother, but essentially they viewed these incredibly resourceful inhabitants of the north as 'foreign'. Yet they would need help from their mother and her people to survive the long journey they planned.

Although these indigenous people regarded themselves as one nation, there were various groups spread across the north. They had different ways of life, spoke different languages and dressed differently. Ingir was a 'forest' Sami. These were Sami who made a livelihood in the forests of the Lapland lowlands. The other main branch was the 'mountain' Sami who lived in the high mountains further to the north and west. Most Sami followed and hunted the wild reindeer herds as they traversed the land. However, the main food source for the forest Sami was fish. The great rivers flowing down from the mountains to the sea were rich in salmon, trout and lavaret. They did not farm the land, but their expertise in forest living ensured that they were able to harvest produce which might not be obvious to southerners. Apart from the autumn berries such as

29

cloudberries and lingon, which were rich sources of vita-
mins, they knew which fungi were edible, they gathered
wild herbs and they even used the bark of some trees as a
food source. These people were entirely self-sufficient,
except for iron, in a most inhospitable wilderness and
survived thanks to their own ingenuity and skill.

From their experience in trading with the Sami, the
brothers had learnt to respect them as hunters and had
tried to adopt their trailing and hunting skills. Most importantly, they had trained to use a bow and arrows from
an early age. The bow, usually made of birch wood, was
essential for hunting deer and other larger animals. But the
Sami hunters had other techniques too. They were expert
at using snares for foxes and smaller animals. Snares were
also used to catch wild birds such as grouse. In the winter
the women and children planted snares in areas where
there was low vegetation, such as birch saplings, and as the
grouse tried to eat the thin stalks they became entangled in
the traps.

These nomadic people often came together in larger
groups at the coldest time of year in places where some
of them had 'winter houses'. It was towards one of these
gatherings that the family from Floga was heading. The
journey across the frozen lake went well in the fine cold
weather and by nightfall they had come to where the lake
ran out into a wide river. They went ashore and found a
flat piece of shoreline where they could erect their tent and
light a fire while they were still warm from the exertion of
the journey and before the temperature plummeted. Here
they would spend the first night of their journey.

During the night they became aware of the wind increasing in strength. Their tent was in an exposed position on
the shore and it was shaking violently in the wind. Arvid
expressed what they were all thinking.

'If this gets much worse the whole tent could blow over.

Gunnar and Torsten go out and move the sled to the wind-ward side of the tent and tie a line from the sled to two of the nearest tent poles. That will stop the tent moving.'

The two men grumbled, but recognising the danger they would be in if the tent was destroyed, they obeyed. The tent flap was facing at right angles to the wind and they had to fight to open it. As they did so, flurries of snow blew inside. A blizzard was blowing from the east, the direction they were to travel tomorrow. Soon the young men returned.

'It looks bad out there. We must remember in future to camp in a more sheltered site.' They put more wood on the fire and then went back to sleep.

By daylight the group had had some breakfast and were ready to move on. The storm had blown over, but the day was dull, with leaden skies which threatened more snow. It took a long time to get the snow off the tent and get it packed on the sled which they had to dig out of the snow. They had planned to follow the river, but now Ingir was worried about this route.

'We had no trouble crossing the ice on the lake. There the water is very slow moving and the ice had set thick, but the river is fast flowing and the ice may not yet be thick enough for us to travel on. With this depth of snow it is difficult for us to see what the ice looks like. I think that we should cross over to the other side of the lake just before where it flows into the river and travel on land, following the river.'

'But that will make pulling the sled really heavy work,' pro-tested Gunnar. The other brothers mumbled agreement.

'Mother knows this river better than any of us, we should do as she says,' said Birna.

Arvid was strangely silent. He plodded through the snow, down to where he thought the lake edge was, and started clearing a small space. He gazed at the ice under his feet. 'It is all right here, but it's impossible to say what it might be like on the river.' He was aware of the expertise of the Sami in surviving in winter conditions and felt that Ingir's advice should not be ignored. He turned and snapped, 'We do as your mother says. Let's get going.'

The brothers groaned, but did as they were told. Finn and Torsten put on the harness, and everyone put their backpacks on. It was much more arduous today; their skis sank into the soft new snow, as did the sled, and their progress was slow. Eventually they reached the far bank and started to follow the river along the shoreline. It was very difficult to keep the sled upright as the riverside was littered with snow-covered boulders, some almost half as high as a man.

'By the gods, this is impossible, it will take us a week to get there at this speed,' Torsten cursed. 'I say we go out onto the river.'

'All right,' said Gunnar. 'Let's see how thick the ice is. We can secure one of us to a safety line, the others hold the other end while he walks out to test the ice.'

Ingir protested. 'That is stupid. If you fall in the freezing water you will never get to see the coast.'

Birna agreed, but Arvid, who was also frustrated at their lack of speed said, 'Let's give the boys a chance to test the ice. If it is safe we could save days of travel.'

Gunnar looked at Finn. 'Now's your chance to show how brave you are, little brother,' he said sarcastically.

'No, not Finn!' protested Ingir.

'Oh dear! Mummy's boy is not allowed to do anything dangerous!' quipped Torsten. Gunnar laughed and pushed the line towards Finn.

'It's fine, I'll do it,' said Finn.

They bound together the two lines which had been binding the cargo on the sled and put a loop on the end for Finn to put round his waist. The rope was made of long strips of elk skin and was very strong.

'Go out about twenty paces and then jump up and down on the ice,' said Torsten.

Finn climbed over the boulders at the edge of the river ice and very carefully started walking out.

'Get a move on! It's cold here,' shouted Gunnar.

Finn moved further out, cleared a patch of snow and stamped on the ice. It held. Then he jumped, and the watchers saw him crash sideways as the ice gave way under him. Gunnar and Torsten pulled on the rope to recover the boy. Arvid joined them, but despite their heaving they could not drag him out of the hole. His head was bobbing up and down as he was desperately grabbing at the slippery ice.

Birna immediately saw what the problem was: the river current was sweeping Finn's body under the ice. He would first have to be pulled in the opposite direction to the flow to get clear of the downstream edge of the hole before he could be pulled shoreward. As the lightest of them, she realised that only she could help. She grabbed her iron-tipped ski pole and ran along beside the rope, holding onto it. When she was almost level with the hole she pushed the pole into the ice for grip and pulled the line at an angle in the opposite direction to the current. Finn's body floated up into the hole.

'Pull now!' she screamed. 'Pull like hell!'

Finn's limp body was dragged across the snow to the river edge, followed by Birna, who was gingerly walking back towards the shore. Gunnar leapt down, picked Finn up and carried him, stumbling, over the boulders. Ingir was busy unpacking the tent cover.

'Torsten, get undressed and lie down on this. Hurry damn you!' Gunnar took off Finn's wet coat and placed him in the middle of the reindeer skins which Ingir had unrolled.

'Lie down here next to him. *Right next to him* you idiot,' Ingir commanded Torsten. She rolled the fur over the men from left and right so that they could not be seen at all, and then folded the top and bottom to make a complete parcel.

'His only chance to overcome death by cold is to get heat from Torsten,' she said.

Gunnar was silent. He was certainly not a compassionate person, but dearly wanted his young brother to live. Praise did not come easily from him so they were all surprised when he said, 'Birna, you did a good thing.' But Birna and her mother were furious with Gunnar for ignoring their advice. He himself was grudgingly coming round to the realisation that travelling in these winter conditions was more of a challenge than even a man of his supreme self-confidence could manage without the benefit of others' experience. And, as regards the longer journey that they had planned, they would have to accept help and advice.

Arvid stated the obvious. 'We camp here tonight and hope that Finn is going to recover. Gunnar, build a fire to dry Finn's clothes.'

They heard a noise from the folded furs and Ingir lifted the top. Torsten's head emerged. 'He is shivering a lot, but I think that he is all right. I thought I would suffocate inside there.'

'Stay there while I make a bed for him with some furs, we need these for the tent.'

Later, they transferred Finn to the bed and erected the tent over the top. Ingir started to feed Finn warm water as soon as the cooking pot was hot and he quickly showed signs of recovery. They all knew that he was feeling better when he cursed Gunnar: 'Damn you, one day you will kill me.'

Around the fire in the tent, while eating their second goose and the blood bread, they discussed their best course of action. It was clear that they could not travel on the river ice and they had seen that following the river on land while carrying their goods was very difficult because of the uneven shoreline.

Arvid spoke. 'It must be possible to find a way through the forest. We are a long way north of the path we take in summer, but there must be other paths, if we can find them.'

Ingir nodded. 'I think that we should continue to follow the river, but keep a way into the forest where the ground is more even. Of course it will be difficult getting through the trees with the sled, but if we are lucky we might find some tree marks where Sami have cut signs in the bark to show a trail.'

Gunnar and Torsten were silent, perhaps because they were a little repentant about their unwise proposal earlier in the day.

That night the wind strengthened again. They could hear the branches of the firs rustling and the low-pitched moan of the wind. This time they were well sheltered by the forest from the icy blast, but the snow found its way through the trees and by morning their tent was once more covered. Clearing the snow and packing the tent again delayed their departure.

Finn had now recovered from his ordeal in the river and was able to take his turn pulling the sled. Because of the late start, the limited daylight and the thick forest, the distance they covered still left them far short of their goal and now Ingir was concerned about whether their food would last. They had taken enough for four days, and this was the third of their journey. She considered suggesting that they should stay on for a day at the camp they made that evening so that the men could go hunting. But if the men were unsuccessful then the family would be in a very serious position. It was impossible to fish on the river as they could not trust the ice. So a hunt was the only chance of boosting their supplies.

Around the fire that evening there was much discussion about the best course of action. The men wanted to move on – they thought that it would be very difficult to hunt in the deep snow. Animal tracks were quickly covered and the snow made it almost impossible for the hunters to move quickly through the dense forest. But Ingir was aware that their journey might take two or three more days and they had to find food. At last the men gave in and agreed that they would go off in search of game.

The next morning was cold and clear when the four men skied off with their bows. While the men were away, Birna and Ingir busied themselves looking for a dead pine tree and felling it for firewood. The work was heavy and tiring, but dead standing pine made the best fires.

As they were dragging logs back to the tent to chop up, Ingir suddenly stopped. It may have been her innate sensitivity to movements in the forest which made her feel uneasy or perhaps she had heard a sound which was not created by the two women doing their work.

Birna looked at her. 'What's wrong mother?'

'Ssh, give me your axe.'

Ingir stood perfectly still and peered into the trees between them and their tent. After a few moments she called out in Sami, 'Greetings, friends.' Suddenly, about fifty paces in front of them the forest came alive as three figures, dressed in brown furs which matched the colour of the tree trunks, each carrying a bow, stepped out from the cover of the trees behind which they had been hiding. They stood on their skis looking at the two women. Ingir whispered to Birna, 'It's a hunting party on their way home.'

'How do you know they are going home?'

'You see the crests on their caps are pointing forward? That means they are homeward bound.'

The three Sami hunters came forward, having overcome

their surprise at finding the two women in the forest. Each was carrying game. Two had hares and one had four grouse. They explained that they had heard the noise of the axes and had come to see who was in the forest. Birna could understand some of what they said, but remained silent while her mother explained who they were and why they were there. After a while, in response to a question from Ingir, the men pointed into the forest and indicated the direction of the settlement where they were living. Birna understood that they were telling her mother about the best way to get to Jokkmokk and how long it would take to get there.

After a few minutes Ingir beckoned to the men to go with her to where they were camping. The men helped to carry the logs and followed her. Once at the camp Ingir delved into the sled and pulled out two axe heads from the bottom of their luggage. She gave these to the men and they gave her the two hares and the grouse. Then they turned on their skis and headed back into the forest.

'Now we have work to do!' said Ingir. 'Can you cut the logs while I skin the hares and gut them, and then you can help me with the birds.'

Birna did as requested and soon feathers were flying in the light breeze as they plucked the grouse and hung them on the side of the tent. They decided to have the birds for dinner and to save the hares for the next days.

Later, much later, they heard the sound of skis outside the tent and men's voices. It was too dark for the men to see the carpet of grouse feathers in the snow. The tent flap opened and Arvid came in. 'The gods were not with us, we have nothing. We have travelled for hours, but –' he stopped short and looked astonished at the birds roasting on a spit. 'How did you get these?'

'Birna and I have been trading. We have enough food for another three days.'

The three sons came in and were about to relate their tale of woe concerning their unsuccessful hunting trip when they caught sight of the feast awaiting them. Ingir and Birna told the story about how they had met the hunters and had bartered two axe heads for the game.

'Two axe heads!' roared Arvid. 'You were cheated! What the hell were you thinking of?'

'I was thinking of avoiding our family starving to death, you ungrateful ogre. If we had relied on you to provide for us we would all have perished. So shut up and sit down to eat. Oh, and by the way, there are two hares in the food store too.'

Arvid was not used to being spoken to in this way by his wife and in other circumstances might have retaliated, but he recognised the weakness of his cause and grumpily sat down and grabbed at the portion of bird Ingir proffered him on the end of her knife.

'The Sami hunters told me the way to a forest trail. They said that it was marked with slashes in the tree bark. They thought that even travelling as slowly as we are we should get to the village in two days.'

And so it was that at midday two days later the travellers saw smoke in the distance and just before dark they approached the village to the yapping of the dogs and the attention of many inquisitive eyes. Ingir realised that they would have to be invited to stay in the village by the village elder or headman, and so they chose a spot just on the outskirts of the settlement and pitched their tent for the night.

Next morning at first light, the boys went outside to look at the village. It was a remarkable sight, the impression of which was heightened by the fact that they had never seen more than three or four houses in one place before. There was a large circle of wooden buildings which the Sami called *kawta*. Each square house had a base made of three or four pine logs lying horizontally, on top of which rested a four-sided pyramid-like structure made from split logs. They could see from one house, which was being repaired, that these logs formed an outer roof under which was an inner roof, covered by several layers of birch bark, to make the structure waterproof. The entrance door was in one side of the sloping pyramid. At the top of the pyramid was a hole to allow smoke to escape, but which could be closed when required. Here and there were some buildings with vertical walls which were supported off the ground by a raft of heavy logs, very much like the store at Floga. In the middle of the circle there were many tents with smoke rising through vents at the top.

Outside some of the houses, two or three reindeer were tethered. These were used to pull sleds, though they could see several of them being milked. They learnt that although the animals did not milk as well as a cow, they provided a small quantity of fat milk each day. There were sleds and skis by the side of almost all of the houses and some had poles, on which fishing nets made of reindeer sinew were stretched for repairing. Outside each house there was a pile of firewood covered by birch bark, with logs on top to stop the bark blowing away. Smoke was curling up through the cold air, indicating that almost all the houses were occupied. One slightly larger building had a great deal of smoke rising from it, similar to their charcoal oven at Floga – this was a smokery where meat and fish were preserved.

Although it was very cold, the weather was fine and there were signs of activity everywhere. Children were chopping firewood, women were shaking out floor coverings, some men were busy repairing or building the houses, a hunting party was packing arrows and getting ready to leave, and two men dragged large chunks of ice past them on a sled. They had probably brought the ice up from the river to melt for drinking water. Dogs were barking, babies were wailing and somewhere unseen a group of women were chanting their traditional music, the *yoik*.

A young man came to their tent and called for Ingir to come out. He invited her and her husband to come to the headman's *kawta* to talk.

'Arvid, we must take a gift. Get a knife from the sled to present to the headman.'

Arvid did as he was bid and the two of them followed the messenger to a building which was slightly larger than the others.

'We must sit outside until we are invited to go in,' said Ingir. They brushed the snow off a bench at the door and sat down. Not long after, they were called into the house.

Once inside, they were invited by the headman to sit on the floor in the traditional guests' place, nearest the door. The room was lit by a brightly burning fire surrounded by large round stones, on the right of which was an old man. On the left side of the fire sat a woman, presumably his wife. Ingir greeted the couple in Sami and handed over the gift. The old man thanked her and started to ask Ingir questions. Since he could not understand what was being said, Arvid's attention drifted to noting the detail of the interior.

The floor was covered by birch twigs, on top of which were several reindeer skins. In the centre of the room a pot hung over the fire, suspended from a beam in the ceiling. There were several shelves bound to the sloping ceiling which were covered with cooking and eating utensils. On a rack below the shelves there were bunches of herbs drying and some dried fish. Under the sloping roof were two sleeping cots. The owner of the house was wearing a fine silver pendant over his brightly-coloured tunic and his wife had a silver chain hanging down over hers. Arvid knew that the Sami believed that silver protected against evil.

Arvid became conscious of Ingir telling what he assumed

to be the story of their journey and the reason for it. She pointed to Arvid several times and the old man interrupted her frequently with questions. Suddenly, Ingir stood up and beckoned to Arvid to do the same. She opened the door and they stepped outside. The bright sunlight dazzled them, but soon their eyes adjusted to the busy scene outside.

'Well, what did he say?'

'He wants to trade with us. He has offered us the *kawta* of a man who died last summer and which is not occupied. He said that it needs some repairs, but it would be possible to live in it anyway. He wants an axe head for rent for the winter.'

'How many do we have left after you were cheated by the hunters?' asked Arvid sarcastically.

'I remind you that if I had not traded with the hunters, you would be a cold corpse in the forest now and so would your sons. So, no more sarcasm. I think that we have five axe heads left.'

Both of them knew that apart from the furs which the boys would need to trade at the coast, and a few small knives, the axe heads were the most valuable currency they possessed. Indeed, the iron was more valuable than the few small pieces of silver which Arvid had in his pouch.

And so it was that the family acquired a temporary home. After a day in the forest to cut timber and three days splitting roofing logs, the house was weatherproof. It was decided that Arvid, Ingir and Birna would move into the house and the three brothers would live in the tent which they pitched alongside.

When the work on the house was complete, the young men were keen to prepare for their long journey, but they realised that they must wait two or three more weeks before leaving so that they could be sure the river was safe to travel on and in particular that the great rapids, which would be last to freeze, were solid ice. Ingir arranged for the men to go out with a Sami hunting party so that they might improve their skill at providing food for themselves on the journey. They were pleased to find that they could shoot arrows as accurately as the Sami hunters, but their hosts were far better at tracking and finding game. However, the most useful lessons they learned were in catching fish. The Sami were expert at locating and catching river fish. They mainly used two methods. The first was the one the brothers were used to for winter fishing in the relatively still water of their lake at Floga. They made a hole in the ice and used a baited fishing line with a hook made of bone. Then they sat absolutely motionless, hoping for a bite. The second method was new to them, but was far more efficient at certain times of the year. The Sami used nets under the ice to catch fish. They did this by breaking a hole in the ice and then making a second hole twenty paces further down-stream. They then dropped a wooden float into the first hole and used the current in the river to drag the float to the second hole. It sometimes took several goes to get the float positioned correctly so that it reached the second hole, but when it did they dragged a fishing net, with the bottom corners weighted with stones, under the ice so that it stretched between the two holes. This method of fishing was particularly successful when the fish were playing and were too engaged to notice the nets. The brothers had understood, using the few words of Sami which they had learnt, that very soon the lavaret would be playing and they should have good catches. And so it was, a week later in the village, that a plentiful supply of the fish was drying and being smoked.

Their experience on the journey to Jokkmokk had taught them that they must travel as light as possible, so they decided to rebuild their tent. Instead of the heavy poles which Finn had cut at Floga, they used birch poles which had been split along their length. These were lighter and not only would they be easier to pull on the sled, they would make the business of raising and lowering the tent quicker. Ingir prepared the reindeer-skin covering so that all the fur was removed. This not only made the tent lighter, but the covering took up far less space in the sled. The disadvantage was that the tent was not as well insulated.

One day, while they were working, they became aware of being watched by an old man who, though dressed in the same kind of fur coat as the other Sami, wore a quite different hat. It was a fur hat covered with large feathers, probably eagle feathers. Around his neck on the outside of his coat he had a long necklace made from many different objects. There were animal claws and teeth, feathers, small wooden figures and pigtails of what looked like human hair. In one hand he had a carved stave and in the other a small skin drum. He spoke to the brothers, but they could not understand what he was saying.

'What's he going on about?' asked Gunnar, irritated by the intrusion.

Finn left the others, walked over to the house and called Ingir. 'Can you come and talk to this old codger and see what he wants?' he asked. Ingir opened the door and walked down the steps while putting her coat on. When she came round the corner of the house and saw the old man she stopped in her tracks. She made a small bow and spoke to him.

She turned to the boys. 'This is the local shaman. You must respect him, he is very powerful and can cause you great trouble.'

The shaman spoke again to Ingir and then waved his stave at them and incanted something while looking at the sky. He then turned and walked away.

'What the hell is a shaman?' demanded Gunnar.

'He is the magic one, the holy man of Sami society. He

can contact the dead and the gods in the spiritual world. He uses the drum to journey into their world. He can tell the future from the visions he has. He said that you must make a sacrifice to appease Horagalles, the god of thunder. He said that he sees great seas and evil in front of you, with much death. Horagalles can protect people from evil spirits with his great hammer or his bow which is made from the rainbow.'

In their isolation at Floga the young men had never come into contact with any form of religious or mystical thinking. Their life was very matter-of-fact. There was birth, work and death, with nothing before or after. Their father had lost his belief in the Norse gods and though Ingir had been brought up with the superstitions and beliefs of the Sami, she had never tried to impress these on her family. The few concessions they made to her beliefs were easy to make – for example, Birna wore the bear's claw necklace and their leather belt pouches were inscribed with Sami runes which only Ingir could understand. Thus the concept of mysticism as described by Ingir found nothing but derision from the brothers.

'Tell him that we look after ourselves and don't need the help of his fantasies!' joked Gunnar. The others laughed in agreement. Ingir was about to say something, but thought better of it, turned from the boys and walked back into the house.

Later that afternoon, just before sunset, Ingir was not noticed as she slipped away to the other side of the village. The bulge under her coat betrayed the fact that she was carrying something. On a slight hillock just beyond the most northerly house was a shelter with two walls and a roof which at the back sloped down to the ground. As the wind was in the north, long before reaching the shelter, Ingir could hear the raucous cackle of birds. As she approached, a flock of carrion crows, which had been feeding on a severed reindeer's head in the shelter, flew off. In front of the shelter was a large polished stone which appeared to have been shaped into the form of a cylinder. This was the holy stone, the *seita*. In the shelter behind the stone there were various animal parts on top of a jumble of bones and antlers which were the remains of recent and ancient sacrifices. In amongst the bones, small pieces of silver glinted in the setting sun. There were many tokens hanging from the roof: feathers, arrowheads, bird skulls, woven figures and strands of coloured wool which must have once been pieces of cloth. At the back, there was a row of small sculpted figures. Ingir looked for the wooden figure representing Horagalles with his cross hammer in his hand. When she found him, she opened her coat and took out a package wrapped in reindeer skin. She unfolded the skin and produced a large lavaret. The fish was heavier than one might have expected, as protruding from its back was part of an axe head which had been sewn inside the fish. Ingir carefully placed the sacrifice in front of the image. She stepped back, looked at the offering, mouthed some words and turned for home. As she walked she considered how she was going to explain to Arvid that she had miscounted the number of axe heads they had left after paying their rent.

But she had something else on her mind which was worrying her just as much. Erke, a young Sami man, had been calling on the family more and more frequently to offer help with various chores and even once presented them with a grouse. Ingir could sense Birna's excitement when the young man called and had noticed how they furtively smiled at each other. She wondered how Arvid would react when he eventually realised that his little girl had interests outside the family.

Chapter 4
From Snow to Sea

The winter was a hard one even by the standards of the Sami. High winds and heavy snowfall caused high drifts which made the prospect of travel in the wilderness danger-ous and ill-advised. Even the three brothers, enthusiastic as they were to be on their way, recognised that they would have to wait longer than they had planned in the Sami village. They used their time hunting and fishing with their father to provide for the family and to lay up a store of smoked fish. With Erke's help they were able to trade some of the food and an axe for a draught reindeer which they would use to pull their sled. Birna proposed that they should call her Siri, and so it was agreed.

They were lucky to find someone willing to make this trade as Sami families had few domesticated reindeer at this time, preferring to follow the herds and hunt them as they wandered over their feeding grounds. The nomadic people carried everything they needed with them and lived in tents, always on the trail of their wild quarry. Life was one long journey for the Sami for three seasons of the year as the animals were constantly tormented by flies and mosquitoes and moved over large areas seeking insect-free places to feed.

Eventually, in the middle of the third month after the

winter solstice the weather settled to a period of intense cold with fine, sunny days. The days were longer now and the cold had caused a crust to form on the snow. It was time to go.

Despite what she had told her husband after the fire at Floga, Ingir realised that she was saying goodbye to her sons forever, but Arvid held the fond belief that they would come back to Floga sooner or later. Thus it was that when they took their farewells, Ingir was emotional while Arvid said goodbye as if the young men were off on a hunting trip. After giving Gunnar and Torsten a hug it was her youngest and dearest son's turn. She opened her coat and untied the leather necklace with the three bear's claws and placed it around Finn's neck.

'These will protect you from death at the hands of strangers who wish you ill; even if they hurt you, they will not kill you.'

She kissed his cheeks and turned away so that they could not see her tears. Finn stared at his feet. Momentarily, he wondered if he should stay to give his mother some comfort. Birna broke the silence and joked with the brothers that they would have to look after themselves now that she would not be around to do so. She gave each of them a kick for luck.

'Come on, let's go!' shouted Gunnar.

Ingir turned round, wiping her eyes. 'Gunnar, I rely on you to look after your younger brothers. I really do, this whole idea was yours, now you have to take responsibility for them.'

'Stop worrying mother, I can take care of them.'

And with that, they were off. They pushed the sled enough for the reindeer to be able to get going and then headed down the track in the snow to the river. The three figures, dressed in furs, each carrying a pack on his back, skied with one in front of the sled leading the reindeer and the other two behind. They turned once and waved before turning a bend and disappearing from the view of their parents.

Once on the frozen river they left the track and headed downstream. They passed a group of Sami fishermen and exchanged greetings. These might be the last humans they would see before reaching the coast. The sled was running well over the frozen snow and the reindeer at first seemed able to manage the load. But it soon became apparent that their enthusiasm was driving them too fast. Gunnar was leading when Torsten dared to admit this.

'Slow down, we can never keep this pace up all day.'

'All right. Finn, we had better remember that Torsten is the weakling.'

Finn was also pleased when Gunnar turned and slowed the animal. However, soon it became clear that Siri too was tiring. She was panting heavily and slowed down even more. Gunnar tried to pull her to speed up again, but the reindeer was having none of it and slowed to a walking pace. And so they proceeded, at her pace, for the rest of the day, apart from when they took several short stops to rest the animal and themselves. This was the pattern which they were to follow for many days apart from when they stopped to hunt or fish.

As well as feeding themselves they had to care for their animal. As a draught animal, a reindeer is very economic. It needs less than a quarter of the food required by a cow to stay strong and healthy. In the winter, lichens make up the bulk of a reindeer's diet. It also eats dried grasses, dormant birch twigs and blueberry bushes. So, each evening the party camped on the side of the river and the brothers had to clear an area of snow to help their animal find fodder. They let her roam on a long lead while they set up their tent and lit their fire. After they had eaten, they tied her up to the side of the sled for the night. They had to unload all their food supplies and take them into the tent to protect them from four-legged thieves. Although most bears would still be in hibernation, there were others with the courage or desperation to approach the tent and steal anything edible.

After a week living on dried fish and smoked meat the brothers decided to stay at their campsite for a day to fish on the river. They hacked three holes in the ice and each of them sat at one of them, huddled in their thick coats, patiently waiting for their dried fish bait on a barbed bone hook to attract the attention of a hungry fish. Gunnar was first to give up. He swore and went back to the tent to get his bow and try his luck seeking prey on land. After a while Torsten followed him.

Not long afterwards, Finn caught his first trout. Then a second, and some time later, a large lavaret. Peering into his ice hole he did not notice the movement behind him. A large male bear, woken from his winter sleep by hunger, had caught the smell of the fish which Finn had gutted on the ice.

The slow, deliberate movement of the starving bear as he furtively approached Finn was quiet, but he could not avoid crunching the snow crust. The sound made Finn spin round to face the bear which was now just twenty paces away. He had seen bears before, many times, but always at a distance, and that was where his father had advised him to keep them. He picked up his knife and glanced round nervously to the tent to see if either of his brothers had returned with their bows. It was deserted apart from the reindeer. He stood up, hoping that when the bear saw him at full height it might be frightened off. However, the bear was three times Finn's weight and was not impressed by the man's stature. For what seemed an eternity they both stood still looking at each other. Then the bear started slowly advancing towards him. Finn bent down quickly, grabbed a trout and threw it towards the brown hunter. It seized the fish in a claw, turned and ambled back towards the shore opposite their tent. Finn quickly gathered up his fishing line and the other two fish and then ran across to the tent. He dived in and grabbed his bow and an arrow. The bear was still on the other side of the river and having eaten the fish was looking towards the bloody fish guts by the hole which Finn had just left. He realised that one trout would not suffice to satisfy the bear for long. If it spotted the reindeer tied up by the tent it would doubtless attack.

The bear loped towards the bloody hole and started licking the stained ice. Finn picked up his bow and took aim at the animal, eighty paces away. He paused. The sheer beauty of the bear made him hesitate. Its coat was in poor condition after the long winter hibernation, but there was something majestic and dignified about the fearless hunter which imbued respect, even affection, in the young man. He lowered his bow, hoping that the bear would now just go on its way. But the bear's curiosity was aroused. It started across the river in the direction of the tent.

Finn raised his bow again, but the bear presented a poor target as it walked towards him. Only the bear's head and shoulders were visible. He knew that if he fired he would have to kill it. If he merely wounded the animal it would either go off into the forest and die a long lingering death or, in pain, it would attack its tormentor.

The wind was blowing from behind Finn towards the animal and clearly it had got the scent of the reindeer. It walked slowly and inexorably towards the tent. Finn could see the ripple of its shoulder muscles as it took each pace. Its snout was lifting, audibly sniffing the scent it had detected. Its black eyes betrayed no fear, and neither did they need to, as the 'father of the forest' was not predated upon.

Looking down the length of the arrow at the animal, Finn

was terrified. He had to get this right, there would be no second chance, and yet he could not get a shot at the animal's body. If he fired at its head the arrow might just glance off. The bear came nearer and nearer until he could clearly hear the animal's breathing, and despite the light breeze being behind him he could smell it.

At just five paces away the animal reared up on its back legs, bared its fangs at Finn and lifted its sharp claws towards him. He was so close that Finn could see that its mouth was smeared with the blood of the fish. It made a grunt and lurched forward, crashing to the ground with Finn's arrow through its chest. Finn sat down on his haunches, supporting himself with his bow, and sobbed. Whether his tears were of relief or of regret for having to kill this beautiful animal only he could know, but probably the truth was that it was both.

He became conscious of the fact that Siri was panicking and tugging wildly at her tether, having been severely frightened by the sight of the bear. Finn got up and tried to calm the animal, but it was clear that he would have to move her out of sight of the dead bear. He untied the reindeer and took her a little way into the forest, where he tied her to a tree.

He returned to the scene of the killing and wondered how he could butcher the animal. Clearly they could not do it in front of their tent as the entrails and blood would attract many unwanted visitors during the night. It would be dark in two hours so he would have to work fast. He could not wait for his brothers so he tied a line to the bear's rear legs and started to drag the animal down the slight embankment and out across the ice. It was very heavy work and he was greatly relieved when he heard the sound of Gunnar cursing his bad hunting luck as he emerged from the forest with Torsten.

'Where the hell is the reindeer?' shouted Gunnar.

'I moved it,' Finn called from below the river bank.

'Why the devil did you do that?'

'Shut up and come and help me,' replied Finn.

The two hunters walked round the tent and there below them saw Finn and his bear. Shocked, they ran down the bank to look at the animal. Finn explained what he was doing and told them what had happened.

Gunnar slapped Finn on the back and said, 'By the gods you are a hell of a lucky man. I hope that you get the power of the bear as the legend says.'

They dragged the bear to the other side of the river and set about the bloody task of butchering the animal. The work went on until long after dark by the light of a fire they had lit. They saved as much meat as they could and removed the beast's claws and teeth to use for trading with later. After cleaning themselves as best they could they went back to the tent and only then remembered that the reindeer had not been fed, so they brought her back to the sled and Torsten went off to find some birch branches in the dark – a task which the other two brothers could tell by the sound of distant curses was not very easy. Finn melted ice in the cooking pot so that they could wash themselves and then grilled the fish he had caught.

They had to take the bear meat into the tent for the night. The next day they would let it freeze on the sled as they travelled so that they could keep it as long as possible and gradually use it as required.

The next morning, Finn walked over the river to the place where they had butchered the bear. In daylight he could see that the once majestic father of the forest was reduced to a jumbled mess of bones and torn fur which was frozen to the ice in tufts where other teeth had dropped it. It had provided food for more than the three brothers. Finn felt a sadness for what he had done; he gazed at the remains for a while and then heard his brothers calling him to help them break camp. They packed and then moved on.

And so the journey continued in a sustained period of settled weather. On the fifth day they came to a place where another wide river joined the one they were on and the way downstream got even broader, but they saw no sign of other people, not even a trace of smoke indicating a settlement. Eventually, after eleven days, they reached the great rapids. These were frozen with an uneven ice cover which left pockets of air between the ice and the water. The under-chilled river water racing seawards underneath the ice made loud gurgling sounds. The going was more difficult on the uneven surface, but the reindeer's hoof pads, which shrink from their spongy surface in the summer to leave a sharp rim in winter, managed the snow and the areas of bare ice on the rapids. The greatest danger was that of the sled capsizing and injuring the animal.

Once they had successfully passed the rapids, they decided to rest Siri for a day and to try some fishing again. This time they took their bows on the ice with them, but there was no repeat of Finn's previous experience. That evening, they enjoyed grilled fresh fish before checking Siri and then going to bed. There was a light wind blowing which caused the tent flap to occasionally make a slight noise, one which they were well used to; otherwise the forest was completely silent. The three of them fell asleep.

Gunnar heard the noise first. Siri was stamping and snorting and then there was a slight thump as something heavy hit the ground. Gunnar rushed to the tent flap and feverishly tried to untie it. Having made a gap just big enough he pushed his head through. In the pale moonlight he could just make out the dark shape of an animal scurrying across the snow leaving the moaning Siri lying in the area where they had cleared the snow.

'Out of bed you two, a wolverine has attacked the reindeer.'

In a while the three of them were standing by the distressed animal.

'Finn, see if you can get a flame out of the old fire so that we can look at her,' said Gunnar.

A few minutes later, Finn brought out some flaming twigs and held them over the reindeer while the other two examined her.

'The damned wolverine has torn open her throat. Torsten, get my bow.'

The other two watched in silence while Gunnar dispatched the animal. They knew what had to be done and fetched their knives to turn the carcass into a source of supply for their journey. They could not leave it until the morning for fear of attracting predators. Finn built a fire and they worked silently, each of them deep in thought about what this would mean to the success of their venture.

By the time they had completed their grisly task it was light. But the morning light was not as bright as it had been on the previous days of their journey. Dark clouds hung low in the sky and it felt slightly warmer.

'What the hell do we do now?' Torsten asked querulously.

'What do mean, what do we do now? We have to pull the sled ourselves and we go on,' said Gunnar tersely between gritted teeth. 'Let's clean up and have some breakfast. Then we strike camp and adapt the reindeer reins so that we can pull the sled like we did on the journey from Floga.'

Two hours later, they were following the river on its journey to the south-east against a bitter wind which was blowing snow in their faces and covering the front of their coats. They took it in turns to pull the sled two at a time, the third one relieving the one who had been pulling longest and so on, so that they all worked roughly the same amount of time. But they were nowhere near as efficient as Siri had been. Their skis slipped under the load, so they had to force their way forward with their sticks. The new snow on top of the old crust made the work even more difficult.

By early afternoon, the two younger brothers managed to persuade Gunnar that the weather was just too bad to make much progress and that they should stop and set up camp in the hope that the next day would be better for travelling.

It was a forlorn hope. The wind continued to blow for three days, piling drifts up against their tent and covering their sled. They busied themselves by attempting some fishing and the interminable job of finding and cutting firewood. On the fourth day, the weather improved and they prepared to dig out the sled and to strike camp. They made some progress during the day, but when they camped on this straight stretch of the river and looked back, they could still see landmarks they recognised, showing where they had been camping the night before.

Gunnar had predicted that their journey to the sea would take them sixteen days. Today was the seventeenth. But their situation was not desperate; they had a good supply of meat and some dried fish. They could feed themselves for another four or five days before they would have to find another source of food. However, they had noticed that although a lot of snow had fallen in the last few days, it was getting warmer. The Sami had warned them that in the fourth month after the winter solstice there would be the first openings in the ice on the edge of the river, although the river ice would not break entirely until the fifth month. It would become difficult for them if gaps in the ice appeared along the shoreline. They must press on as fast as they could.

Two days later, all three of them were finding that long before they lost daylight they were very tired and they agreed readily when one suggested that it was time to stop for the day. Apart from the tiredness, they had developed painful sores on their shoulders from pulling the sled. They were glad of the relief that resting for the night gave them. After they had pitched the tent, they sat on the sled and Gunnar expressed what they all knew.

'Our progress is too slow; we do not have food for more than two or three days. If we stop for a day to hunt and fish and are unsuccessful we will be in a worse situation.'

'It is still light now and will be for a couple of hours, I could go into the forest and see if I can find a hare run and set snares,' suggested Torsten.

'Good idea. Finn, you get more firewood while I start the fire.'

Finn nodded, took the axe and plodded off through the snow parallel with the river bank. He looked over his shoulder and saw Torsten heading into the forest with his bow over his shoulder and snares on his back.

Later, with the fire blazing and reindeer meat grilling, Gunnar and Finn waited for Torsten.

'Where the hell is he?' said Gunnar. 'It's getting dark.'

'I'll go look for him. Maybe he has too many hares to carry,' joked Finn.

Finn took his bow and a quiver of arrows and opened the tent flap. The dusk was gathering as the last trace of the sunset showed over the forest to the west and a light wind was driving broken low cloud across a rising half moon. He walked across to where prints in the snow betrayed Torsten's route into the forest. Following the route was easy by the increasing light of the moon. There seemed to be some kind of track, perhaps made by elk following a regular path to the river from the forest. As he got deeper into the forest the quiet was broken by the faint call of a distressed human voice.

'Gunnar, Finn!' The voice, which was definitely Torsten's, came from some way ahead through the trees, the way the trail and the footprints seemed to lead. Finn hurried his steps and climbed a small hillock. Immediately on the other side he could see a deep indentation in the ground, a kind of pit.

'Torsten, where are you?'

'In the damned hole, where do you think?'

Finn looked over the side of the pit and saw two dark figures lying side by side.

'Are you all right Torsten?'

'No. I've hurt my back. I can't get out.'

Finn recalled that his mother had told them that the Sami sometimes hunted by digging pits towards which they drove reindeer and that sometimes the pits were dug on a regular animal run to catch deer or elk. The pits were marked by putting warning slashes on nearby trees so that other hunters would not fall into them.

'What's that in there with you?'

'An elk calf, frozen solid. They've placed sharpened stakes at the bottom of the pit. The elk must have fallen through the light brushwood covering and impaled itself. The snow had covered the hole and I fell through, fortunately on top of the elk, so I missed the stakes. I guess the animal is still here because no other animals dared to get down into the hole to eat it.'

'I'll go back and get Gunnar and some ropes.'

'Right, but hurry, I am damned cold.'

Finn hurried back to the campsite and quickly explained the situation. They both returned to the pit and threw a line down to Torsten.

'Tie this round your chest under your arms and we will pull you out,' said Gunnar. The two onlookers heard Torsten cursing as he tried to do as requested.

'I have devil of a pain in my back, I can't lift myself up to do it.'

Gunnar thought for a moment and then said, 'Finn, go and get the axe, we will have to make some kind of ramp to pull him up on.'

After an hour, by the light of the moon, they had felled two small pines and put them side by side, sloping down into the hole.

'Finn, take the rope and slide down the poles to Torsten. Then put the rope around him. You lift him to the bottom of the ramp and push him up while I pull.'

'But that will leave me down in the hole!'

'Don't be such a damned fool. You have work to do there. I want you to hack the legs of the elk. We can never get it up here in one piece, but we can get some meat from it! Don't worry little one, I won't leave you for the wolves.'

Finn did as instructed and as gently as he could moved Torsten over to the poles. Gunnar took the strain amid howls of pain from their burden, while Finn pushed him up. The hole was deep, about the height of a man, but after a few minutes Torsten's cursing stopped and he lay flat on the ground at the top of the pit with the pressure taken off his back.

Gunnar passed Finn the axe. 'Get on with it little brother. I'm going to get the sled to put Torsten on so that we can pull him back to the tent.'

Finn swung the axe and gradually chipped the frozen flesh away on the animal's uppermost hind leg until he came to the thigh bone. This took more effort, but after an hour he had severed the frozen limb. By this time Gunnar had spent some time impatiently watching him from above.

'Pass me the leg. We'll do the rest tomorrow. We'd better get Torsten to the tent to warm him up.'

Gunnar threw the rope down to Finn, who tied on the elk leg for Gunnar to pull up. Then Gunnar threw the rope to Finn again to help him up the ramp. They removed the poles so that no animal could use them to venture down into the pit. Together they lifted Torsten onto the sled and placed the elk leg on top of him.

'Hold on to that brother, and we will take you home.'

'About damned time too,' growled Torsten.

It was clear that Torsten had severely strained his back. He had trouble standing and could not walk. They had no idea how long it would take him to recover. He rested in the tent while the other two were busy with their chores. Gunnar beckoned Finn to come over to where he was standing, out of earshot of the tent.

'Right, we've got plenty of meat now, but we can't stay here.'

'But Torsten can't walk, we can't leave him,' Finn replied.

'No, no, I don't mean that. We will have to continue with just you and me pulling the sled. It looks as if we will have to put Torsten on it until he gets better.'

'Why are we in such a hurry?'

'We can only follow the river while it is safe; once the ice starts to thaw we will be back on the banks. You remember how difficult that was, when we did it before.'

'But we're going to get to the coast before the ice breaks and the trading ships arrive.'

'I know, we will just have to wait.'

Later they struck the tent and placed Torsten on top of the cargo.

'This is going to be impossible,' said Finn.

'Shut up and pull!'

With that the two brothers heaved the heavy sled into motion. It was very hard work and they were forced to have many rest stops. Early in the afternoon they travelled round a great bend in the river. As the icy waterway straightened again Torsten suddenly shouted, 'Smoke!'

The two skiers had been concentrating on the snowy surface in front of them as they dragged the sled and had not been looking ahead. They stopped.

'It's coming from behind the trees on the left side of the river,' said Finn.

'Come on, let's move,' replied Gunnar.

60

They set off in the direction of the smoke. As they got closer they could see that the forest had been thinned and there was an area of open land. About sixty paces from the river bank there was a *kawta*, the source of the smoke. Next to the house there were some low huts, probably for animals. There was also a fishing net hanging from three poles.

The travellers turned off the river and onto the bank where the house stood. During their long stay in Jokkmokk the three brothers had learnt some basic Sami. Gunnar shouted a greeting. They stood waiting for a response, but got none. They moved closer to the house and Gunnar tried again. This time the door opened and a frail looking old woman dressed in a Sami tunic stood looking at them. The house was clearly in bad condition, the door hung on one hinge.

She shouted nervously in a shrill voice, 'Who are you?'

'We travel to the coast,' replied Gunnar hoping that she would understand him.

They pushed back their hoods so that she could see them better. She peered at them curiously and then looked at Torsten who was trying to prop himself up with his arms.

'Who is he?'

'He is my brother. He sick.' Gunnar's Sami was now being really stretched. Finn interrupted.

'He ...' Finn mimed having a pain in his back by placing his hand on his back and jerking his body up.

'Go away!' shouted the old lady.

Gunnar turned to Finn. 'Cut some of the elk meat and take a piece to her. Old ladies love your blue eyes.'

Finn gently lifted Torsten's head and pulled out a package from under the tent skin. The old lady watched him intently as he unwrapped the skin and pulled out a cut of meat. He held out his gift and walked towards her, smiling to try and allay her suspicion. She took the meat and looked at it. She beckoned to Finn to come up the step and follow her into the house. The dilapidated door slammed shut. Gunnar went back to the sled and sat on the edge next to Torsten.

'The old hag will be able to tell us how far we are from the coast. If it's not too far we could rest up here for a few days for you to recover.'

'I damned well hope so, this pain is bad enough without being dragged on a bumpy ride.'

'You ungrateful sod, I should have left you to the wolves.'

They both waited with increasing impatience for Finn to reappear. Eventually, the door creaked open again and Finn emerged.

'By the Gods you look happy!' shouted Gunnar.

'Yes, just had a bowl of porridge and some bread!'

'As I said, old ladies like you. What did you find out?'

'We're in luck! The trading post on the coast is only a day's walk from here.'

There was a whoop of delight from the two men on the sled.

'We've done it! We've damned well done it!' shouted Gunnar.

'Ssh, Gunnar don't frighten the old girl.'

'So what do we do now?' asked Torsten.

'We push on of course,' answered Gunnar.

Torsten was clearly irritated. 'You said just now that we might stop here for as while.'

'Hold on, hold on,' said Finn. 'The old lady has said that she will help Torsten recover if we will work for her. We could stay here until the ice breaks and then walk to the trading post when the ships are there.'

Gunnar was silent. He resented plans being made by someone else, but could see the sense in the idea.

'What does she want us to do?'

'You should see the state of the house, it won't last

another winter. If I have understood correctly, her husband went out hunting in the midwinter and never came back. She is alone. She wants us to repair the house and to lay up logs for next winter. She says she can make poultices for Torsten's back.'

'Then that's decided,' shouted Torsten.

'Its all right for you, you lazy son of a bitch. You're on your back and Finn and I will have to do the work.'

Finn sighed. 'Gunnar, what will we do at the trading post for many days, waiting for the ships? And anyway, we will have to buy food there; here we can provide for ourselves and Torsten will get help.'

Gunnar pretended to be considering the matter when really he had made up his mind – there really was good sense in staying.

'Right, for Torsten's sake, we camp here.'

They unloaded Torsten and placed him on the snowy ground for a moment while they got the tent off the sled, then they put him back again to wait until the tent was erected. They chose a spot near to the *kawta* and settled into what was to be their home until the following full moon.

Each day, Finn and Gunnar spent time in the forest choosing and cutting timber for the repairs to the house or working on replacing the rotten wood. They knew that it would be better for the timber to age and dry out after they had cut it, but they did not have time to wait. The old lady's husband had left a good supply of tools which they were able to use for their work. At the beginning of their stay the old lady went to the tent each day to put poultices on Torsten's back. Whether it was her cures or the natural healing process was not clear, but Torsten gradually recovered and towards the end of their stay he was able to help his brothers.

The old lady had a supply of oats which she had grown

on the pasture where the trees had been felled. Porridge was a favourite with the brothers and she also provided them with various Sami foods. She had some chicken in the coops they had seen when they first approached the house and occasionally they had eggs. From time to time they used the fishing net with some success and the old lady showed them how to trap grouse. Later, when the first birds of spring appeared, the snow bunting, these were added to their diet.

As time went on, the widow's woodpile grew, patches of grass appeared through the snow cloak, the ice melted along the river banks, and the brothers became fond of the old lady, as she did of them. But they were itching to get going. One morning they heard loud groaning sounds coming from the river. These were replaced by cracking and grinding noises. The three of them stood by the bank to see the remarkable spectacle as the ice parted in places and the current of the river dismantled it with terrifying force. Sheets of ice piled on others which were stationary, forcing them in their turn to break loose and join the exodus to the sea. And not only ice succumbed to the huge pressure. Branches, whole trees and here and there even boulders were borne by the icy progression downstream. A day later the river was open water, up to almost 1,000 paces wide where the torrent was swelled by the snow melt.

Fortunately, the widow's house had been cleverly placed to avoid the broadened stream. She assured the brothers that her sons would be coming to see her in the spring and they would help her to prepare her field before they went off following the reindeer. Two days after the breaking of the river ice they packed their backpacks and left her. They abandoned the sled and their skis at the house and carried the tent slung on a pole between two walkers as they followed the trail pointed out to them by the old lady.

After a long day's march, they gradually became aware of

a new sound and saw birds they had not seen before; they were white and circled around the sky in front of them where the source of the sound was. Just before dark they came through a thicket of low fir trees and bushes, and there, ahead of them, was the sea.

Chapter 5
Life and Death on the Coast

The three brothers stood mesmerised by the sight before them in the gathering dusk. To their right the river, now nearly 1,000 paces wide, was rushing to join the sea carrying with it great chunks of ice intermingled with logs and branches. At the point where the river lost its identity there was a huge jumble of debris swirling in the current. Further out, in the last grey light of the afternoon they could see several small islands, each covered by fir trees, and beyond them the wide-open sea. Waves, encouraged by an easterly wind, spent their energy on the sandy shore, which here and there was strewn with boulders.

Torsten was first to speak. 'Well, thank the gods we've made it!'

'What do we do now?' queried Finn.

'Now little brother, we have to use the sea to carry us south,' answered Gunnar. 'I guess the trading post must be to the north of here.'

They all looked to their left, but in the poor light they could see no sign of any buildings.

'All right, let's camp here tonight and tomorrow walk north along the shore,' said Gunnar. They found a flat piece of land and pitched their tent for the night.

They were woken in the morning by the squawking of

seagulls and immediately became aware that the sea was more disturbed than it had been the evening before. Large waves were smashing onto the shore and then, as each receded, they appeared to be trying to pull the sand seawards. At sea the waves were decorated with many white caps as they made their inexorable journey to land. Again, the three brothers stood looking out to sea, fascinated by what they were seeing, each of them secretly feeling some anxiety about travelling in a small boat on such a huge expanse of turbulent water.

'Come on, let's have something to eat and then set off,' said Gunnar.

They tramped along the beach for half an hour and then in the distance saw smoke being driven inland by the onshore wind. As they approached the source of the smoke they were disappointed not to see any ships. The shore turned around a bend and headed inland. Following it, on the other side of the inlet, four wooden buildings with grass covered roofs came into view. There was smoke rising from three of them. The inlet curved around to form a bay which was protected on one side from the open sea. There were two small boats pulled up on the foreshore in front of the buildings.

The houses were clearly not of the same sort that the Sami used and were likely to be occupied by southerners. A dog started barking; their presence had been noted. The door of one of the houses opened and a man came out carrying a bow. He looked around and spotted the three strangers. He pulled an arrow out of his quiver and put it in the bow.

'Who are you?' shouted the man in their language.

'We are the sons of Arvid the blacksmith at Floga,' shouted Gunnar.

The man with the bow was suspicious. At this lonely place, many days' journey from the south, there was no government, no law, no protection by right. These pioneers lived on their wits. Strangers were always a threat and people were accepted only when the settlers were convinced they did not pose a danger. Survival in this wilderness depended on protecting lives and property from the weather and from those with ill-meaning, be they four- or two-footed. Two more men appeared from the other buildings, each armed with bows.

'What do you want?' the first man demanded.

'We have furs to trade and we want to get a passage on a boat to Birka.'

'Two of you stay there and one come round here. Leave your weapons there.'

Gunnar looked at Finn and said, 'Now you can see if you inherited the power of that bear you killed. Take your knife and show them the mark of father's forge on it.'

Finn hesitated.

'What are you afraid of, you have your mother's magic bear's claws round your neck,' mocked Torsten.

Finn put his pack on his back and started walking round the bay towards the houses. As he did so, Torsten and Gunnar pulled their bows from the package they had been carrying the tent in and moved into the cover of the shoreside trees. If Finn were murdered, they would wreak quick revenge.

Finn was ten paces from the three men when one said, 'We said leave your weapons over there!'

'I want to show you my knife to prove who we are. Arvid's forge mark is on the knife.'

One of the men advanced towards Finn with an axe in his hand, the other two pointed their arrows at the younger brother. The first man was fair-haired with an untidy beard which had grown unevenly on his face, like a field with a patchy crop. His front teeth were missing and his bent nose betrayed the fact that he had had an altercation with something hard in the past.

'Give me the knife, slowly, handle first.'

Finn did as he was told. 'Yes, it's Arvid's work all right,' the man with the axe shouted to the other two. They lowered their bows. 'Stay here while we talk,' the man said to Finn. He went back to the other two. Finn could hear them talking in lowered tones, but could not make out what they were saying. He noted that the axe man seemed to be the dominant person in the discussion. All three of the men were dressed in conventional southern clothes which were very worn and had been repaired clumsily. None of them wore reindeer-skin clothing like the brothers. Then he noticed that there were some children at the door of one of the houses looking out inquisitively. They were poorly dressed and looked frightened.

'Leave your bows over there and come round here,' the blond man shouted to the two brothers on the other side of the inlet.

Torsten and Gunnar walked round the bay and were soon by Finn's side. 'You sods, you would have let them kill me, wouldn't you!'

'But they didn't, did they?' joked Gunnar.

The man who had looked at Finn's knife came up to speak to them, still holding the axe.

'It is too early for the trading boats to come; it will be another two weeks at least before we see them. If you want to stay here you will have to work for us. You get food in exchange.'

'What kind of work?' asked Gunnar.

'The jetty which the boats berth on was destroyed by a storm in the winter. We have to repair it. You will have to fell trees and split the logs to use in building the jetty.'

The brothers looked to where the man was pointing. About a hundred paces away where the water looked deeper they could see that the upright posts for a jetty were intact, but all the other timbers had disappeared.

'All right. We will work for you. We want good food and plenty of it. I am Gunnar, this is Torsten and this is my youngest brother Finn, but you have already met. He would like his knife back.'

The man roared with laughter. 'A child like him should not have a knife. You are responsible if he cuts himself.' He gave Finn the knife despite the fact that the young man was bridling with anger about this comment.

'I am Sverker, this is my land. These are my brothers Olof and Jan. And those brats in the doorway are Olof's kids.'

'Where can we put our tent?' asked Gunnar.

'Best choose a good spot inside the trees over there, away from the shore. When the wind blows hard off the sea it's very exposed near the beach. In the next few days the Sami traders will begin to arrive and they will be pitching their tents over there too. There is a forest stream which runs into the sea over there too and you can get water.'

'When can we eat?' asked Gunnar.

'When you have done some work; we eat at sundown. Pitch your tent and come back here to get tools.'

The brothers put up their tent and strolled back to the settlement. They were intrigued by the way the settlers had organised themselves. There was a well with a large pole balanced on a pivot. On one end there was a bucket and on the other a counterweight to make lifting the water easier. They could see fish traps a few paces out in the water and further out there were birch floats which betrayed the fact that there were fish traps in deeper water too. Adjoining the back of the buildings there were animal enclosures from which they could hear a grunting sound. They went over and looked in one of the sties. The top half of the door was open and they could see a sow with a litter of piglets. This was the first time they had seen pigs and the strong smell, which was new to them, made them recoil. 'These must be pigs! They smell worse than you Finn,' joked Gunnar.

At the back of the buildings there was a forge and a charcoal burner. Behind these was a large clearing which was obviously for growing crops; it was partly flooded by the snow melt. Here and there they could see heaps of stones, large and small, where the ploughman had cleared them from the field. Three of the buildings were dwelling houses, but the fourth appeared to be some kind of store. They walked towards it and saw that here too there was a door which was split horizontally so that that top and bottom could be opened independently. Gunnar opened the top of the door and was surprised to come face to face with Jan who was just about to come out.

'What do you want?' asked Jan.

'I was just interested to see what was in here,' stammered Gunnar, for once caught off guard.

'This building has many uses as you will see in a few days. At the moment our sheep are lambing in here. Time you lazy beggars started work. Come with me.'

And so they were put to work. They collected hemp ropes, long axes, hand axes and wedges from a store and were taken to the forest edge by Jan.

'Make sure you look after the tools, you'll pay for anything broken,' he told them sourly.

He was a slightly built individual who made up for his lack of stature by the volume of his voice, a physical attribute which allowed him to curse longer and louder than most about the inadequacies of others. A risky strategy perhaps, but he lived under the protection of his bigger brothers. He showed them an area of trees adjoining the clearing.

'We want to enlarge the clearing, so cut the pines parallel with the field from here. And no damned slacking, make the stumps as low as you can so there's less for us to clear later. Best you wedge and split the timber here so that it's not too heavy for you puny half-breeds to carry to the jetty.'

Uncharacteristically, it was Gunnar who calmed his brothers by sternly eyeing the other two to stop them from reacting to this braggart's taunts. Later he murmured to them, 'Steady lads, we need these people, we will get our chance one day.'

The three brothers started the job and continued for several days, felling pines. After they had felled each one, they trimmed the branches off and then squared off the thick end of the log. Next they made a deep axe cut and finally drove a wedge into the cut to start the splitting of the log. This could take many hours as the wedges had to be driven in deeper and deeper until the whole log split. They used the hand axe to make the surface of the split timbers as even as possible.

While they were working on this task, Sverker, Olof and Jan were about their chores. Jan was the fisherman. Each morning he checked all the traps and then rowed out to the floats and pulled up the baited cages, which were made of split birch wood, to see if they had lured any fish in through the funnel-shaped entrance which made escape for the fish difficult.

Sverker worked the forge, but from time to time he stopped to direct the work on the jetty. Olof seemed to be the farmer, he tended the pigs, sheep and their two cows. He also had the unpleasant job of rendering seal blubber to produce oil. Behind the buildings there was a vat where the blubber was boiled. The smell was awful, but didn't seem to bother Olof. Several times the three men had gone off seal hunting. They killed grey seals which at this time of year gathered with their pups on the small islets just off the coast. It was easy hunting with a bow and arrow or a club. The seal meat was nutritious, but the animals also provided useful by-products such as oil, which the settlers used for their lamps and for candle-making. They had several wooden barrels of oil which they would be using to trade for other products when the ships arrived. The seal skins were used for clothing or for making ropes.

There were no women in the settlement. It seemed that Olof's wife had either left or had died, and he was bringing up his children, two boys and a girl. Despite their ages they too had jobs to do each day, such as collecting firewood, tending fires and general household duties. They looked unkempt and generally uncared for. Life was harsh for the children as well as the adults.

After several days some Sami families arrived and pitched their tents near to the forest edge. The tent nearest to the brothers' was occupied by a Sami woman with two small children. They understood that her husband was hunting and she had come to trade his furs. The brothers asked around to see if any of the Sami families had news of their parents and sister, but none of them had come from the same area where the three had wintered.

Then the great day arrived when, early in the morning, a ship was seen making towards the shore. Propelled by an onshore breeze the freighter came closer and closer to the bay, its square sail filled by the wind over the stern. About a hundred paces offshore the sail dropped and the crowd which had gathered on the shore saw men adjusting lines before two oars appeared on each side and the vessel started to move slowly towards the opening of the bay. Once inside the bay they could see the crew preparing berthing lines before guiding the ship alongside the refurbished jetty. The three children were already on the jetty with their father and Sverker to take the ship's lines and make them fast. The sailors put a gangplank ashore and one of them walked across it and shook hands with Sverker.

The ship, known as a *knar*, was built of pine and oak in the style of the classic longship, but was wider and had decks in the bow and the stern with a hold for freight amidships. It was about fifteen paces long and five paces wide.

The hold was full of barrels, bales and boxes, but also, with their legs tied together to prevent them struggling, there were two calves.

Gunnar was the first of the brothers to arrive at the ship. The sailors, a rough-looking group of seven men, most of them wearing heavy cloaks with cowls, were already unloading cargo. Two of them dragged the calves ashore. Gunnar could see from the stinking mess in the bottom of the hold why the sailors wanted the animals off quickly. One of the crew, who was better dressed than the others, was directing operations in between conducting a conversation with Sverker. Gunnar pushed through the crowd and learnt from Sverker that this was Leif, the merchant captain.

'Get your brothers to help you move this cargo to the storehouse before the rain starts,' ordered Sverker.

'I want to talk to Leif,' said Gunnar.

'He's busy at the moment, wait until this evening. Olof, take the calves to the cow shed.'

Gunnar did as ordered and the three brothers and the crew started to carry the goods to the storehouse. It was while this work was going on that they heard the screams. The children had been playing on the jetty, climbing over the boxes piled there. The girl, Sif, had lost her footing and tumbled into the water. Olof ran down to the jetty and frantically searched to see where she had fallen. The sailors peered into the water, but showed little interest in getting involved. Finn was not far from the boat and dropped the bale of wool he was carrying to join Olof in the search. There was no sign of the girl, but Finn realised that the current might have carried her under the jetty. He jumped into the freezing water and swam under the wooden platform. In the half light he could see a disturbance in the water where her arms were flailing. He grabbed her and tried to drag her out, but she was panicking so much that he could not easily hold her. He grabbed her hair and swam backwards towing her by the hair until he reached the daylight and then staggered on the uneven stony bottom to pass her up to her father. Gunnar and Torsten helped Finn out of the water.

He stood shivering on the shore. 'You stupid devil, you seem to like cold water,' quipped Torsten. 'You can warm yourself up this time!'

Later, when the ship had been unloaded, Olof came to the brothers' tent.

He looked at Finn and said, 'I am in your debt and beholden to you. Sif is well, I have punished her and she will not be playing on the jetty again.'

'Go easy on her, she's only a child,' said Finn.

'But she has to learn,' he retorted.

By the afternoon, the brothers could see what Jan had meant when he had said that the store had many uses. There was a queue of Sami trying to get into the store to barter with the traders. They carried bales of furs, wood carvings and some even had walrus tusks. The latter could only have come down the trade route from Northern Norway as there were no walrus in this sea. The merchant captain stood on a raised platform doing deals with the Sami. After a trade had been made they would leave the store carrying iron pots, knives, axes or packs of wool, whatever they needed that the southerners could supply. Sometimes the merchant used his scales to weigh out silver in exchange for furs, but generally the system was based on barter. The atmosphere was generally friendly, but occasionally there was some shouting when someone was not satisfied with the deal they had been offered. The sailors stood ominously by, ready to use force if an argument got too heated. Each of them carried a *seax*, a large knife in a holster, on their hip, and several had cudgels.

Later in the afternoon, Gunnar approached Leif.

'We want passage to Birka, we can trade furs to pay for the journey.'

'How many of you are there?' he asked.

'Three.'

'No, not possible. It takes seven men to work the ship and with the load of cargo we carry there is not space for three more. Maybe we could take two of you, but you would have to work for your passage.'

'No, it has to be three. We don't want to split up.' Gunnar was acutely aware of his mother's last words to him about being responsible for the other two. 'We'll have to wait for the next ship.'

'I think that you will find that they have limited space too. We left port with another *knar* which was a bit smaller than this one. I guess that it will arrive here in the next few days. If you are going to be stuck here you might as well enjoy it. Come back after you have eaten, you can have some wine with us.'

'Thanks, I will.'

'Let's have a look at the furs,' said Leif.

Gunnar rolled out the packs of furs and after a few minutes they agreed a price in silver. Leif carefully weighed some pieces of the metal and Gunnar put them into his pouch.

Gunnar was troubled by what he had learnt about the chances of getting a passage south, but decided not to say anything to the other two yet. When he got to the tent, Finn was boiling fish which Jan had begrudgingly given them earlier in the day.

'The captain has asked us to come for some wine this evening. You want to come?'

Torsten looked puzzled. 'What is wine?'

'It must be a drink from the south. They obviously had some with them to trade. I'm staying here tonight, I want to dry my coat, you go with Torsten,' said Finn.

77

Later that evening Torsten and Gunnar walked over to the storehouse. As they approached they could hear the sound of laughter. They pushed the door open and there, by the light several candles, they found the three settlers, Leif and five of the crew sitting on packing cases and boxes with wooden tankards in their hands. They were laughing and joking and had obviously been drinking for some time.

'Come in northlanders and enjoy a drink from the south!' yelled Leif.

The brothers took a wooden mug each and held them under the barrel tap. They were surprised to see how red the liquid was.

'Do southerners make this?' asked Torsten.

There were peals of laughter from the crew. Leif spoke. 'This drink my friend is made far south of our land. Ask Ivar, he has been to the far south to trade, and to fight. Though you could say that most of the trading he has done has been with the blade of an axe.'

They all laughed again and looked at one of the crew with a livid scar on his forehead which was clear even in the dim light of the candles. 'By thunder, it was a hell of a hot place to fight, but the plunder and the women were worth it!' roared Ivar.

And so the evening went on, with much banter, a lot of it with the brothers as the butt of the jokes. Jan teased them and referred to them as 'Sami mongrels'. Gunnar whispered to Torsten, 'One day he will see that these mongrels can bite.'

The two brothers became more and more aware that the world they had been living in was a very small one and that they lacked knowledge of many things which the southerners took for granted.

Finn was sitting in the tent stoking the fire to dry out his coat when he became aware of a noise outside, coming from the direction of the Sami woman's tent. It sounded like an animal whimpering. He put his head outside and in the dark could just make out two writhing shapes on the ground. He grabbed a lighted branch from his fire and went outside. He saw that one of the crew of the ship was sitting on top of the Sami woman holding a knife at her throat with one hand and loosening his belt with the other.

Finn grabbed the long axe which they had left outside their tent, took hold of the blade and swung the handle hard across the back of the man's neck. The man fell sideways on to his back, dropping the knife. The woman jumped up, straightened her skirt and scurried into her tent.

The man was recovering from the blow. He looked up at Finn and said, 'You are going to be very sorry you did that son.' He struggled to his feet, hunted around, found his knife and stood facing Finn. By this time, Finn had changed his grip on the axe so that he could defend himself with the blade. The sailor, aware that Finn was better armed, turned and walked away in the direction of the settlement. Finn put the axe down and went back into the tent. He was shaken by what he had seen and done and sat thinking about whether they were doing the right thing leaving their secure northern world to put themselves at the mercy of such villains.

The two brothers hardly noticed when the sailor who had threatened Finn entered the storehouse. He went quietly over to Ivar and whispered something to him. Ivar got up and left the building with him.

Finn was about to prepare to go to bed when he heard a noise outside. At first he thought it was his two brothers returning. But then the tent flap was thrown open and one of the crew pushed his way in.

'Quick! Your brothers need your help!' he shouted.

Finn grabbed his almost dry coat, pushed his feet into his boots and went outside. As he tried to put his coat on his arms were grabbed from behind. In front of him in the dim light he saw the sailor who had threatened him.

'Gunnar! Gunnar!' Finn screamed.

'No good calling for big brother, he's drunk and probably too frightened to help you anyway,' growled Ivar.

Before he could duck Finn felt the thud of a fist on his cheek. He struggled to get free and kicked out at the man in front, but could not reach him before another blow broke his nose. As he lost consciousness he was aware of another blow to the face, then another before the man behind him dropped him to the ground. Thankfully, he was not aware of the kicking as he lapsed into deeper unconsciousness.

The two sailors went into the tent, leaving the body outside. While they were rummaging around looking for anything of value they did not hear hurried footsteps passing the tent in the direction of the store.

The door of the store opened and a Sami woman stepped in. There was a roar from the men. 'Now the fun starts,' shouted Leif. The woman went straight to Gunnar and whispered something in his ear. Gunnar looked across at Torsten and shouted, 'We've got to go!'

'Oh yes, it's all right for some! Have a good time!' bellowed Leif.

Torsten followed the other two out amid catcalls and jeering from the crowd.

'Keep an eye on big brother! He's up to no good!' joked one of the crew.

Outside the woman spoke as slowly as she could to try to make the men understand what had happened.

'Where are they now?' asked Gunnar.

'In your tent,' she replied.

The cold air was sobering the pair fast.

'Let's go and get the bastards,' said Torsten.

'No, revenge is a dish best eaten cold,' answered Gunnar.

He continued, 'Woman, go and tend to Finn as soon as they have gone. Torsten, they will have been through our things and probably stolen the best furs. My guess is that they will go straight back to the boat to hide our stuff. We will catch them when they don't expect us. Go round to the back of the cowshed and get some rope, I'll meet you just past Sverker's house where the path is narrow.'

Gunnar went as fast as he could in the dark to the jetty where there was a pile of timber which they had not used in the reconstruction. He selected two pieces just over half the height of a man, returned to the meeting place where Torsten was waiting and gave him one of the pieces of timber. They stretched the rope across the path at knee height, Torsten holding one end in the shadow of the house and Gunnar crouched gripping the other end behind a bush.

They did not have long to wait before they heard voices approaching. One of the speakers they recognised as Ivar. The men were hurrying as fast as they could, side by side in the poor light. There were two loud thuds as they both tripped and fell to the ground. Gunnar leapt on the nearest face-down figure, put the timber under his throat, his knee in his back and forced his head up. There was a dreadful crack and the body went limp. Torsten tried to hit the other man over the head with his timber, but his aim was not good in the dark and the man was shouting and struggling. Gunnar grabbed the man by the throat and dragged him to his feet as Torsten sank a blow to his head. The man sagged and Gunnar took his weight.

'Help me get him to the jetty,' panted Gunnar.

They dragged the man to the back of the ship and threw him into the water. They then returned and did the same with the body of the other man.

'Clear up the stuff they have dropped on the path and put the timbers and the rope away. I'll see you at the tent.'

Back at the tent they found the Sami woman had dragged Finn inside and was bathing his dreadfully battered face to clear the blood.

'Is he alive?' asked Torsten.

Gunnar felt his neck. 'He's still warm and there's a pulse, but it looks very bad.'

'What the hell do we do now? When the crew find the bodies they're going to murder us!'

'Calm down, Torsten. What they're going to find tomorrow is that two of their crew have fallen into the water and drowned. You saw this afternoon that none of them could swim, only Finn dared to jump into the water. That's what gave me the idea. If they fish them out they won't find a mark on them apart from the bump on the head you gave one, and that won't be too obvious. But we had better keep Finn away from them; they might get suspicious if they see what he looks like.'

Finn started to stir. One of his blue eyes opened under the badly swollen lid.

'Finn, can't we leave you alone for an evening without you getting into trouble?'

Finn's mouth moved slightly as if he was trying to smile, and he spat out a tooth.

They thanked the Sami woman for her help before she left for her tent and then started to tidy up the mess made by their nocturnal visitors.

Next morning, as Gunnar and Torsten were going off to work, the older brother noticed two yellowish cubes pushed into the mud outside the tent. He bent down and picked them up. They were two dice made out of bone. The dots on the dice had been made with black burn marks.

'It looks as if someone dropped these last night,' said Gunnar as he put them in his pouch.

The two of them walked on down to the settlement to

find out what Sverker wanted them to do today. They met him walking towards them.

'Where's Finn?' he asked.

'Oh, I think he drank too much last night, he's ill.'

'I don't remember seeing him in the store, but then I had had a few and he's a quiet lad. You're in luck, two of the stupid sods got so pissed last night that they fell off the jetty and drowned. Leif needs two new crew. You might persuade him to take the three of you.'

Chapter 6
A Sea Voyage

Gunnar and Torsten were told to go to help Jan who was extending the cowshed to accommodate the new calves.

'We're feeding three of you lazy devils; why are there only two of you here?' demanded Jan.

'Finn's not well, he won't be working today,' answered Gunnar.

'Then don't expect us to feed him. What's wrong with him anyway?' asked Jan.

Gunnar realised that Jan was ruthless enough to go to their tent and drag Finn out of bed. If Finn was seen in his present state there might be some awkward questions.

'He has a fever. I think it might be caused by fleas.'

'Best the weak little brat stays away from me. You will have to share your food with him.'

With that Jan assumed his usual position of standing watching them while they worked and his irritating habit of interjecting with unneeded advice and sometimes criticism.

It was while they were splitting logs for the cowshed wall that Leif came to see them.

'We fished two of my crew out of the sea this morning. I can't understand it. They were both experienced sailors who had survived storms, shipwrecks and all manner of danger and for some obscure reason, they just fell into the sea.'

'Perhaps they had drunk too much,' ventured Torsten.

Careful Torsten, thought Gunnar, *just keep quiet.*

'Ragnar didn't drink, I know him well, he was one of my kinsmen, and Ivar could empty a barrel by himself given the chance and still climb the mast.'

'It makes no sense, does it?' interjected Gunnar before Torsten had a chance to speak.

'It's an ill wind that blows no good for someone. I'm now two crewmen short and we have a long journey ahead of us. Are you still looking for a berth?'

'If you can take the three of us,' answered Gunnar. 'Er, when are you going to leave?' Gunnar realised that if the Leif saw Finn in his present state, suspicions would be aroused about who had beaten him so badly and that could lead to Leif putting two and two together.

'We have to load yet and check the trim of the vessel. We came up with heavy goods and are going back with lighter stuff, I may need to add ballast. But in any case, I want to see the other boat in, as then I can report its safe arrival to the owner when we get back. I guess that we will leave in a week or so, depending on the second ship's arrival, and the wind.'

'That suits us well, I wouldn't like to leave the settlers here before we have done all we can to help them,' lied Gunnar. 'But can you take all three of us? Finn is unwell at the moment, but he is a strong lad and learns fast.'

'All right, but you'll all need to learn fast, life on a ship is very different from what you are used to. It is cold, wet and dangerous and I expect every man to do his full share of work.'

'Don't worry, you can depend on us. How long will it take to get to Birka?'

'Sailing boats don't have schedules; they get there when they get there. It took us six days to get here. But we were lucky, we had good winds and our water just lasted us so we didn't have to stop. And by the way, haven't you heard about Birka?'

'What?' asked Gunnar.

'By the gods you are isolated up here aren't you! It was four years ago. The once proud centre of the Viking world, the biggest manufacturing and trading centre in the country, is in ruins. Good thing I say. It was getting more and more difficult to get a boat in there as the water level went down. King Erik had just returned from the Land of the Danes where he had taken the new religion, Christianity, and he decided that Birka should become Christian. There were some Christians there, but most people believed in the old gods. They were having none of it. The chieftain of Birka owed fealty to King Erik, but he thought he was too powerful for Erik to argue with him. Eventually, Erik's patience was exhausted and he attacked the island, burnt down the garrison fortress and slaughtered most of the inhabitants. The chieftain's head is on a pole on the top of a hill on the island as a warning to those who defy King Erik. Those they didn't kill they took as slaves and made Christians of them. But now Erik has gone back to the old beliefs and sacrifices to Odin again.'

'So where do you sail to then?'

'We sail to Sigtuna; old Sigtuna that is. King Erik made the place his new capital, all his chieftains from around the country have houses there which they live in while he is around. But he doesn't like the place, thinks that it's not fine enough; so he's building a new Sigtuna an hour's sail east from the old one, on the other side of the channel. The harbour is not finished so we still use the old one.'

Four days later, the *knar* was ready to leave, apart from filling the water barrels. This they would leave until the last moment so that the water was as fresh as possible. The crew had chosen a number of large round stones from the beach to add to the ballast in the hold, and on top of them the cargo was stored and lashed down under the cover of skins which had been greased to make them waterproof. Finn's wounds were healing and the swelling on his face was diminishing, but he was still being kept in the tent to avoid him being seen by the crew or the settlers. Two days after the boat was ready for sea, the second trading vessel was sighted coming into the bay. Gunnar and Torsten happened to be on the berthed boat where Leif was giving them some basic training in seamanship. There were two other crew members on board.

'Einar, cast off the lines fore and aft,' ordered Leif.

'Clear the oars to move out!' he shouted to no one in particular, but it was clearly an order for all to obey. They needed to move their boat so that the smaller one could get up to the jetty to unload.

Gunnar and Torsten watched what the other crew were doing and tried to emulate them by grabbing an oar each and opening the oar ports, which were blocked on the outside by an infill board to stop heavy seas coming in. Leif could see that they were dithering with an oar in one hand and trying to open the port with the other.

'Do one thing at a time, open the port first and then put the oar through!' he shouted. Gunnar tried to push the oar through the port from the inside of the boat. 'The other way you damned fool! The blade is wider than the port. Push the handle of the oar in from the outside.'

And so began their practical sea training in earnest. They were used to rowing with two oars on the lake at Floga, but now they had a long oar each, one sitting behind the other, and they had to pull in unison. They quickly got the hang of it and the ship circled round the bay, steered by Leif. The newly arrived ship moved up to the jetty and made fast. Leif's vessel then moved alongside the newcomer and one of the crew threw lines over. 'Get those oars out Gunnar and Torsten, so that we can get alongside.'

They did as they were bid and then sat mesmerised by the teamwork of the two crew as they made fast lines and put two sacks of straw between the two vessels to stop the hulls scraping against each other. They seemed to know the crew on the other vessel; there was much shouting of greetings and questions about their voyage.

'Where did you get to?' asked Leif ironically.

A tall, thin, distinguished looking man who was obviously the captain of the smaller vessel shouted, 'We had to pull in to Eagle Bay to get water. Those damned savages wanted the usual tribute to give safe passage. Cost us a fortune.'

Later, Gunnar asked Leif, 'Who are the savages?'

'At some places down the coast, there are some fishing settlements. Each one is a law unto itself. At best they demand payment to allow a ship to refill their water barrels safely; at worst they will seize the ship and kill the crew.'

'Why don't the ships carry more water with them, so that they don't need to stop?'

'This is a small cargo vessel; the more cargo we carry the more profitable the journey. Water barrels take space and they are heavy and weight slows us down more. We carry water, beer and food for five or six days; if the voyage takes longer we have to stop. Now, get your things, but keep them to a minimum, and bring your brother. We sail in the morning if the wind is right.'

Gunnar and Torsten went back to the tent. The days were much warmer now and Finn was sitting outside, preparing fish for supper.

'Time to go, Finn. Get your stuff packed. We can only take clothes, and our bows. We have to leave in the morning.'

'What are we going to do with the tent, the tools and all our cooking stuff?' asked Finn.

'I'm going to see Olof, I'll leave it all for him.'

Later Gunnar went to see Olof. 'You told us you are in

our debt. Well, I want you to do something for us.'

'What's that?' Olof asked.

'Well, two things really. Firstly, when the Sami come here to trade, tell them all that if they pass Floga they should visit our parents and tell them that their sons are well and that we have left for the southlands on a ship.'

'I'll do that. And what was the other thing?'

'Could I borrow your wood bore? I have a little job to do this evening. I can put it back in the tool shed when I've finished.'

'Yes, that's fine, do you know where it is?'

'Yes, I can get it. Oh yes, we've left the tent with some tools and cooking things which you can have.'

'Thanks, and have a safe voyage. And by the way, I'm sorry about Jan, he can be a real sod at times, he's the same way with Sverker and me.'

The two men clasped wrists in farewell. Gunnar wondered how such a pleasant man could have such a swine of a brother.

The brothers reported to the ship just before sunset. Leif looked at Finn. 'What the hell's happened to him?'

They had hoped that he would not pay any attention to Finn's appearance. It was impossible to hide the bent nose and the eye which had now turned from being black to a yellow and blue bruise.

'That bastard Jan took a dislike to him. There was nothing we could do about it. He was our boss.' Leif looked at Finn and then to the other two. It was easy to detect that Leif found it difficult to believe that the two brothers would not have taken revenge on Jan, but he said no more about it.

Later in the evening, after they had moved aboard the ship, Gunnar told the others that he needed to go ashore for a while. He clambered over the ship next to theirs to reach the jetty and, checking that the settlers were in their houses, made his way to the tool shed. After fumbling in the dark for a while he found the wood bore. He quietly walked down to the foreshore and found the rowing boat which Jan used each morning. A few turns of the wood bore and there was a neat circular hole through the boat's hull below the water line. Gunnar rubbed some mud and grass into the hole so that it would not be easily noticed. He walked back to the tool store and replaced the bore.

On board the ship they slept in their fur coats; the nights were still very cold. At first light, there were sounds of movement on board as one of the crew tried to get the fire basket alight. Cooking on a ship was a dangerous matter and could only be done if the weather was fair. There was a metal basket for the coals hanging on chains on a tripod over a hearth of stones. Once alight, a cooking pot was hung, also on chains, over the fire to heat water. They were about to get their first meal of porridge, a dish which, together with salted or dried fish, would be repeated every day for the entire voyage.

There was no wind inside the bay, which was protected from the north-west by the forest. But from the appearance of the sea outside there was a light wind blowing in a useful direction for the start of their journey. They cast off and the oars were put through the ports to carry them out through the bay entrance and out to sea. Although only four oars had been used yesterday, there were three ports on both sides of the ship. Four rowers sat on the foredeck and two on the afterdeck. By each port was the seat for the rower. The seat was a chest in which the crewmen kept personal belongings. Leif had his own chest which was chained to the mast. The seventh crew member had a chest under the foredeck, and this Finn shared with Torsten.

Gunnar and Torsten were keen to show the rest of the crew that they were not complete novices and they grabbed an oar each and tried to match the stroke of the third oar on their side.

Once outside the bay, the brothers immediately became aware of the unfamiliar motion of the ship as it rode over the slight waves. As they stood to ship the oars, their sense of balance was confused and they had to hold on to the gunnels when not sitting. Leif noticed the northerners' discomfort. 'You'll soon get used to it. You'll have to because it will get a whole lot worse than this. Hoist the sail, take it to the top!'

The brothers watched as two of the crew unstrapped the sail and another two started to hoist the heavy cloth. The sail itself was made of wool and linen and was waxed to make it windproof. Leather straps were sewn in a crisscross pattern on the sail to help it keep its shape. The size of the rectangular grey sail could be altered according to how high up the mast the top spar was hoisted. In light winds such as these the whole sail was raised.

The ship gathered pace as the sail went up and Leif carefully kept the wind exactly behind them so that the top spar did not get twisted. He steered with a handle which was slotted into the end of a long oar and held in place by raffia rope made from lime bark. This steering oar swivelled on the right side of the ship not far from the stern. This oar was known as the *styrbord*, and thus this side of the ship was called the 'styrbord' or starboard side. The other side was the 'barbord' or port side, that is, bareboard, the side where there was no oar. The brothers were bombarded with new nautical terms throughout the voyage and it was clear from the first day that no allowance was going to be made for ignorance. Worse still was that the crew found constant amusement in trying to confound the landsmen by giving few explanations.

'Gunnar and Finn, coil the warps and stow them. Torsten, get those fenders aboard!' shouted Leif.

The brothers realised they would have to accept some

humiliation and tried to keep in good humour as their mistakes were laughed at.

Once the ship was in order, they were given cleaning and tidying tasks to do as were other members of the crew. They had a chance to talk between the three of them.

'So, it's goodbye northlands,' said Torsten. 'I only wish that I had had a chance to give Jan something to remember us by before we left.'

Gunnar winked at the two others. 'Today he will have discovered that the Sami mongrels have bitten.'

'What do you mean?' asked Finn.

'Let's just say that while his fishing boat is made of wood and won't sink, he will have a cold and wet morning.'

They were interrupted by Leif.

'There are eight of us. While we are at sea we will have four, six-hour watches, two men on each watch. The first watch starts at midday and goes on until I say, roughly sundown. The next watch until midnight. You have to judge yourselves when that is. The night watch is until daybreak. Every two days we change the watches round so you all get night watches. Finn, you go with Einar for first watch, Torsten with Gudmar, Ahl with Botvid and Gunnar with me, morning watch. The night watch cooks breakfast, the afternoon watch cooks dinner. Any change in the weather, all hands help.'

The ship was almost on a dead run, with the wind right behind. It was rolling from side to side as well rocking as it traversed the waves. This was the most efficient point of sail for the *knar*, but not one that they could expect every day. When Finn and Einar started their watch, Leif called the three brothers over to the steering position.

'Right, we have a good wind in the right direction, get the feel of the steering oar and see the effect if you make changes. We want the sail to fill evenly and not to flutter and flap.' Each of them spent some time trying to get used to steering the ship. 'As you can see, it is hard work holding the oar. It is a lot harder when the wind is strong, so you have to share the steering with your partner on the watch.'

'But how will we know which way to steer when the wind changes?' asked Gunnar.

'For the whole journey we sail in sight of the coast on our starboard side. But we must not get too close as in many places there are rocks and small islands.'

'And at night?'

'We use the Polaris star to navigate by. If we can't see the stars then we keep the oar on the daytime course and shorten sail so that we move only slowly. Always listen for seabirds or the sound of surf. If you hear these then we are too close to land.'

'And in fog or rain?'

'I'll show you if and when it happens.'

The three brothers were keen to learn about boat-handling and had many questions about parts of the ship and the different tarred hemp ropes which spread out from the top of the mast to different parts of the vessel. As they were gathered around the stern of the boat talking to Leif they became aware that the ship was beginning to roll more violently. Spray was now flying over the sides of the high prow, forcing the two crew members who were attempting to sleep to seek refuge under the foredeck. Torsten was the first to admit that he was feeling unwell. Leif was waiting for this moment.

'Torsten and Gunnar, the best cure for sea sickness is to keep busy. Take two wooden scoops and start baling out the cargo bilge. Finn, you are on watch with Einar, take over the steering oar. The wind is strengthening so take a firm hold.'

As the wind increased, so the waves built in size and the ship responded by yawing and rocking ever more violently.

Surely, Finn thought, *we can't go on like this much longer before the sail splits.*

94

Einar grabbed the oar as Finn leant over the gunnels and brought up his breakfast. Leif had noticed that the other two had each taken a break from their work to hang over the side for the same purpose.

'Come on you two, bale faster, we don't want to have to slow down, we're making very good time.'

Late in the afternoon the wind started to abate and the movement of the ship became less pronounced. The brothers started to feel better and Torsten even had some porridge before he went on watch with Gudmar. As dusk fell the wind dropped off completely, the waves diminished and the crew had a very quiet night drifting with the weak current. When Gunnar and Leif went on watch in the morning the sea was like a mirror; yesterday's waves had been transformed into nothing more than ripples. The sun started to rise on the left side of the ship, auguring a fine day.

Leif was grumpy. 'This is not going to get us to Sigtuna in a month. Finn, Torsten, Gunnar and Gudmar, out with the oars. I'll steer, let's make some progress in the right direction. Ahl, drop the mainsail.'

They rowed until mid-morning. The speed they could achieve was less than half that of the boat under sail even with a light wind. 'That will do, I think we have a breeze coming up from the south.'

The rowers shipped oars. Gudmar rubbed grease on his sore hands and the three brothers copied him. The breeze increased, effectively blocking their way south.

'Now we are going to be more busy lads. We will tack south. Ahl and Gunnar, up with the sail. Gudmar, pull in the port mainsheet for a starboard tack.'

A few minutes later they were heading out to sea with the land behind them. They stayed on this tack until it was almost impossible to see the wooded hills beyond the stern.

A laden ship with a rectangular sail could not be safely

tacked by turning the bow through the wind even in good weather, so at Leif's command the ship was veered to port so that the wind was first behind the vessel and then coming across the port side. The port mainsheet was eased off and the starboard sheet pulled in. They were now heading towards the distant land. After going through this procedure all afternoon the dilemma facing Leif was what to do at night. If they continued tacking there was a risk that they could run into the unseen shore on the port tack. As dusk fell and they were approaching land he announced his decision.

'Take her up to the shore and we will look for a place to anchor.'

An hour later they were riding at anchor fifty paces from the beach. The night watch was given the job of attending to the anchor ropes, listening for any groaning sounds which would betray that the anchor was not holding, and checking that the wind did not shift to the east and thus risk putting them on a lee shore.

When the other crew woke for breakfast, there was an eerie stillness. The sea was blanketed in fog and they could only just make out the trees on the shoreline.

'I was afraid this would happen. The warm southerly wind blowing across the cold sea is a recipe for this murk. It's going to be rowing today lads. After breakfast I want all six oars pulling us south.'

Those who had rowed yesterday groaned, their hands still sore from their efforts. But their protests were ignored by Leif. They raised the anchor and set off south. Once away from the land, the fog was completely disorienting and they could have been rowing round in circles, but for the sun stone. Leif had unlocked his sea chest and taken out a piece of crystal. He held it up to his eye and slowly rotated it in his hand. He gradually turned around, facing different directions from starboard to dead ahead and then to port.

He turned back again and then stopped, facing the starboard bow. Unseen by the crew, he had lined up two black dots in the crystal. He knew that when the two dots were together, the optical property of the crystal had detected the brightest place in the sky, the sun above the fog. Since the sun was indicated to be off the starboard bow, they were heading too far east. He corrected the steering to keep the sun on the port bow until he judged that it was midday, when the sun should be directly ahead of them if they were travelling south. And then, in the afternoon, he would expect the sun to be on the starboard side.

They continued rowing until what they judged was early afternoon when the crew gave a loud cheer for the sun breaking through the fog bank. A little later a light breeze which sprang up from the north-east gave them even more pleasure.

'Ship oars, raise the sail!' bellowed Leif.

The exhausted rowers were quick to find energy to obey this command. Finn went on watch with Einar and the others found whatever comfortable places they could to rest.

'Gudmar, do you want to play dice?' called Gunnar.

'All right, best of ten games. The loser takes one of the winner's watches!'

The off-duty crew gathered round to watch. Gunnar pulled the two dice he had found outside the tent from his pouch and put them on the sea chest.

'They look like Ragnar's dice; look, the six on one of them is all crooked, just like his.'

Leif moved over from the stern to take a look. 'Where did you get these, Gunnar?' he asked.

'I found them in the mud near our tent,' he replied.

'Come on then, roll the dice, Gunnar,' said Gudmar.

Leif remained silent. He looked at the dice closely and

then at Gunnar before moving back to the stern where he sat, deep in thought.

The breeze held for two and half days and they made slow progress in the right direction. But the journey was taking far longer than Leif had hoped. It was during the morning watch that Gunnar saw Leif looking anxiously up at the sky. He looked up to see what the captain was observing.

'You see those rows of high cloud with the curved tails across the western sky?'

'Yes.'

'We can expect a big change in the weather, perhaps by this evening. I think that we might get a westerly gale. We are now on the sixth day of our voyage. Water is getting scarce. It doesn't please me to say so, but I think that we will need to go ashore to refill our barrels. If we go in tonight we might find shelter in case there is a storm.'

Gunnar had mixed feelings. He was in a hurry to reach their destination, but the prospect of riding a storm in this laden little ship, which might be driven a long way off course by a westerly, did not appeal to him. In any case, they would have to get water somewhere very soon.

Leif eased the steering oar south-westwards so that they might get closer to the coast to find a suitable place to anchor later in the day. He did not need to explain to his crew what he was doing or why – they had sailed with him many times before and had had the same thoughts, especially when they saw the signs in the sky.

By mid-afternoon, they were very close to land. It was flatter than the terrain they had seen the day they anchored. Ahl had climbed up the mast and was sitting on the spar keeping a lookout for submerged rocks. Einar was standing by the prow with a light rope with a stone attached. Each time he was ordered by Leif he swung the line into the sea and called out the number of marks on the line that were submerged.

There was a shout from Ahl. 'Captain! There is an inlet ahead.'

All the crew peered over the starboard bow. There were several small wooded islands and beyond them a narrow inlet.

'Drop the sail and man the oars!' ordered Leif. 'Steady, let's take a look at the opening.'

When they came level with the opening they changed course and headed towards it. The channel was narrow, but deep, and allowed them entrance to a small bay the shores of which were completely wooded apart from a flat piece of land on one side of the entrance. They dropped anchor close to the western shore where they would get most protection from a possible storm.

'Ahl, let out more line on the anchor. Torsten, Gudmar, row us slowly back towards the shore. Einar, take soundings over the stern.'

They found that they could almost reach the shore before the water was too shallow for the *knar*, which needed less water than the height of a man to float in even when loaded.

'Finn, we've seen that you can swim. Strip off and take a line ashore. Put it round one of the trees and bring the end back to the ship.'

Finn started to undress while Botvid tied a tarred hemp line to a post in the stern. Torsten and Gunnar, highly amused by their brother's embarrassment, picked him up and threw him over the side. Botvid cast the line down to him and Finn quickly waded through the cold water to the nearest pine tree and ran the rope around it. Soon the ship was moored securely fore and aft.

After Finn had dried himself and dressed, Leif spoke.

'You three landsmen, go ashore and see if you can find a

stream with good water while it's still light. If you cling on to the stern rope and climb along it, you won't get wet.'

They did as ordered and clambered ashore. Once there, they had a curious feeling of lacking balance.

'After six days of the ground rocking under us, it's difficult to stand on firm land again,' remarked Gunnar.

They set off around the bay and soon found a stream which was emptying into it from the forest. They went back to the ship to report to Leif.

'Let's see if we can fill the barrels before dark, then we'll be ready to leave first thing tomorrow morning if the weather is reasonable.'

The crew lowered three barrels over the side of the ship and they were floated to land. Botvid and Ahl went ashore to help and before long the barrels were filled with forest spring water. They floated the filled barrels along the shore edge, wading through the water to push them to the boat where all hands pulled them aboard with the help of ropes.

'Supper time, and then we can get some rest. We keep the watches as at sea, but let's change the schedule. Gunnar and I will take the watch after supper, then Finn and Einar take the night watch, Gudmar and Torsten take over in the morning.'

The evening was dark, very dark, with no sign of stars. The wind was moaning through the trees from the west. All was quiet on the ship apart from the usual creaking of the timbers as the vessel moved gently in the light swell.

'Leif, did you hear something?'

Clearly, the captain was using the privilege of his rank to obtain the benefit of a catnap despite the fact that he was on duty.

'Hear what?'

'It sounded like voices on the shore.'

'All hands!' Leif went forward and kicked the recumbent forms to get their attention.

'All hands!' he repeated. 'I want to pull her further from the shore, we may have company.'

Ahl went forward with Botvid to pull on the anchor rope. Gudmar tied a line on the end of the shoreline to lengthen it. He slipped the rope to allow the other two to pull the ship out while still keeping a line to the shore.

'Hands off duty, I want you to sleep with your bows beside you in case we get visitors.'

The crew were now so wide awake that they all sat quietly staring towards the shore, even though it was in complete darkness. Suddenly, they heard something thumping the ground some distance off. The noise continued intermittently for some while and from time to time they could make out a splashing sound.

After a while, all was quiet apart from the wind, which by now was blowing strongly. Those off duty dozed, while the two watch-keepers nervously fingered their bows. When Leif decided the time had come for the watch to change, the night watch were woken to take over just as the rain started. Together with the two coming on watch, they stretched the sail over the cargo hold to protect it and to provide cover for those crew who could not creep under the fore and aft decks.

'Gunnar, you and one of your brothers can use Ragnar and Ivar's rain cloaks. They're in the two forward chests on the starboard side.'

Gunnar took one and gave the other to Finn, as he was on watch. The heavy, greased cloaks with a cowl were effective at keeping the wearer dry. This was just as well, as by mid-watch the rain was torrential and being driven by a strong westerly wind. Even in the protected bay, the ship was pitching on the swell.

At first light, the rain had ceased, but the wind was still strong. Finn roused the crew to show them what they had heard in the dark. On the flat piece of land there were three large tents and in the dawn light they could make out figures moving about around them. The crew had breakfast and watched the strangers on the shore.

'What the devil is that?' said Gunnar, pointing towards the opening of the inlet.

'They've blocked us in with a log barrier, damn it!' said Leif.

The crew could now see that there were five logs, tied end to end, across the entrance. The tents were pitched about fifty paces from the log barrier. They could see a number of men with bows leaving the encampment and walking around the shore in the direction of their ship.

'It looks as if there about twelve of them,' said Gunnar.

'Ready with your bows, lads,' commanded Leif.

The men stopped at the point where the boat's shoreline was looped around the tree. They were dressed in some kind of deerskin clothing and looked wild and strangely primal.

'Captain! Welcome to our territory. You were wise to shelter from the storm.'

'The storm has blown over and now we are wanting to leave. So kindly remove the barrier.'

'But captain, you are in our territory, you have to pay the price.'

'What price?'

'Unload your cargo and we will spare your lives, you can sail off today.'

'Damn you! If anything happens to us you can expect that our king will send warships and retribution will be merciless.'

The men on the shore laughed. 'Even if they could find this place, they would not find us.'

'If you don't remove the barrier, we will,' threatened Leif.

'Then you would be in danger. We guard the barrier and no one can get near without an arrow in the neck. Think about it, you are few, we are many. We are in no hurry. We will come back again this afternoon.'

The men laughed and joked between themselves and then wandered back along the shore to their encampment.

'Who are these people?' asked Torsten.

'They are brigands, mainly escaped criminals and slaves. There is no authority or law here. I think we have to give them what they want,' said Ahl.

'Ahl's right, why risk our lives to protect what doesn't belong to us anyway?' said Botvid.

'We could fight them,' ventured Torsten.

'Now that's a brilliant idea. There are at least twelve of them, probably more, and we are eight,' said Ahl.

'How many of you can fight?' asked Gunnar.

'They are just seamen, never trained as warriors. I don't suppose they could hit anyone with an arrow even if they stood next to them. Now, if we had Ivar here he would make a good account of himself,' said Leif.

It seemed that there was nothing more to be said; they were in an impossible situation. Gunnar beckoned to Torsten and Finn to come to where he was sitting alone on the hold cover. He addressed them in lowered tones.

'If we give in to this bunch of ruffians, I think we will all get our throats cut.'

'But it doesn't look as if the crew are up for a fight with them, and the three of us can't take them on alone,' said Finn.

'We might if we could surprise them in some way and attack when they don't expect it,' answered Gunnar.

'What about at night?' asked Torsten.

'Yes, that would be the best time, but how do we arrange it? If we hand over the cargo this afternoon then we could all be dead by this evening anyway. There has to be some way of delaying satisfying their demands until tomorrow.'

Gunnar called across to where Leif was discussing the situation with Gudmar.

'Well, we didn't travel this far to get killed by a bunch of piratical savages. I have an idea.'

'It had better be good,' said Leif, 'because they will be back this afternoon.'

'Do you have any more of the wine which we drank in harbour?'

'Yes, about half a barrel.'

'And you have beer?'

'Yes, we keep a barrel of beer in case the water goes sour. It's our reserve for emergencies.'

'Right, tonight you are going to have a feast with the savages.'

'Are you out of your mind?' asked Leif.

'When they come back this afternoon, tell them that we will unload the ship tomorrow morning, but tonight we will come to their camp with beer to show our friendship. It seems that only Torsten, Finn and I can use a bow to any effect, so we're not coming to the party. You can tell them that we're doing jobs on the boat. They will be suspicious that we're trying to poison them so let them see you take a drink of wine and beer. Then leave off, and let them drink as much as possible, then wander off back to the ship.'

'So, what will you be doing Gunnar?' asked Leif.

Gunnar remembered his mother's words as they watched the fire at Floga.

'Fire is a good servant, but bad master. We are going to take a keg of seal oil and while you are keeping them occupied we will douse the side of the tents where they can't see us. Each of us will set fire to a tent; hopefully they will be inside at least one of them. If we hold ourselves back in the darkness while they're silhouetted against the fire we should be able to account for a few of them. When the panic breaks out, two of you run over to the log barrier and

cut the rope holding the end to the shore and then run for
it. The rest of you get back the ship fast, raise the anchor,
man the oars and hold the vessel as close to the land as
possible for us to climb on when we've finished our work.'

'You must be mad,' said Leif. 'If we fail we will be in
a worse situation than before. They may kill us.' He was
resentful of Gunnar taking the initiative, but felt helpless, as
he did not have any suggestion to come up with.

'Face it, they're probably going to kill us anyway, once
they have the cargo. This boat might be very useful for
them,' Gunnar replied. 'Has anyone got a better idea?'

'I say we give them the cargo,' mumbled Ahl.

Leif spoke quietly. 'Gunnar is right. If they slaughter us
and take the ship, no one will ever know what happened to
us. We could have been lost in a storm or stolen the ship
and the cargo and gone to another port.'

There was silence while they all pondered these words.

'It looks as if our only chance is to trick them in some
way, we can't fight them on equal terms,' said Botvid.

'Right,' said Leif. 'Let's see if they fall for the bait when
they come round this afternoon.'

Heads were nodding, though thoughts were turning to
the dangerous nature of their proposed evening activity.

Chapter 7
First Blood

'Well captain, will you start to unload your cargo for us?'

Halfway through the afternoon, the gang had returned to the ship and were standing in the same place as before. Their attitude was so confident that it was clear they were totally unafraid that the crew might attack them.

'It's late now, we will unload tomorrow morning. Do I have your guarantee that you will not harm the crew and that we can sail away unhindered?'

'Of course captain. But why don't we start unloading now?'

'We thought that we would have a drink with you. We have beer and wine with us.'

Whoops of delight went up from the scruffy warriors on the shore.

'We have a few things to do to the ship to get ready to leave tomorrow. Later we will bring the beer and the wine over to your camp,' said Leif.

'Come as soon as you can then,' replied the gang leader.

After they had left Gunnar said, 'So far, so good.'

'Can you explain when we should cut the barrier?' said Ahl.

'It's difficult to say, but the idea is that when the gang are distracted by the fire and by being shot at, the rope should be cut. Who is going to do it?'

'I think that Ahl and Botvid should. They are younger and can move faster to get back to the ship without delaying us,' said Leif.

The crew manhandled the barrels over the side and into the water, then pulled them ashore. Three of them carried the beer barrel and two the wine. In a while, as darkness was falling, the three brothers could hear sounds of merriment from the encampment and see figures moving around the camp fire. Each of the three filled their quivers with arrows and prepared to go ashore.

'All ready boys? Have you got your tinder and flints?' asked Gunnar. 'I'm taking a hand axe with me. Let's go.'

They carefully carried the keg of seal oil and handed it to Finn who was standing thigh deep in the water. As quietly as possible they walked around the bay and keeping low sneaked behind the tents, each hiding as best he could. They had a very anxious wait as the crew were staying too long, much longer than they had agreed. They had to be out of the way before the tents were set on fire. Gunnar scurried from tent to tent, coating the greased woollen material with the oil.

One of the gang left the camp fire and walked past where Finn was hiding. He had not seen him and walked on a few paces. He started to relieve himself. Gunnar saw his chance. Before the man could react, Gunnar plunged the hand axe into the back of his skull. The man collapsed with a thud.

Gunnar whispered to the others, 'We have to get started, they may miss him. The crew will just have to run when the flames start.'

Each of them started striking their flints against the back edges of their knives. Finn's tinder was quickly alight. He put the flame against the oil and it flared immediately. The other two brothers were trying desperately to get a light, but with no success. They saw some figures leaving the party and dashing off in the direction of the boat. There was no time for Gunnar and Torsten to continue with the flints. They ran back out of the light from the flames and joined Finn.

'Spread out, so they can't detect where the arrows are coming from, and start firing!' commanded Gunnar.

The element of surprise was in their favour, but not as complete as they had hoped, since only one tent was on fire. In the camp firelight, they could see that one of the crew was struggling to free himself from the gang. Several of the gang were trying to beat the flames on the tent and presented a fine target. The brothers fired almost simultaneously. There were loud screams as two of the gang fell. As and when a figure could be seen silhouetted, they loosed off more arrows.

Finn was trembling with excitement and fear. He was closest to the camp fire, but realised that if he fired at the group still struggling with the crew member he might kill one of their own. He needed to get closer. As he walked closer to the burning tent he noticed two more of those trying to save the tent fall, as Gunnar and Torsten continued firing. He saw one of the gang running out into the dark in his direction with a sword – had he been spotted? The man was screaming curses and heading directly towards where Finn was standing. It was easy shooting at anonymous figures silhouetted against the fire; he wasn't even sure if he hit anyone, but here coming towards him was a man he could see clearly in outline and whose features would soon be clear. Flesh and blood and real. He remembered the bear and how difficult it had been to take a life. He could turn and run or fight the man. He had no chance against the sword; he must fire. He drew back the bow and hesitated a few seconds; if he missed he had no chance. The bear had been a slow-moving target, this man was bounding towards him over the uneven ground. And there he was, sword raised with both hands, almost as close as the bear had been, when Finn fired. There was a scream as the man took the arrow just below his right shoulder and dropped the sword. He stumbled and fell at Finn's feet. Finn dropped his bow and grabbed the man's sword. He brought the blade down heavily on the man's head, picked up his bow and stood trembling with shock. He became aware that Gunnar was calling his name.

He ran in the direction of his brother's voice and found him crouching with his bow.

'Where the hell have you been?'

'I wanted to see if we could free the crew member.'

'No chance. I guess that it's old man Gudmar, he was just too slow. I hope they've cut the barrier loose. We must get back fast before this lot recover enough to get organised. We must have killed or wounded at least half of them.'

'Where's Torsten?'

'He'll have to look after himself. He knows the plan.'

They ran off around the bay. The ship was lying as instructed with its stern within wading distance of the shore. As they arrived they saw the figure of Torsten in front of them, wading to the boat. The crew pulled them aboard.

'The barrier is cut. We're waiting for Gudmar,' said Leif.

'We saw someone was trying to escape, but the gang were struggling with him.'

'That must be him. We can't leave without him,' said Leif.

'We have to, we all took our chances, and he was too slow. Let's go before they discover what's happened to the barrier. Now! Row!' shouted Gunnar.

'I am the captain of this ship and I give the orders. Stand by your oars.'

'You fool, you'll get us all killed!' bawled Gunnar.

'We wait,' said Leif.

Gunnar leapt across the after-deck and swung a heavy

punch on Leif's cheek. The man collapsed to the deck. Gunnar took the hand axe from his belt and shouted, 'Row or I split his skull!'

Ahl, Botvid and Einar grabbed their oars and Finn grabbed the fourth one to balance the rowing. The crew needed no second bidding and pulled quickly away towards the entrance to the bay which they could clearly see in the starlight. Gunnar steered, the axe in one hand and the steering oar in the other. As they got closer they could see the obstruction was still there, but the severed end had floated slightly seawards in the weak current. As they got level with the barrier they could hear shouts from the encampment and an arrow thudded harmlessly on the hull. Among the shouts they could hear a voice they recognised. 'Leif, Leif wait for me! Aghh!' And then they heard it no more.

The ship struck the barrier and slowed down as they pushed against the logs. Gunnar shouted, 'Pull, pull, we are nearly out!'

The end of the log barrier was moved out further and further until it slid along the port side and the boat started moving more quickly. Leif sat up and spoke.

'And just what do you intend to do now in shallow water with rocks and skerries all around?'

'Captain, I intend to hand the ship's command back to you. I am sorry about the punch,' said Gunnar.

'It won't be forgotten, or forgiven. Take her out slowly. Einar, take soundings. When we're out of bowshot, we anchor until morning.'

Einar stood in the bows feeling the knots on the sounding line, the only way to judge the depth of the sea under them in the dark.

The crew were deep in their own individual thoughts. Every man was coming to terms in his own way with the violent happenings of the evening. None less so than

Finn, who was justifying in his own mind the killing of his adversary. Gunnar, who was not given normally to deep thought, was mulling over the fact that this evening he had saved the ship, most of the crew and his brothers, but that he had made a very dangerous enemy. Leif's words to him had been full of menace.

As dawn broke the next morning, the crew and the brothers found themselves looking over to the entrance to the bay which they had left so dramatically the night before. They breakfasted and then Leif gave the order, 'We row slowly back to the inlet to see if we can rescue Gudmar.'

As they approached the inlet they saw that a pole had been erected on the seaward side of the encampment. On top of the pole was a head; they all knew whose it was.

Leif steered the ship out to sea. The wind was blowing gently from the north-west. 'Soundings, Einar. Stand by to raise the sail.'

They set off south with a fair wind which held for two days. Whenever the sun appeared Gunnar had seen Leif using a triangular board which he held vertically in the direction of the sun.

'What are you doing?' he enquired.

'When we left the land channel I measured how high the sun was at midday. Now if I can take the measurement around midday I can see how far south we are and if it is time for us to head inland on the channel to Sigtuna.'

The time must have been right, for Leif gave the order for the ship to remain on the starboard tack and to head for a large group of islands to the west. As they travelled, the islands they passed became bigger until it was clear that on one side there was a large land mass. As night fell, he gave the order for them to drop anchor in a place he seemed familiar with.

Finn asked Ahl where they were.

'This is the main channel up to the great lake which

112

leads to Sigtuna. With a good wind we will reach home tomorrow.'

At first light, they used the north-east wind to sail further westwards. Here and there they saw small boats with fishermen laying nets. Smoke rising from some islands betrayed the fact that there were small settlements. Just after midday they reached a narrow channel and lost the wind. The sail was lowered and they started to row.

'Stand by with the mooring lines!' shouted Leif.

As they glided onto a quay, the starboard side rowers shipped their oars. Einar and Ahl threw their lines to two men waiting on the land.

'What is your business and where are you bound?' called one of the men.

'We are subjects of King Erik arrived from the north country with trading goods.'

'What is this place?' Gunnar asked Leif.

'This is the place of poles, *staket*. Here the channel runs between those two hills which are defended by King Erik's men. The waterway is made narrower by the poles standing in the water. All ships are checked here before permission is given for them to proceed. This is the only way to Sigtuna, so *staket* prevents enemies making a surprise attack.'

One of the guards came aboard the ship. Botvid and Ahl untied the cover on the cargo hold and lifted it for the guards to see what they were carrying. They moved some bales and looked underneath them.

'How many crew did you sail with?' asked one of the guards.

'Seven, same number we have now,' replied Leif.

'Where are you bound?'

'The old harbour at Sigtuna.'

'Ships are forbidden to use it now. You must sail into the new town. King Erik's orders.'

'But my men live in the old town.'

113

'Not for much longer they won't; the king is going to force everyone to move.'

There were some moans from the crew, but they were careful not to argue with these men, who could delay their departure.

'Cast off, you have permission to go through the channel,' said the guard.

They pushed off from the jetty and the crew manned the oars. They pulled out into the channel and continued as it gradually got wider until their way was apparently blocked by a spit of land stretching across in front of them. Leif steered to starboard and they rounded it through more narrows. Ahead of them was a wide opening to starboard between the land and an island, but Leif ignored it and swung the boat to port into a very narrow channel. He saw Gunnar looking surprised.

Leif pointed to the shallows. 'That's a nasty shock for any strangers trying to get to Sigtuna. The opening to starboard hides submerged rocks which will tear the bottom out of any craft moving at speed.'

The channel they now entered was even narrower than *staket* and bowmen could be seen on the land side guarding the fairway which led to Sigtuna. The oarsmen continued through the narrow waterway and then Leif decided to use the north-easterly wind to speed their journey. They sailed for an hour and then, rounding the bend to port, the brothers could see across the bay a mass of wooden houses stretching along the coast in front of them. As they got closer they could make out that they were looking at the back of the houses. Each one had a garden running down to the shore side, many with fences between them. Behind the houses, up the slope, there were more houses facing in the other direction. There seemed to be a long straight street between the two rows of wooden buildings. Everywhere they looked there was activity. There were pigs and other livestock in many of the gardens, children playing, builders working on some of the houses, horses and carts going up and down the access road to the town.

The ship rounded a point with a small hill, on which was a huge wooden structure, the biggest the brothers had ever seen. They stared in wonderment.

'That is the king's mansion,' said Leif.

On the other side of the point, they dropped the sail and started rowing in to the town quay. Their arrival had been seen by the town's merchants. Theirs was the first ship this year to arrive back in harbour after a trading voyage and there was much jostling among the well-dressed traders hungry to do business. As soon as they had berthed, a middle-aged man jumped on board. He was wearing a fine tunic, long leather boots into which were tucked the legs of his trousers and a hat of beaver skin.

'That's the ship's owner,' whispered Ahl to Gunnar.

'Well Leif, what have we got?' the man said as he clapped the captain on the back.

Leif threw back the covers from the cargo hold to reveal the barrels, packs of furs and walrus tusks. A gasp went up from the spectators on the jetty who were precariously craning over the ship's side to get a look at the goods on offer.

'Here's the inventory, master,' said Leif.

The owner scrutinised a wooden board on which Leif had carved notches and scraped signs indicating various types of cargo. He beamed as he ran his finger down the list. He looked up and noticed Finn.

'Have you got some new crew?' he asked.

'We lost some men. I'll explain what happened when we get ashore, but the good news for you is that you won't have to pay the new crew. They have worked their passage.'

The owner looked at the three brothers and said, 'You don't sign off until the cargo is in my store. Let's get unloaded before dark.'

The crew started to unpack the hold and together with some stevedores used barrows to move the goods into store. No one noticed that Leif was not helping, indeed that he was not on the ship, until he arrived on the quay with six armed men.

'Those are the three!' he shouted, pointing at the brothers. The armed men first grabbed Finn and then made towards Gunnar. He put the pack of furs he was carrying down and looked round desperately for a means of escape. Behind him was the sea, each side was blocked by onlookers. He aimed a punch at the first of the men who tried to grab him, but the man was too quick and dodged deftly, drawing a large knife from his belt. Gunnar saw that resistance was useless and raised his hands to his shoulders to indicate that he was not going to draw his knife.

Torsten, too, saw that he had no chance of escape and allowed himself to have his hands bound. The three of them were stood in a line.

'Leif, what is this?' screamed Torsten.

'I am charging you in the people's court, the Ting, with the murder of Ragnar and Ivar and with mutiny on my ship.'

The three were roped together and dragged through the main street, which separated the rows of houses they had seen from the sea, to the large building on the hill. The guards opened a door at the back of the building and dragged the brothers down some wooden steps into a dark cellar room.

'I hope that you are comfortable,' scoffed one of the guards as the brothers were bundled into the room. Finn, the last one, was shoved in unceremoniously. The door was slammed behind them as the guards left.

Part 2

The Southlands and Beyond

Chapter 8
The Hammer of Thor

The brothers spent a miserable night in the cold cell. They were able to undo the ropes which bound each other's hands, but when they attempted to sleep on the straw-covered floor, the noise of the rats scavenging and the snores of another prisoner in an adjacent cell kept them awake and gave them plenty of time to consider their position. It was not long before the recriminations began. It was an indication of the severity of their situation that Torsten and Finn dared to question their elder brother's actions.

'By the devil Gunnar, you have got us into a mess here. Why the hell did you hit Leif? You humiliated him in front of his crew. Did you really expect him to let you get away with that?' asked Torsten.

'Think, Torsten! If we had not left that bay quickly, we would probably be floating in the sea now with our throats cut.'

'And why does Leif think that we had anything to do with the death of Ivar and Ragnar? He said himself that they had drowned,' asked Finn.

Finn had gained in confidence since they had left Floga. He had also gained in strength. The rigours of their long journey to the coast, the forestry work and the hours of rowing had done much to improve his physique and his many experiences had made him surer of himself.

'There is no way Leif can connect us to the death of those two. The sea killed them,' Gunnar answered.

Torsten was prepared to let Finn believe this half-truth and said no more, although he was tempted to mention Gunnar's carelessness in taking the dice on board.

At daybreak, there was some light coming through a small window high up in the wall and they could see their surroundings. The wooden cell walls were scratched with bleak graffiti. A cartoon-like figure depicted a beheading, another showed a skull being smashed by a hammer. On one wall there was a series of marks which seemed to indicate the number of days a prisoner had been in the cell. The marks started strong and deep and became progress- ively weaker, until after about twenty they terminated. The window faced east and they could tell that the morning was well advanced when they heard the rattling of a metal catch and light streamed in from the door to the outside of the building.

'Time for your banquet,' the gaoler joked. He pushed a loaf of bread under the wooden door and passed Finn a small wooden pitcher of water carefully through the bars in the upper part of the door.

'The Ting is gathering this afternoon. If they decide to execute you, then this will be a waste of bread and water!' he quipped, and then moved on to the next cell where he said to the prisoner, 'And you, you thieving sod, don't need food, because the king has turned down your plea for mercy.'

'A pox on all of you!' exclaimed the prisoner, and spat at the gaoler. It was clear from the way he spoke that he was a foreigner.

Gunnar called out to the gaoler, 'What is this Ting?'

The gaoler came back to stand outside their cell. 'Where

have you been living, on the moon? To judge by the way you speak the language, you could have been.'

The northerners had been aware that their manner of speech was different from that of the sailors and some jokes had been made about it, but they had no trouble understanding or being understood. Of more concern to them was that they felt foolish not understanding many of the institutions and concepts of the southerners.

The gaoler, full of his own importance, continued. 'This country is run by King Erik. His kingdom stretches to the coast, up country past the town of East Aros, inland past West Aros, and way down south to the Land of the Danes and Raunrike. Once he was friendly with the Danes, but now they constantly fight about where the border is.'

'Is the king in this building?' asked Gunnar.

'Yes, you might see him later; he likes to inspect the progress on his new capital – and beware any worker who is not busy. They could end up in here.'

'Does he go to the Ting?'

'What him? No, he leaves justice to his stewards, chieftains and the freemen. Whenever he's in town, the chieftains come in from their country estates and stay in their houses in Sigtuna. He only gets involved if someone pleads for mercy, but little good does it do them!'

Torsten interrupted, 'Who are the freemen?'

'They are citizens with rights, like me. Some slaves who become favourites of their masters become freemen too. A freeman must have arms so that the king can call on them to help defend the town. Look, there are three levels of society here. Slaves, who belong to freemen or chieftains, or of course to the king, then above them are the freemen, and then the chieftains. There are big chieftains with great estates the king has given them and small ones who may just own a big farm. At the Ting meeting, the king's steward or the most powerful chieftain available will preside and all the others are minor chieftains or freemen who have been chosen as members. Of course, some of the freemen are fat, important and wealthy, some of them are warriors too, but most are ordinary people full of their own importance.'

The gaoler spat on the floor. They were not sure if he did so of necessity or as a mark of his view of the Ting.

'Enjoy your food!' he said scathingly. 'It might be your last meal.'

After he had gone, Gunnar broke the loaf into three pieces of as equal a size as he could. The fact that the loaf was stale made this difficult. They ate their portions and spent some time discussing what the gaoler had told them.

The time passed slowly. They tried to converse with the other prisoner, but he had little language and they had trouble understanding him. After some time, they understood that he was a slave from the eastlands; he had been captured by the Rus and sold to a builder in Sigtuna. He seemed to call the people who lived in Sigtuna the 'Rus'. But they could not discover why he was in the gaol.

The sun was on the other side of the building when they heard the outside door open. Six armed men squeezed into the corridor outside the cell.

'Out you come. You first,' they said to Finn. They grabbed his hands and tied them with some kind of raffia. Next came Torsten and then Gunnar.

One of the guards gave Gunnar a push in the back which was the signal for them to leave and go through the door. Although it was the end of the day, the light was blinding. They were pushed down the slope towards the main street of the town. It was surfaced with planks and was a hive of activity. The street was marked with hurdles running on both sides, the whole length except at the corner of each small street crossing the main one. Behind the hurdles there were workers engaged in all manner of handicrafts. As the brothers were marched along they saw small artisans' workshops. There were carpenters busy with tools the like of which they had never seen before, shaping timbers for furniture or details of houses, a blacksmith with the type of small forge with which they were familiar, another forge which was being used to heat glass for bead-making and some weaving looms which were taller than the women working them. The houses themselves were of two types. Some were constructed from horizontal timber logs, such as they had had at Floga, and others had smooth walls which looked as if mud had been spread out evenly to cover the woodwork. Some had wooden roofs, but most had earth and grass covering them. Some of the houses were still being built or altered to suit the owners' needs.

As they passed, people looked up at them enquiringly before resuming their work. They passed several men on horseback, dogs, cats and even one pig being guided along the street by a boy with a stick. They came to a corner and on their left was a large open square with round cobble-stones where some traders were selling goods. At the back of the square was a bigger building of a different type of construction. Here the timbers were vertical and the roof was made of wooden tiles. On the roof was a carved dragon's head peering down at those who entered the single door in the middle of the long wall.

The guards stopped and one of them went into the building. He soon came out. 'We have to wait a while, the king's steward is busy,' he announced.

The brothers surveyed in detail the amazing town they found themselves in. On one side of the square there was a group of warriors, all dressed in the same type of grey cloak, each with a metal clasp at the neck, and tight-fitting trousers. They wore a belt round a tunic under the cloak, on which a sword hung. They were standing with wooden beer mugs in their hands, talking loudly to each other. On the other side of the square a group of slaves were digging a drainage trench under the supervision of an armed guard. Merchants were calling out to the crowd, trying to sell their goods. What really caught the northerners' attention and reminded them of their far-away home was a small metal caster's workshop. The metalworker was pouring bronze into a mould in his forge. In front of him were displayed bronze brooches which were for sale. They also saw, standing by the side of the large building, a thick pole, to which were tied two men with raw sores on their bare backs.

Suddenly the door to the building opened and a woman, hands tied, was dragged out screaming followed by a man with a long whip. She was tied to the pole next to the men. The brothers realised what had caused the cuts on the other men's backs.

'Come on, in you go,' commanded a guard.

They were shoved through the door one by one. Inside, by the light of many candles, they saw a formidable audience. At the end of the room on a raised platform sat an elderly man dressed in fine robes, wearing a large silver pendant. In front of him, on the table, were some small wooden figures. On either side of him there was a guard with a spear in his hand and a sword on his belt. They were dressed in the same fashion as the soldiers they had seen outside.

Around the room there were tables, each with a bench on the far side. On the benches closest to the guards, there were wealthy-looking men, each with a tankard in front of them. At each successive table running down the room, past them and behind them, the occupants of the benches looked decidedly less well dressed. Looking behind, Gunnar could see that at the tables furthest away from the front the men were simply dressed, indeed some looked very untidy and scruffy.

The walls were decorated with shields with different

motifs, probably the marks of different chieftains owing fealty to the king, thought Gunnar.

'Who are these men?' asked the king's steward.

Gunnar was about to answer, when a figure they recognised stepped forward from the shadows.

'They are peasant ironworkers from the north country,' said Leif.

'And what is their crime?'

'I charge them with killing two of my crew by drowning them. Further, that the man Gunnar led a mutiny on my ship and struck me a blow.'

There were gasps from the onlookers and a babble of comments.

'Silence! In the case of the killings, what proof do you have?'

'I have taken these two dice from the belt of Gunnar. They belonged to one of my crew, a kinsman of mine, one Ragnar.'

'Gunnar, how came you by these dice?'

'I found them in the mud outside of our tent, sir.'

'Which god do you sacrifice to?' asked the steward.

Gunnar was fooled by the unexpected question, but quickly collected himself and said, 'Odin the god of wisdom, sir.'

'Step forward and take the god Odin in your hand.'

Gunnar walked forward to the table. The guards readied themselves in case he should be unwise enough to defy the authority of the steward. There were several wooden sculptures in front of the steward. He recognised the one representing Odin by the two ravens, one on each shoulder. These were Hugin and Munin who roamed the world and brought back wisdom to Odin. He took the wooden figure given to him.

'Do you swear by the god in your hand that you found these dice in the mud, recognising that if you lie, then Odin will smite you and take away your strength so that you will be at the mercy of your enemies and grave illnesses?'

'I do, my lord.'

The crowd once more broke into muttering and gossip.

'Silence! Return to your place. What other evidence do you have that these three murdered your comrades?'

'The man Finn had a beaten face when he came onto my ship.'

'What proof is that? Have you never heard of brothers fighting with each other?' said the steward.

'Men of the Ting, are these men guilty of the murder as accused?'

There was a roar of 'No!' from the benches.

'And what of the mutiny, captain?'

'We were in a bay in the wild country up the coast and were held prisoner by pirates. When we managed to trick the pirates into letting us go, the accused brothers refused to let me wait for one of my crew who was held captive. Gunnar struck me and issued orders to leave.'

There were gasps of shock from around the room and a general hubbub of conversation. At the same time Gunnar shouted, 'Tell them how we tricked the pirates!'

'Silence!' shouted the steward, ignoring Gunnar's comment.

'Gunnar, is this true, did you hit Captain Leif?'

'Yes, my lord, but ...'

'No, no, I ask for no excuses. No matter what your reason in doing so, you admit to committing an act of mutiny.'

'But my Lord ...'

'Silence! What say you, Tingsmen?'

One of the men near the steward's table stood up.

'The northerner has admitted mutiny. This is an act where the perpetrator must be punished by death.'

There was uproar around the benches and shouts of agreement. Finn looked across at Gunnar and urged him

126

on. 'Tell them if we had not risked our lives, the ship would never have got free.'

'Gunnar, have you anything to say?' said the steward.

'My lord, we are three skilled ironworkers who wanted nothing more than to come to the southlands to serve King Erik. We have much to offer. But if you decide that I must die, at least show mercy to my brothers who had nothing to do with the so-called mutiny. Let me explain what happened.'

'Enough! I have heard enough!' barked the steward.

'But hear me out,' pleaded Gunnar.

The steward held up his hand. 'I said I have heard enough.'

There was silence in the room while the steward scratched his beard and gazed at the floor. He looked up.

'The town has few enough men, especially in the summer while the Viking are in the eastlands. Here we have three strong men with skills which are badly needed by the king.' He paused, scratching his beard again and gazing at the same spot on the floor. His head quickly jerked up.

'Captain, in compensation for the humiliation you have suffered, I give you these three men to be your slaves. But in the name of the king I command you to sell them to me at a price of one piece of silver each, this being a fair price.'

Once more the men on the benches turned to each other and exchanged comments.

'Silence! You three northerners shall be taken from here to the king's estate to work in the iron foundry and the charcoal burners. You will be branded as slaves with the mark of the makers of iron – the cross hammer, the hammer of Thor. Take them away!'

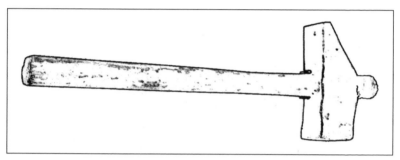

Outline drawing of a Viking blacksmith's iron hammer, discovered in
Mästermyr, Sweden, in 1936.

Chapter 9
Slaves in Sigtuna

The three brothers were marched back through the streets by the guards towards the king's mansion. They passed it on their left and saw that behind it there were several long buildings outside of which there were warriors training. They understood that this must be the garrison of the town. Soon, they found themselves walking along a deeply rutted cart track which had obviously been used often by heavy wagons. Still in sight of the mansion, they arrived at a small settlement with two long, low and windowless buildings. Women were milling around outside one building and men around the other.

Smoke rose from behind the buildings and they soon saw why. There were several charcoal-burning clamps. These were circular ovens, perhaps ten paces across. Inside the clay-covered humps, wood was charred at a slow controlled rate around a central fire, to produce charcoal. No other combustible material than charcoal could produce the intense heat required to forge metals.

'This is on a very different scale to Floga,' said Torsten.

'Father would love to see this,' added Finn.

Gunnar was silent. The decision of the Ting to put the three of them into slavery angered him immensely and he was hugely resentful of the fact that he had not been permitted to explain their part in saving the ship and most of the crew.

They were directed to the building with the men outside. 'Here my lads, this is your new home.'

They were pushed through the door. The building was lined with rows of wooden beds. If they had counted them they would have seen that there were twenty of the roughly-hewn bed frames and beside each of which were piles of clothes, presumably the property of whoever slept in each bed. A rough-looking man in a worn tunic with cruel features looked them up and down.

'What have we here then?' he snarled at the guards.

'Slavemaster, by order of the king's steward, they are to work in the iron foundry or with the charcoal clamps. They must have the hammer mark. Look after them, the king has paid three pieces of silver for these creatures!' joked the guard.

'What language do they speak?'

'Roughly the same as you and me,' said the guard.

'That makes a change, almost all the other slaves are from the eastlands.'

The guard took out his knife and cut the bindings on the brothers' wrists. They stretched their stiff hands and arms which were painful after being tied for most of the day.

'Right, slaves, the rules are simple. You get food at day-break and again in the evening. In the summer we stop work for a drink of water in the middle of the day. Any fighting gets you a whipping and time in the town gaol. Any thieving gets you a spear in the chest. If you try to run away, we have slower ways of killing you. Understand?'

The brothers nodded. They were led to the far end of the building. The weather had been warm and it seemed that every stench which humans could produce prevailed in the house. The ends of the building had least ventilation.

'As you prove your worth to the king, you get a chance to

move to beds nearer the door, where there is more air,' said the slavemaster. Looking at Finn, he pointed. 'Here, you take that bed, and you two take the ones over there. The previous occupants left us in a hurry this morning; you may have seen them in the market square.'

'When do we eat?' asked Torsten.

'When all the working parties are back, at sundown. You can get water for drinking and washing at the well at the front.'

The three brothers sat on Finn's bed and looked around at their new quarters. Two men walked into the building and walked down to where the brothers were sitting. One spoke, but he was using a language they did not understand. The two looked disappointed; it seemed that they had hoped to find that the new slaves were from whatever country they had lived in.

The brothers were surprised that the two men had been quite well-dressed, though they were dirty from whatever they had been doing during the day. Gunnar walked back to the door and saw the slavemaster there.

'Are those two slaves?'

'Yes, why do you want to know?'

'They have some kind of uniform.'

'Everyone starts with a uniform here. In the summer, trousers and a shirt and in the winter you get a cloak. You will get your clothes tomorrow.'

The brothers went outside and saw that some of the women from the other house were laying food on the long table in front of the men's building. The women too had some form of similar dress. Most of them had a white shirt, a long skirt and an apron.

The northerners were ravenously hungry now and watched the food preparation with great interest. Men started appearing from different directions; some came along the cart track, some, covered in black dust, from the direction of the charcoal clamps, and some came in from the forest carrying tools and ropes. The latter had a guard with them, but the majority were unsupervised. There was much activity around the well as they washed and took the chance of a drink. Those who lingered longest were shoved out of the way by others who were waiting.

Just before it got dark, they all sat down around the tables. Some showed interest in the newcomers, but their main concern was the food which was placed in the middle of the table in surprising quantities. It was clear that many of the men did not understand each other's languages and tended to sit together with others from the same country. Their appearance also betrayed the fact that they came from different parts of the world. One group was fairly short with dark skin and black hair; some had high cheekbones similar to the Sami; a few of them were tall and fairhaired. There was no fighting for food; everyone had plenty of meat and bread and each had a wooden tankard with weak ale which was poured out by the girls serving at table.

'This is too good to be true,' said Finn. 'We can eat as much as we want.'

'It's certainly better than I had expected,' answered Gunnar.

Later, the men filed into the house. Some went straight to their beds and others sat around talking to each other. Several came over to talk to the brothers, but only one could speak a little of their language – he was one of the tall, fair-haired men. He introduced himself as Siward.

'Where are you from?' he asked.

'We come from the north country,' answered Finn.

'What have you done to displease the king? You are of his own country.'

'We have been treated unfairly.'

'Yes, everyone could say that. In my case I am here because I am not one of the Rus.'

'Who are the Rus?' asked Finn.

'It's what the slaves from the eastlands call the citizens of this country.'

'Where are you from?'

'I am a Frisian sailor. I was captured when wild men from Daneland attacked my village. They sold me to a Rus merchant who sold me to the king. I have been here for five summers.'

'What do you do here?'

'I work in the shipyard building the king's ships. It is good work, at least in the summer it is.'

'You are treated well?' asked Gunnar.

'Oh yes, a master is judged by his peers on the quality and appearance of his slaves. And remember, slaves are valuable. We get good food and plenty of it, and you won't see any of the king's slaves wearing rags. You are lucky that you were bought by the king and not a poor freeman.'

There was a shout from the doorway. A loud voice commanded all men to go to their own beds.

Siward whispered, 'That is one of the night guards. Two of them stay in here all night to make sure that there are no fights. Some of the eastlanders hate each other and they will not be happy that you of the Rus are here either. Sleep with one eye open!'

By daybreak the slaves were shuffling out to use the latrines and to wash before breakfast. Finn had Magyar slaves sleeping on either side of him while the other brothers were side by side at the end of the building. The night had been uneventful and the three of them were now anxiously waiting to see what would next happen to them. They joined the others at the long table outside the building and, once more, plentiful food was brought to their table by the women. They sought out the Frisian man they had spoken to yesterday.

'How do we get a job in the shipyard?' asked Torsten.

'The slavemaster decides where you should work. Everyone starts with the charcoal burners or the forge. The charcoal workers get very dirty, you see them there.' He pointed to several men having their breakfast. 'No matter how you try it is impossible to get rid of the blackness of the soot. The forge isn't too bad. There are several ovens, each with double bellows which have to be operated all day. It is not so bad in winter when the days are short, but now, at midsummer, the work day is very long. The other job they might put you on is working with the smelting.'

'Who collects the bog iron?' asked Gunnar, anxious not to find himself doing the job he hated at Floga.

'They don't use bog iron. They use ironstone which is brought from up country on horses with baskets on each side of their backs. The stone is yellow before it is dried out and then you get a reddish powder. Terrible stuff, you get it all over you when the wind blows.'

'How do they get iron from this?'

'They fire it with charcoal in equal proportions and produce iron blooms which they can work with in the forge.'

'You northerners, come over here!' shouted the slavemaster. 'Come with me.'

The brothers followed him to a workshop at the end of the building. Three guards followed them. Pointing at Gunnar he said, 'What are you called?'

'Gunnar, son of Arvid.'

'Follow me, son of Arvid,' he commanded sarcastically.

Gunnar and the three guards went into the workshop. Inside there was another man sitting at a table with some implements in front of him.

'Take your shirt off and sit down.'

Gunnar did as he was bid and immediately the guards moved forward to hold his arms. Gunnar did not resist, realising that since he had value to his master they were

134

unlikely to do anything which would limit his capacity to work. A rope was tied around his wrists while the man who had been at the table moved forward with a bone needle. Gunnar winced as the man started to jab the needle into his upper right shoulder. The painful process continued for about a minute before the man wiped Gunnar's shoulder with a rag and then opened a wooden box containing some black powder. He dipped the rag into the powder and rubbed it fiercely into his back. After a while he stopped and washed the area of the operation.

The slavemaster gave Gunnar a bundle of clothes. 'Here are your summer work clothes. Leave your shirt off until I tell you.' The guards undid the rope and pushed Gunnar outside.

'Don't worry lads, they won't kill you,' said Gunnar to Torsten and Finn.

Torsten went through the same procedure. When he came out Finn looked pale and said quietly, 'They are not doing that to me.' He turned and started running alongside the building. The guards chased after him until he reached the breakfast table. One of the eastlander slaves stuck out his foot and Finn tripped and fell heavily to the ground. The guards were quickly on him, but he was not giving up easily and threw punches at them before he was over-powered and his hands were tied.

Finn was dragged back to the workshop, his brothers looking on helplessly. As he was pushed into the room he kicked at the slavemaster.

'Damned idiot! You don't make it easy for yourself, do you? Lay him down!'

Finn was dragged to the floor and the guards held him tightly. 'Put it on his face, over the beard,' the furious slave-master commanded the tattooist.

When Finn was released into the sunlight his right cheek was bloodied and swollen, but it was clear to see that he now bore the mark of the ironworkers, the hammer of Thor, on his cheekbone under his right eye.

'Gunnar and Torsten, you are to work with the charcoal burners. Go with the guard,' ordered the slavemaster. 'Finn, let's see how much fight you have left in you this evening after working on the smelters' bellows all day.'

The brothers were taken off to their workplaces and it was these jobs that they kept for the whole hot summer. Each evening Gunnar and Torsten returned to the slave village black from the charcoal and Finn, red from the coating of ochre from the ore dryer.

As the days and weeks passed, the northerners got to know their fellow slaves, but communication was difficult because of the fact that they spoke different languages and they knew little of the language of the country they were forced to work in. Five of them came from a country they called Wallachia. They did not mix with the slaves from Rossija, Magyar, Hrvatska or Frisia, and tended to be aggressive towards them. They were detailed to work in the forest on timber-felling together with two Rossijans, Vanja and Pasha.

As summer turned into early autumn, there was a new urgency to produce more timber. Wood was needed for ship production the following year. It could not be used green, so the ships' carpenters needed to lay up pine planks to season and dry through the winter. There was also pressure on iron production. At least 8,000 iron rivets were required to produce one longship and to forge these an amount of iron the weight of six men was required. And at the beginning of the production chain was charcoal. So, extra supplies of timber for the charcoal clamps were needed before snow seriously impeded the possibility of transporting logs out of the forest, which was usually done by small horses.

Gunnar and Torsten were pleased to be transferred from

working on the charcoal fires to increase the timber-felling work force. But they quickly found that the atmosphere among the forestry workers was soured by the attitude of the Wallachians to the others. Frequently, they jostled and pushed the others and generally asserted the fact that they were the majority. At first, Gunnar was particularly incensed by their behaviour as they picked on him to show off to their friends. The northerner was clearly the physically strongest-looking member of the team and they enjoyed trying to provoke him as a dog might bait a bear. Gunnar knew full well that if his temper got the best of him he would have to deal with five adversaries, though hopefully with the help of Torsten.

As a team they were taken out to the forest each day by two guards, shown which area to work on and then left to choose and fell young pine trees for the charcoal burners and mature trees for the shipbuilders. Sometimes the guards left them to get on with the work while they foraged for wild mushrooms and autumn berries and sometimes hunted for small game. They knew full well that the slaves would not run away; the deep forest offered no hospitality to fugitives. And the slaves knew what punishment awaited if they were caught trying to escape. When they were left to work alone, the Wallachians dictated the allocation of tasks. Frequently, they let the rest of the team do the heavy work of felling the trees while they rested or did the lighter work of log trimming.

In the sleeping quarters, the Wallachians all had their beds in one area of the house near to where the guards spent the night. Although they were noisy and frequently shouted what were presumably insults at the other residents they were careful not to invoke the displeasure of the guards. However, if at night they detected that the guards had fallen asleep, they would prowl around the building trying to steal from the other slaves.

One morning in autumn, Gunnar was using a short-handled axe to trim a tree which had just been felled. One of the Wallachians walked up to the tree and pulled back one of the branches just behind Gunnar, which was not yet cut and released it so that it flicked hard against Gunnar's back. Axe in hand he turned to the Wallachian.

Torsten leapt forward, 'No Gunnar, you kill him and that's the end for us. If these bastards don't kill us our master will.'

Gunnar glowered at the Wallachian. His landsmen were by this time behind him, one with the long-handled tree-felling axe. The man who had caused the incident undid the top of his shirt and to the northerners' astonishment he flaunted a leather necklace with three bear's claws.

'By the gods, that's Finn's isn't it?' said Torsten.

'These thieving sods must have stolen it, why hasn't Finn told us that it had been stolen?' said Gunnar. 'They are going to pay for this.'

'Yes, but not just now, Gunnar. Calm down and let's get back to work.'

Gunnar shouted a curse at the man with the necklace and went back to his work. When they returned to the slave encampment, Gunnar and Torsten waited impatiently for Finn to come back from his work. When he appeared Gunnar grabbed him by the arm.

'Show us mother's bear-claw necklace!' demanded Gunnar.

'I've lost it,' lied Finn.

'Why didn't you tell us?'

'I was going to, but I forgot.'

'Lies! It was stolen, wasn't it?' shouted Gunnar.

'Er … I was going to tell you, but I know what your temper is like and I didn't want you to get into trouble. By the gods, we only just escaped with our lives last time.'

'When was it taken?'

'Three nights ago, when the guards were asleep. The Wallachians beat me, but they were careful not to hit me where it would show.'

Finn lifted up his shirt and showed them bruising on his back and chest. By this time Vanja and Pasha had joined the brothers, and their faces indicated concern about the injuries they saw. It was not clear if this served to increase their fear of the Wallachians or to stimulate their fervour for vengeance. But on the other side of the compound they were also being observed by the perpetrators of Finn's discomfort, who were laughing and commenting loudly.

Gunnar whispered to Finn, 'Don't worry brother, we'll get your necklace back for you at a time of our choosing.'

For the moment, Gunnar was prepared to endure the taunts and humiliation of the Wallachians and to see Torsten, Pasha and Vanja suffering the same treatment.

Autumn ended abruptly with an early first fall of snow. The snow was being driven by a cold east wind which twisted and contorted the tops of the pines where the timber workers were labouring. The guards had gone off into the forest with their bows in the hope of finding game. The Wallachians had built a makeshift shelter with branches trimmed from the felled trees and were sheltering in it. Gunnar and his three companions were selecting their next tree to fell. There was a fine full-grown pine of the type the shipbuilders required, about fifteen paces directly to windward from where their unwilling work companions were sheltering.

Gunnar saw his chance and without speaking indicated to Torsten what he had in mind. Pasha and Vanja quickly understood the strategy. Gunnar took a long-handled axe and heaved it into the side of the trunk facing the snow shelter. Torsten stood on the other side of the tree and as Gunnar detached his axe, he swung his into the cut.

Gunnar continued in a frenzy while Pasha and Vanja took it in turns to relieve Torsten. It was vital to complete their work before either the guards returned or one of the Wallechians looked out of the shelter.

After what seemed an eternity the wind took charge and began to bend the tree, closing the axe cut. The axemen started to widen the cut to weaken the trunk, but as they did so, one of the men in the shelter stepped out. He looked towards the tree fellers and at first did not grasp the magnitude of danger he was in. When the reality hit him he shouted to the others and leapt aside as the mighty tree groaned, and then started to lurch forward, the movement accelerating with every blast of the wind. Two of the other men in the shelter tumbled out, looked up, and totally ineffectually put their arms up across their heads to defend themselves.

The tree crashed down with a resounding thump. The sound was replaced by screams from injured men. Gunnar leapt forward, axe still in his hand, and went to investigate the remains of the shelter. It was covered by branches from the fallen pine which had hit the ground slightly to the left of the shelter. The other three joined him and started to hack off branches to access the shelter. When they had cleared enough to look inside, they saw that two of the occupants were still alive, pinned down by branches, and two appeared to be dead. The fifth, who happened to be the one with Finn's necklace, was watching nearby, completely unharmed.

'Drag that man out,' said Gunnar, pointing at one of the dead Wallachians.

Torsten, the only one who could understand what Gunnar had said, pushed Pasha and Vanja towards the recumbent body and indicated for them to cut off some more branches to permit access. They dragged the dead man back to the foot of the tree.

'Torsten, while we lift the trunk you push the body under the tree.'

Gunnar and the two Rossijans heaved at the colossal weight of the tree trunk, but they could not lift it high enough.

'Torsten, get one of the saplings we cut this morning and let's try to lever the trunk up.'

Torsten dragged the trimmed sapling to them and they lifted the trunk just enough to get the pole under. Gunnar and Torsten collected some timbers and put them under the sapling to make a fulcrum to form a lever. They tried again, this time three of them pushing the lever down. The trunk was raised about knee height and Torsten pushed the dead man underneath. They let the lever down, pinning the man under the tree.

'Give me the long axe Torsten,' said Gunnar.

Gunnar took the axe, placed it in the man's right hand and clenched his fingers over the handle.

Despite the cold, sweat was running down Gunnar's forehead. He turned to where the unharmed survivor was standing and waved at him to bid him come closer. The man, shaking with fear, stepped towards Gunnar. Gunnar put his hand out with his palm upwards. No words were necessary; the man reached for his neck and took off the necklace. Gunnar put it in his pouch.

'Let's see if we can save the two injured men,' said Torsten.

'That's right, they have had a terrible accident.'

It was while they were trimming back branches to get the two men free that the guards arrived.

'By the devil, what has happened here?' shouted one of them.

The situation was soon clear to them: the feller of the tree had misjudged the direction it would fall and he had paid for his foolishness with his life.

141

'Don't just stand there, help us to get these men free,' said Gunnar, and the guards came running over to assist.

That evening at supper, which was now taken inside the building where some beds were temporarily pushed to one side to allow the table to be erected, Gunnar and Torsten took Finn aside.

Little brother, you had better believe in this charm, it really does seem to protect the wearer, though in this case it was a pity.'

Finn had already noticed that only one of the Wallachians was at the supper table.

'Gunnar, what the hell have you done?'

'Don't worry, there will be no trouble for us, he can't speak our language.'

Finn put the necklace on self-consciously, looking across the table. Gunnar glanced round and noticed one of the serving girls was watching intently. She looked away when she was noticed. Gunnar looked back at Finn and saw that his face was almost the same colour as his hair and he realised that it was not caused by the red ochre.

Chapter 10
At War with a King

As winter progressed, the snow made work more difficult in the forest and Gunnar and Torsten were transferred to new duties at the shipyard, where many slaves from other encampments by the harbour were working on the construction of new ships. Their work involved the splitting of logs with wedges, trimming them with an axe or an adze and then cleaving and hewing the wood into planks. It was slow work; a smooth pine plank could take up to four days to produce. Finn stayed at the ironworkers' settlement and was moved to the blacksmith's forge where he was able to use some of the skills he had learnt from his father.

By the standards they were used to, the winter seemed relatively mild and the days were not as short as those at Floga. The decimation of the group of Wallachians meant that the beds were rearranged in the slaves' sleeping quarters and the brothers now occupied beds beside each other, nearer to the fresh air from the door. Other slaves had arrived to fill the empty spaces, but the brothers were no longer bothered by aggressive neighbours. The word had got around that these three were not to be trifled with.

But for all the improvements in their lifestyle, they longed for their freedom. Finn and Torsten were becoming increasingly restive and frequently complained to Gunnar.

'Soon we will have been here for a year; this is not the way we had planned to live,' commented Torsten.

'What happened to your promises that we would become rich and travel to far lands?' added Finn.

'Patience brothers, we live well here for the moment. We will leave here when the chance comes, I promise you.'

Gunnar had seen at the boatyard that there were many longships and other craft which had been pulled onto land for the winter to avoid the ice damaging the hulls. Among them was a fine-looking craft which was an exact replica of a longship, but just fifteen paces long and with oar ports for four oars on each side. The hull was painted in rich colours and at the prow was a carved raven, the symbol of Odin, ruler of Asgard, the home of Valhalla, and ritual god of wisdom and war.

As he was walking back to the slave quarters with Siward one evening he asked, 'What is that small ship?'

'It is the royal boat, the king uses it for short journeys when he visits parts of his kingdom around the lake. His royal bodyguard man the oars. It only needs a small crew.'

'Have you seen it sail?'

'Yes, of course. It's not as fast as the longships, but it's light and does not need as much wind as they do to start moving.'

Gunnar stopped and looked back at the craft. 'When do they relaunch the ships?'

'It depends on the ice, but usually two weeks before Walpurgis.'

'What is Walpurgis?'

'It is a celebration to mark the end of winter and the beginning of spring. We celebrate it in Frisia too, we are of the Christian faith. When the king was a believer in the Christian way he learnt in Denmark of a woman teacher from Britannia, Walpurga, who was a teacher of that faith. He followed the tradition of celebrating an important occasion in her life. But the celebration today is for the Norse gods, the king now sacrifices in the old way and celebrates the sacrifice of Odin, the Allfather, on the Tree of Yggdrasil.'

'What's the celebration like?'

'The king has all his chieftains at the mansion and they have a mighty feast which goes on most of the night. There are so many people that the slave women at our settlement have to help with the cooking. Even the guards in the garrison and the people of the town eat and drink to show their happiness that winter is over. Children decorate the houses with the new spring greenery at twilight. The belief is that Odin dies for an instant and all the light of the nine worlds around the Tree of Yggdrasil is extinguished. Then at midnight the light returns with dazzling brilliance. At this time the king lights a great fire to symbolise the return of light.'

'But the slaves have no celebration?'

'No, only the guards; some of them get so drunk that we start work late the next day.'

They walked on towards the slave quarters, Gunnar deep in thought.

Over the next few days, Gunnar considered and reconsidered his strategy for escaping from Sigtuna. Clearly, if they managed to elude their master, they would have to travel far to ensure they were outside his realm. There were only two options. Either they flee overland, through the forests and over the mountains to Norvegia or they cross the lake and find their way to the great sea on which they had sailed from the north.

To travel overland through the vast forests they would have to rely on providing food for themselves, something they had tried to do on their last land journey and found very precarious. The main risk after avoiding capture by the slave settlement guards would be to keep clear of the lands of chieftains loyal to the king. It would be obvious to

145

anyone who saw them that they were escaped slaves, especially as Finn had the mark on his face. And what of the people of Norvegia? Would they find themselves in slavery there instead?

The other alternative would require a boat which was big enough for them to sail on the great sea, but small enough for them to handle with a small crew. But before they reached the sea they would have to escape from the lake. Gunnar remembered how complicated the route had been from the sea to Sigtuna. And where would they sail to? Gunnar would definitely not consider going north. To go east they would follow the trading route of the king's longships and might be found by them. The only other way would be to go south to the lands of the king's enemies. What reception might they get there? They would have to somehow ingratiate themselves with the enemies of King Erik.

The days were getting longer and the thaw had set in when Gunnar decided to confide in his brothers. 'When the geese fly north, we sail south.'

'What do you mean?' said Torsten.

'I mean that the time is coming for us to leave this place.'

'How?' retorted Finn.

'We steal a boat and sail for the lands of the king's enemies.'

'You make it sound very easy. How do we do that?' scoffed Torsten.

'In a few weeks, the ships which are on land for the winter will be launched. We need a boat which is strong enough for us to sail on the great sea, but it must be one which does not need a large crew.'

'And how do we get away from here to the quay? We are watched all night by the guards.'

'Soon after the ships are launched there will be a great feast here and Siward tells me that the guards get drunk and there is great merriment in the town. Over there at the end of the building where Torsten and I first had our beds, there are holes in the wall where slaves have tried to get air; the holes are badly patched. On the night of the feast, we break open the holes and escape through them.'

'And then?'

'We run to the town and go to the quay where a boat will be waiting.'

'What boat?'

'Trust me, there will be a boat there.'

Gunnar did not want to tell them of his plan to steal the king's boat, the venture was risky enough and he was afraid that he might already have trouble persuading his brothers to take part.

'Finn, how well do you know the serving wench who keeps finding your eye?'

'None of your business, Gunnar.'

'We could arrange to take her with us if she would help us.'

'What help do we need?'

'We need food. She must steal food for us for the journey.'

Finn was silent for a few seconds. 'How would she escape?'

'It will be easy for her, they cook food here for the feast. She and the other women will have to take the food to the mansion which is very close to the quay. And the women don't usually have guards with them.'

'Gunnar, this is too fanciful! It will never work,' said Torsten. 'It depends on too many different factors.'

'Look, I don't intend to spend the rest of my life here. If you have a better plan, then I will listen to it.'

There was silence.

'What happens if we get a boat, how do we find our way out of the lake in the dark?' said Finn.

147

'Yes, that is a challenge, but if we get away quickly after dark, we should have many hours' start before we're missed. We will have time to go slowly and find the channels.'

'And what about if we get to the open sea, could the three of us and a girl sail a ship to the southlands? Never. Not possible. Remember what it was like when we sailed here. You need a crew to share the work.'

'Yes, I suppose you are right Torsten,' admitted Gunnar reluctantly. 'But what if we took Siward with us, he's a sailor. We could take Vanja and Pasha too, they're strong lads and we get on well.'

'How would you explain what you are planning? They can hardly understand anything,' quipped Finn.

'I can get through to them and I'm sure they would jump at the chance of leaving this place.'

'So, that would be six of us plus the girl?'

'Wait a minute, I'm not sure I want her to take the risk,' said Finn.

'Well, stay here with her then, but you will never get the chance to touch her!' scoffed Gunnar. 'By the gods, you two are cowards. Do you want to be slaves here for the rest of your lives?'

'It would be better than being blood-eagled in the market square. That's the punishment for escaped slaves.'

Blood eagling was an extreme form of execution where the victim's ribs were broken and spread out like blood-stained wings. And it got worse. An escaped slave had to be made an example of to deter others.

'Think about my plan, we'll talk again in a few days,' said Gunnar.

The plan was not spoken of for over a week. In the meantime Gunnar sometimes noticed Finn was furtively exchanging some words with the girl during and after mealtimes.

'Who is she, Finn? Where does she come from?'

148

'Her name is Aneka, she is from the Land of the Danes.'

'Why is she a slave?'

'She is from the borderland in the south and kin to a chieftain who owes fealty to King Harald of the Danes. Her family were captured by Erik's men.'

Gunnar had been wondering how it was that the two managed to converse with each other; now he realised that their languages were very similar. He also understood that Aneka could be of value to them in winning approval from the enemies of King Erik.

Aneka herself was a privileged slave. She had spent three years in captivity after the dark day when raiders had attacked her father's estate and burnt buildings after putting many of the inhabitants to the sword. She had been lucky to escape with her life and had only done so because the raiders knew the value of slaves in this sparsely populated country. She had been dragged away from her home and, together with some other young men and women, had been forced to walk for many days across the country through deep forests to the east coast where they had embarked on a ship to Sigtuna. Her mother had trained her well, and as a slave in the royal kitchens she had soon found favour with her mistress and she was treated well. But she longed to be free and to return to the estate on the hill from which she could see the sea to the north and the south, and far across the water, the Land of the Danes. And now there was a chance that she might do so. She enthusiastically agreed to help the three brothers with their plan and she did this not just to escape, but to be with Finn.

*

The snow lingered only in shady parts of the forest, the sunny glades were decorated with white forest anemones and the ice on the lake had broken along the shoreside when Gunnar spoke to his brothers again of their deliverance from slavery.

'Siward has told me that they will start to launch the ships tomorrow and the feast is in fourteen days.'

'Have you talked to Siward about your plan?' asked Torsten.

'No, but I think he suspects that I don't intend to stay here much longer.'

'What about Pasha and Vanja?'

'No, I don't want to risk them talking to others otherwise we might have all the slaves trying to join us or the guards might get to hear about it. I would tell them the day we intend to go. That is, if you intend to join me.'

'We are getting short of iron in the forge and I heard they are going to start lighting the charcoal clamps soon, so I expect that I might be moved back to work on that confounded job again with the ironstone. You two might get put to work on the clamps.'

'Never, not again. I'm with you, Gunnar,' said Torsten.

'And what about you, little brother? Are you going to stay here for the rest of your life just talking to your girl when the guards aren't looking?'

'Aneka wants to join us if we're going south. She has been here for three Walpurgis Eve feasts and says that there are many strangers from the islands and the country in town for the celebration. If you have cloaks, it would be possible to move unnoticed in the crowds. She takes food in baskets to the mansion with the other women and could wander through the crowds to the quay.'

'Gunnar, we are going to need more than a basket of food for a crew of six, and her too of course.' protested Torsten.

'Yes, but it would keep us going until we get through to the sea. Then we will have to fish.'

'With what?' asked Finn.

150

Gunnar fell silent. He remembered how close they had come to starvation when they had travelled from Floga to the coast.

'When we came through the sound from the great sea to the lake we passed some fishing settlements, you saw the smoke. We will steal nets.'

'Stop, stop! This is getting more and more fanciful. I don't want to hear any more. Let's just plan our escape and then take it as it comes.' Torsten was resigned to the fact that his brother was not going to be deterred, and he himself did not want to be left behind.

On the afternoon of Walpurgis Eve, Gunnar and Torsten were still working in the shipyard. As the day had progressed, the atmosphere had become more and more excited. They had seen distinguished guests arriving at the quay by boat from different parts of the lake. They were dressed in fine clothes, the like of which the two brothers had never seen, and many wore chains of office with large medallions. The guests were escorted to the mansion by servants and in some cases had bodyguards.

But there were also many of the less wealthy visiting Sigtuna. Freemen with their womenfolk rowed ashore in simple craft and made their way into the town. From the shipyard the workers could hear the playing of musical instruments; the *lur*, a long willow pipe, and sometimes panpipes could be heard above the hubbub of the crowds and the calls of street vendors.

And, to Gunnar's satisfaction, the guards were entering into the festive spirit of the occasion, standing around with wooden tankards in their hands and occasionally disappearing into a shelter from whence they reappeared with replenished drinking vessels. He decided that this was the time to tell Siward of his plan.

Siward listened intently, now and then asking questions. He was excited about the plan and agreed to join in.

However, he realised that there was a major problem.

'But there are no oars in the boat, Gunnar! When we launched it, we put the sail on board, but we didn't need oars.'

'Where can we get oars?'

'Well, the longship oars are too big. I don't know where they keep the oars for the king's boat.'

'Can you find out before tonight? The guards are not very observant this afternoon.'

'I'll try. Otherwise we will have to steal oars from several of the visitor's rowing boats, but they will be too short really.'

As they were marched back to their quarters, the guards were more loudmouthed than usual. Some broke into song, but others became aggressive and shoved the slaves with their staves.

Before supper, Gunnar met Pasha and Vanja who had just returned from the forest where tree felling had resumed. Torsten and Finn observed Gunnar gesticulating and drawing in the mud, trying to explain to the two what was afoot. They looked at each other, smiled and then turned to Gunnar and nodded with beaming faces.

Gunnar sat at supper with Siward and his brothers.

'Right, as soon as it's dark, we all creep down to the end of the building and break open the patches. Judging by the state of the guards already, they're not going to be watching us very carefully tonight.'

And so it was: the building was in darkness apart from the light of a fire outside the open door. The guards were outside, their loud conversation punctuated by raucous laughter as they commented on the women in the constant stream of basket-carriers going to and from the mansion. Occasionally there was a scream as one of the women protested about being molested.

The group of escapees had all taken their winter cloaks

and were hurrying down towards the mansion, following the route taken by the women. Gunnar and Siward had got through the hole in the wall first and arrived at the quay, which was in darkness save for the pale light of a quarter moon rising beyond the town. The music, laughter and shouting coming from the same direction indicated the fact that the festivities would continue for a long time yet.

'The oars are under the covers by that store,' said Siward.

They walked towards the store, but stopped quickly when they heard voices from inside.

'There must be some guards in there,' said Siward.

This was confirmed when the door opened and in the candlelight from within, they saw a man lurch out and with great difficulty remove enough of his trousers to relieve himself. Gunnar jumped forward and gave the man such a blow in the back of the neck that he fell straight to the ground. He grabbed the man's knife and drew it across his throat. Glancing into the store, he saw that there was one man inside with his head and arms on the table.

'He won't hear much,' said Gunnar.

They dragged back the old sails that were covering the oars and took two each.

'By the devil, these are heavy,' said Siward.

'We need six; we'll come back for the others.'

When they got back to the edge of the quay the others had arrived.

'Where the hell have you been Gunnar?' asked Torsten nervously.

'Shut up and get these in the boat.'

'Which boat?'

'This one,' indicated Gunnar.

Siward and Gunnar went back to collect two more oars and then the group climbed on board the king's ship. Aneka passed a large basket to Finn who helped her aboard. She climbed over the thwarts and sat in the stern with the food.

'Torsten, Finn, cast off and push us out.'

They had difficulty extracting the ship from the quay as several of the guests' rowing boats were crowding the area at the bow and the stern. They prodded at the other boats, cursing the people who had put them there, but eventually made enough space for the brothers and Siward to be able to use their oars to propel themselves out onto the dark lake.

Pasha and Vanja were in the way, not understanding the necessity of making space for the oarsmen to work. Gunnar got up and pushed them towards the bow, where there was a seat. As he did so, he stumbled and fell on the sail which was stored amidships, not yet attached to the mast. The heavy sail appeared to move under him. He put his hand down and immediately realised that he was putting his weight on a man's leg. There was someone asleep under the sail!

Gunnar took the knife which he had stolen from the dead guard and held it in one hand while he pulled the sail off the recumbent form below him. By the light of the moon, which by now was much brighter, he could see that the man was a warrior; he had a broadsword on his belt, a *seax* and a hand axe too.

'Torsten, give me your belt, quickly.'

'What the hell for?'

'Shut up and give it to me.'

Torsten paused in his rowing and passed Gunnar the belt. Gunnar grabbed the man's hands and wrapped the belt several times round his wrists before passing the leather through the buckle.

'What is it?' asked Finn.

'We have an unexpected passenger, must be one of the bodyguards of a chieftain, but he's as drunk as his master probably is at the moment.'

'What are you going to do with him?'

'Wait until morning; let's concentrate on getting away from here. Maybe I'll have to slit his throat and throw him to the fishes.'

By this time they were well out into the lake.

'Where now?' asked Torsten.

'We came into Sigtuna from the south-east, so that's the way we go.'

'And which way is that?' asked Finn.

Gunnar was looking up and trying to remember what Leif had told him about finding the Polaris. Eventually he found the Great Bear.

'There is the Great Bear,' he said, pointing up. They all tried to find it with varying success. 'Following the line of the last two stars, look five times the distance between those two stars beyond them and there you see Polaris. So east is over there and we follow the waterway in that direction.'

They followed the broad lake, passing two headlands before it turned south.

'Now we have to be careful when we see an island in front of us. You remember that Leif took the very narrow channel, the broad one being blocked by rocks. But we have to keep up our speed as we must get through *staket* before light. Let's hope that the guards there are celebrating too and won't see us in the moonlight.'

It was difficult to navigate and row at the same time, with their backs towards the direction of travel.

'Wait, we have to man the steering oar. Stop, lads. Pasha!'

The Rossijan reacted and came over to Gunnar who stood up and directed him to his seat. Gunnar put the oar into Pasha's hands and as far as he could in the dark without the benefit of a common language, he instructed the man how to use the oar. After a few collisions with Finn's oar being worked from behind him, the Rossijan got the technique. Gunnar went astern to the steering oar and they set off in the direction of the narrow channel.

This close to the middle of the Nordic summer, the time between sunset and sunrise was just eight hours. By the time they had reached the narrow channel between the island and the land it was three hours before sunrise. Once through the narrows they rowed faster as the moon dropped nearer the horizon and they approached *staket*. Soon, Gunnar caught sight of the gorge between the high hills on either side of *staket*. On their port side, the reddening of the sky was a portent of the beginning of a fine day.

'Quiet everyone, no talking, keep rowing slowly.'

The bound warrior started to stir and began to curse loudly. Gunnar dropped the oar and grabbed a mooring warp. He went forward to the man and wrapped it twice round his neck and across his open mouth, fastening it tightly so that the man could not make more than guttural sounds.

'Put your hoods up everyone.'

Back at the steering oar, Gunnar made for the quay, trying to avoid the side where all the poles had been placed to restrict the width of the channel. The daylight was increasing alarmingly quickly as they slid through the water just more than an oar's length from the land.

'Hellooo!' shouted a slurred voice. A guard left the cover of a shelter and started waddling down the quay towards them. He suddenly stopped and stood erect.

'What's the matter with him?' asked Finn.

'He's showing respect,' answered Gunnar. 'Pull as hard as you can, let's get going.'

Pasha's oar clashed with Finn's, not having understood the import of Gunnar's command.

'Damn it, wake up man!' shouted Finn. 'What do you mean, he's showing respect?'

'Well, he knows who is usually on board.'

'And who is that?'

'The king.'

'The king! Do you mean we have stolen the king's own boat? Are you mad?'

'Well, if we get caught, we get executed anyway so we might as well get executed for a goat as for a kid. This is the best boat for our purpose.'

'By the gods, Gunnar, we are at war with the king!' exclaimed Torsten.

They rowed in silence for a while, contemplating this news.

'When do you think they'll discover that the boat has gone?'

'At first light, same time that the guards discover that seven slaves are missing.'

Siward spoke. 'They will send longships after us, they could be here by mid-morning. They will know that we are going to the great sea and will easily catch up with us.'

'You are right, we have to find somewhere to hide,' said Gunnar.

'How can you hide a boat?' Finn retorted.

They continued rowing for a while and passed a pointed headland on their starboard side.

'They will expect us to be travelling south for the channel to the open sea. Let's see if we can fool them. There might be a good place for us on the other side of this headland.'

Gunnar steered the boat to starboard and they soon found themselves travelling north up the other side of the headland. Eventually, they entered a narrow channel about three times as wide as *staket*. There were wooded hills on both sides and no sign of a settlement. At the end of the channel, their way was blocked by a low piece of land. On the starboard side there was a tiny bay with good cover on three sides. They slowly entered the bay and found that the water was deep enough for them to go alongside the shore, almost under the overhanging trees.

157

'In the water with you, Finn. We'll throw you bow and stern lines to make off round the trees and then we take a midship line over to the other side of the inlet to hold us off the shore.'

By the time this manoeuvre was complete, the sun was high in the sky. For the first time they could see the detail of the ship. As well as a carved prow, there were other ornate details betraying the fact that this craft had been made for a person of exalted position. But what was most striking to Finn, who was ashore and could see the outside of the boat, was the colouring of the hull. The ship was bright red with patterns of yellow and blue running round the area above the waterline. Compared with the dull colouring of seasoned wood typical of other vessels this ship was very distinctive.

'Siward, take Pasha and Vanja with you and cut low branches for us to cover the boat and see if you can find a stream where we can get water. Torsten, try to get through the trees to the headland to watch for the longships and see where they go. Finn, you go with him.'

The three men took the warrior's axe and climbed ashore over the stern line while Torsten climbed over after them and joined Finn. Gunnar took the gag off the warrior.

'Who are you and what the hell are you doing?' he demanded.

'First, who are you?' said Gunnar.

'Give me a drink of water.'

'You'll have to wait, we haven't got any yet.'

'I am Hacun, bodyguard to King Erik.'

'Oh, that may shorten your life, Hacun. We are fleeing from King Erik and heading south.'

'Thanks to you bastards, I too must flee for my life. If I am caught, I will be hung for dereliction of duty. I was the guard on the boat.'

Gunnar transferred the rope to Hacun's ankles to stop

him kicking. He had already removed the man's sword and *seax* to a safe distance. He thought for a while.

'How can I be sure that I can believe you? Our lives are at stake.'

'If you mean to travel to the Land of the Danes, you will need help. I have been there before with my master, before there was war between him and Harald. What weapons do you have?'

'Your sword and axe.'

'You fool, you may have to fight your way to the sea and when there, you will be at the mercy of pirates.'

'But why would you want to go to the Land of the Danes?'

'There is nowhere else for me, thanks to you. I will offer my sword to King Harald. He will employ a man with my training and experience. Do you have food for a voyage?'

'No, we expect to steal from the fishing settlements.'

'Armed with one sword and one axe! Don't you realise that these fishermen are used to defending themselves? Some of them are warriors.'

Gunnar was glad that his brothers were not hearing this conversation. He decided to leave Hacun bound up until the others returned.

'Aneka, what food do we have?'

'Bread and pig's ribs. We must eat the meat before the sun spoils it.'

'All right, we save the bread and eat meat. Give Hacun some. Put it down in front of him, don't get too close.'

The girl nervously pushed the food along the thwart in front of where Hacun was sitting. He grabbed the meat with his tied hands and hungrily gnawed at the bone.

Soon after, the shore party returned, dragging the first batch of branches.

'We have found water, but we have nothing to put it in.'

Hacun looked up. 'Captain, if my memory serves me,

there will be an empty ale flagon and my tankard under the sail.'

Gunnar fished out the fat leather flagon.

'By the gods, no wonder you slept well Hacun.'

Gunnar passed the flagon to the crew and they went off for another load of branches which they brought back together with the filled water container.

Now the sun was at its full height. From a distance, the boat looked like a fallen fir tree. Gunnar had stood the branches up against the rigging, stretching from the bow to the top of the mast and back to the stern, and draped more around the hull.

'Come and eat, lads,' said Gunnar as he poured a drink of water from the flagon into the tankard.

When they had finished, Finn appeared with Torsten.

'We saw four longships with full crews speeding south. They were rowing faster than a man can run.'

'It will be a while before they realise we have tricked them. That's when we really do have to be lucky.'

Gunnar took his brothers and Siward to the stern and explained to them about Hacun.

'Can we trust him?' asked Torsten. 'He's a big man to have to fight.'

'Maybe he will trick us and deliver us to the king's men.' suggested Finn.

'Well, we can't let him go. If we keep him tied up on board, we will have to feed him and he won't be able to help with the work. We either have to trust him or I will dispose of him.'

Gunnar wondered if Hacun had heard what he had said because the warrior called out, 'Captain, I have an idea. I can help you to get weapons and food.'

Gunnar moved forward to where Hacun was sitting.

'How can you do this?'

'Do you think that I will tell you while my hands and feet

are bound? No, if you want my help, you have to trust me. And if you kill me, you will starve. And now, I badly need a pee. Undo my hands!'

Gunnar went back to the others, 'What do you think?'

'He could slit our throats while we sleep,' ventured Torsten.

'If you kill him, we will get no help from him,' said Siward.

Gunnar went back to Hacun. 'You must agree that each night we can tie your hands while we sleep.'

'Agreed.'

'So what is your idea?'

'That remains my secret, but I can tell you that instead of heading for the great sea where we are expected to travel, we go to Birka.'

'But Birka is destroyed!'

'Yes, but in the destruction there is a secret which only King Erik and his bodyguards know.'

Gunnar removed the belt from Hacun's wrists and the rope from his ankles. The warrior stretched his arms and legs, stood up and walked to the side of the boat, pushing aside the fir branches.

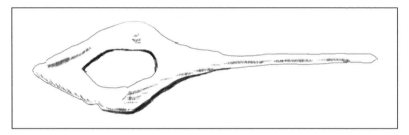

The type of fire arrow recovered from the ashes of
Birka Ceremonial House.

Chapter 11
Birka

Hacun came back through the fir branches and sat down in front of Gunnar.

'Soon, the captains of the longships will return. They will realise that they would have caught us by now if we had headed straight for the sea. And they will spend the day hunting round the bays and islands looking for us. But it would take them weeks to search every possible refuge in this lake, so I think they will soon give up and, instead, maybe one of the ships will anchor out of sight along the channel to the sea, just waiting for us to make our move.'

'So, how long do you think we should stay here?'

'We could leave early in the morning the day after to-morrow.'

'Shouldn't we travel at night?' asked Gunnar.

'No. There are many islands and narrow channels; we need light to travel safely.'

'Are you sure the longships will not be still searching?'

'King Erik has much bigger problems than us. His dead brother Olof's son, Stybjorn the Strong, is raiding the king's land in the south. He was causing trouble here before. He killed a member of the king's household when he was just sixteen, and the Ting ruled that he was too quarrelsome and unruly to share power with his uncle. So the king gave him sixty ships as payment for him to leave. That is why we are so busy building ships in Sigtuna and other places, to strengthen the king's navy.'

'Why is he called "the Strong"?'

'He leads the Jomsvikings, the most terrible and fearsome fighters. They have their base in Jomsborg on the Island of Wolin in the southlands near to the Land of the Danes.'

'You said that we should go to Birka – why?'

'This boat gives you the king's authority; that is, until people know it has been stolen, but news travels slowly around the country. When Birka was destroyed, most of the inhabitants were killed, but a few remain. Remember, the king was a Christian then and he spared those islanders who could prove they too were Christian. When they see the king's ship arrive and I step ashore in my tunic of the royal bodyguard, they will assume that we are representing the king. They know that he no longer embraces their faith and they will be fearful of persecution. We shall plunder their food stores.'

'But there must be other places which are closer where we could do this.'

'No, Birka has another attraction which I will keep to myself as insurance that you do not slit my throat when my hands are tied.'

Gunnar smiled wryly. This man was clever as well as strong. Hacun had given him much to think about. He spent a while considering what had been said before he called his brothers and Siward over to report to them. Later he tried to explain to Pasha and Vanja what they were going to do, but wasn't certain that they understood. What they all did understand was that they were short of food.

'Aneka, how much bread do we have?'

She showed him the remains of the food in the basket. This confirmed to Gunnar that they had no choice but to follow Hacun's plan.

He called the crew together and showed them the food. He took half of it out and shared it round, keeping the remainder for tomorrow. After their meal, Gunnar strapped Hacun's wrists with the rope.

Although they were not at sea, it was decided that they should have a watch system with one member of the crew in the stern of the boat looking through the camouflage to see if the longships appeared. Anxiously, one after another, through the night, they kept watch, but to their relief there were no sightings.

The next morning they took it in turns, two at a time, to go ashore and drink and wash at the stream where they had obtained their water supply. There was some debate about whether Hacun should be allowed ashore and the question was resolved when Gunnar volunteered to take him to the stream with the man's hands tied.

That evening they finished the last of their food. They had no fishing equipment and the brothers had had no luck when they tried to trap hares. Their situation was desperate, they had to make a move soon. And so it was that at dawn on the third day they set about removing the fir branches and attaching the sail to the mast so that they had the option of sailing should the wind be fair.

'The wind is certain to be favourable in some direction,' said Hacun. 'The way to Birka is not straight. First we must go south for two hours in the same direction that the longships travelled, before we can turn to starboard and through a group of islands which will give us some cover. So, these first hours are the most dangerous.'

They set off soon after dawn. Hacun stood with Gunnar in the stern and Aneka took one of the oars. The lake was like a mirror, there was not a breath of wind and apart from the cawing of some distant crows, it was eerily silent. No one spoke as they rowed as quietly as they could, but from time to time each one of them cast nervous glances around the horizon. Gunnar steered as near to the starboard shore as he could to avoid being seen in the main channel.

Aneka, not surprisingly, found herself in a difficult situation. She was surrounded by rough men who had been denied the company of women for a long time. The lascivious glances of some of the crew made her feel uncomfortable. But she was not afraid of them, she knew that her relationship with Finn and in turn his protection by his brothers guaranteed her safety. There was little privacy on the boat but with the curious mix of cruelty and chivalry which was typical of the warrior class, Hacun had rigged a line in the bow on which she could hang her cloak to hide behind when she needed to use the slops bucket. Yet, she was aware that having fulfilled her task of providing food for the beginning of the journey she would only retain the crew's respect if she shared the work on board on equal terms with them. The drudgery of heavy kitchen work had given her strong arms, and thus when they had set out that morning she readily volunteered to share the rowing.

Eventually, they reached a group of six small islands and turned to put the sun at their backs. After rowing for another two hours following the north-west channel their way was blocked by a large headland.

'Turn to port and when we get round this corner our course is south-west. Then we are no longer in sight of the longships if they are patrolling the main route from *staket* to the sea,' Hacun said to Gunnar.

After they had turned, Gunnar called out to the rowers, 'All right crew, take a rest and have a drink of water, but go easy on the flagon, it's all we have.'

The boat slowed and the crew hung on their oars, resting after the effort and anxiety of the first part of their passage. A breeze had been developing from the north-west as they rowed, making their progress more difficult.

'Can we sail from here?' Gunnar asked Hacun.

Siward had overheard the question. 'It looks as if there are a lot of islands ahead of us. Safest to carry on rowing until we get to open water, Gunnar.'

Gunnar had forgotten that Siward was a seaman and knew more of boats and seafaring than the rest of them.

Hacun agreed with Siward's suggestion and volunteered to take his place at the oar so that the Frisian could stand in the stern and steer the boat.

'Aneka, stand at the bows and look out for rocks,' shouted Siward.

Gunnar took Aneka's oar. They set off, nervously weaving their way through four narrow channels where unforgiving-looking jagged fingers of rock pointed seaward. When they had passed the fourth channel Hacun called, 'Stop a while. I must look around to see if I can remember where we should turn south.'

Gunnar called to the rowers to take a break and Hacun went up to the bow where Aneka stood. He turned round. 'It is confusing, there are two channels heading south-east, we should take the second one.'

'We passed a southbound channel a while ago, this must be the one you want,' called Siward.

'Then we can use the wind and run south-east!' shouted Hacun.

Siward turned the boat towards the sun and gave the order for the rowers to ship oars. Gunnar and Pasha raised the sail.

Finn and Torsten were forward of the sail watching it unfurl.

'By the gods! Gunnar have you seen this?' shouted Torsten, pointing to the front of the sail.

'What?' answered Gunnar, coming forward to look.

Anyone seeing this ship coming towards them would be in no doubt that the vessel was on a mission for the king for there was a huge black raven, his emblem, painted on the front of the grey sail.

The rowers rested and took in the view of the islands on both sides of the long channel as the billowing sail powered the boat through the calm water. After half an hour Siward steered them close to the starboard shore to avoid some small islands and rocks. As they came near to the shore they saw some buildings which appeared to be badly damaged.

'This is the island of Adel and the big ruined building was the great hall of the chieftain of this island and of Birka. We came here two summers ago with the king's army to teach him a lesson. He did not escape, nor did his kinsmen.'

The crew looked in silence at the devastated village. King Erik clearly showed little mercy towards those who offended him.

'And there is Birka,' announced Hacun, pointing to an island dead ahead of them. 'There is a harbour on the north-western tip of the island. Don't go too far south because I remember we lost some boats on sharpened poles which had been driven into the seabed to defend the town.'

'Lower the sail!' shouted Siward.

The crew were beginning to work well together and the rowers took their oars without needing to be told. They rowed gently towards a row of jetties. Siward chose one of them and steered the boat alongside. They tied up the craft and surveyed the scene in front of them.

The first things they noticed were signs of life. There were several rowing boats tied to the jetties next to piles of nets, and smoke was rising from the other side of a long earthen wall with a broken palisade on top. But they could not see any people.

Hacun broke the silence. 'They will have seen us coming and have run to hide in their homes, they are not allowed to carry arms. You see the high hill over there, they probably had a lookout posted there who will have recognised the sign of the king's raven. Now, let me take command and do the talking. I am going to treat you as slaves.'

'Anything to get some food, we are starving,' said Siward.

'Give me my sword and axe so that it looks believable that I am the king's emissary.'

Gunnar looked at the other brothers, wondering what to do.

'Give them to him Gunnar, anything to get some food,' said Torsten.

Gunnar reached under the short after-deck, pulled out the weapons and passed them to Hacun.

'Torsten, you stay here with Vanja to guard the boat and keep a lookout for any sign of the longships. Here's my *seax*. Bring Aneka with us, we need to get some new clothes for her.'

'Clothes! Man, we are starving!' shouted Siward.

'I will explain later, but our lives may depend on her clothes.'

They asked no more questions and the landing party disembarked. They walked to the shore and up the incline to the town wall. The gate had been destroyed and hung at a drunken angle on one hinge. Dogs started barking and they saw some children scampering to hide. There was great dilapidation in the once proud town. Many of the wattle and daub buildings were roofless through neglect and only the outer walls remained, but here and there some had either been repaired or had not been damaged. Most of these had a fence of laid branches around a garden in which chickens scratched the topsoil or, as in one case, a goose was fussing around her goslings. But all the doors to the houses were closed.

'Gunnar, grab that kid, when he starts screaming his parents will soon appear.'

Gunnar chased after a little boy and seized him by the neck. Sure enough, a door opened and an anxious looking woman appeared.

'Where is the house of the headman?' demanded Hacun.

The woman came out of the house and pointed up the street towards a large house by a pond. They saw that smoke was rising from a cooking fire in the house and a horse was tied up outside.

'Let the boy go,' Hacun ordered Gunnar gruffly. The lad ran to his mother and they watched as the visitors walked up the street as she had directed them. Hacun pushed down the garden gate, drew his sword and banged on the door of the house with the hilt. There was the rattle of a bolt being drawn and the door opened slightly. Hacun put his shoulder against the door and sent the man inside flying.

'Are you the headman?' demanded Hacun.

'I am, officer.'

'In the name of King Erik I want three things and when we have got them we will leave and harm no one.'

'Yes sir, what is it you need?'

'First, food for my slaves. You will prepare food for us immediately and send a servant to take food for my two men on our boat.'

'But sir we are poor and last year's harvest was bad.'

Hacun grabbed the man by the neck and threw him to the ground. There were screams from women standing in the dark interior of the room whom the intruders had not seen.

'Outside, you have a horse. We shall have him for dinner and roast the steaks on the ashes of your house.'

A woman stepped forward and held her hands imploringly towards Hacun.

'Please leave him, he is an old man. You shall have supper, we will prepare it straight away.'

Gunnar noticed that she had a silver cross on a chain around her neck. He looked her up and down. She was a comely woman.

Hacun was standing slightly to the side of Gunnar and noticed where Gunnar's eyes were straying. He reached over and cuffed him with the back of his hand.

'You are a slave, take your eyes off of this freewoman!'

Gunnar bridled and Finn rushed forward ready to grab his arms, but Gunnar controlled himself and feigned a look of hatred at Hacun.

'We want baskets of salted or dried fish and a side of smoked meat as well as bread and a barrel of ale.'

'But sir, we do not have all of these things,' the woman pleaded.

'Then get them from the other citizens or I will turn my slaves loose on the town and you have seen that they are not without vices.'

'When do you need the foodstuffs?'

'Tomorrow morning.'

'And what were the other things you want?'

'I want a fine gown, the best you can find for the lady behind us.'

The woman's eyes fell on the slender figure of Aneka standing outside the doorway and waved at her to come into the house. The woman looked Aneka up and down and then turned to Hacun.

'We will have to alter one of my gowns. And the third thing?'

'The third thing I will tell you tomorrow morning, but I will need two strong men with axes and a shovel here tomorrow at sun up.'

'It shall be.'

The next day, it was raining. The crew had been sleeping under the sail, which they had detached from the mast.

'Come on everyone, we go ashore for breakfast,' commanded Hacun.

The news of the king's emissary's demands had spread in the town. Clearly the inhabitants were keen to be rid of the crew. As they walked up the main street they passed people hurrying in the rain to deliver items of food in baskets to the headman's house. The group pushed their way into the house. Hacun looked at the assortment of food waiting for them.

'Take some bread and fish each. Woman, we want porridge.' Hacun was aware that they would not be having hot food for some time if all went well for them, and here was a chance for them to enjoy some.

By the time they had eaten, the rain had stopped. Two men waited outside the door with axes and a shovel as requested.

'Outside, slaves, we have work to do,' Hacun ordered. 'Aneka, you stay and make sure that you like the clothes.'

'You will leave me alone with these people?'

'Do as I say, they won't hurt you, they just want to help, isn't that so, Christian woman?' said Hacun cruelly.

'Yes sir, the lady will be safe with us.'

Hacun grabbed the woman by the arm. 'You have seen what can happen to those who offend the king!'

'Yes, sir.'

Aneka reluctantly agreed to stay alone at the house while the women measured her and took out clothes from a chest in the corner of the room.

Hacun went outside with the others and signalled to the two men with the tools and the rest of the party to follow him. He led them towards the high hill they had seen from the jetty. It was surrounded by another rampart in which they could see one opening.

Out of earshot of the men with the tools Hacun whispered to Gunnar and Finn. 'This is the king's gate to the fort. That ruined building was the ceremonial house dedicated to Odin and next to it was the garrison. We had good sport there. Not one of the guards escaped us. Our victory was so complete that the king refused to accept the arms of the garrison as they were tainted by the blessing of Odin. As a final insult to the defenders of the town, he had them blessed by the priest and commanded his bodyguard to case the weapons after greasing them with pig's fat and to bury them under the floor of the desecrated and damned ceremonial house as a sacrifice to his Christian god. The king doesn't want them, but we do!'

'How did you destroy the garrison?'

'Our archers used fire arrows. They have arrow heads with a small hole in which they place lighted linen. They came close to the shore with their ships and unleashed a hell storm on the defenders. Once the garrison and the hall were on fire, we came ashore at the place where we have our boat and put the town to the sword.'

'But now the king embraces the old beliefs again,' stated Finn.

'Yes, and these Christians know that they are in danger if they displease him.'

They walked over to the burnt out remains of the ceremonial hall. Parts of the walls were still standing and on the western end the scorched woodwork bristled with arrows which must have been fired from the sea. Finn walked over to the wall and examined the arrows. He managed to detach three of them and saw the specially shaped heads which had carried the flames to destroy the building. He broke off the heads and put them in his pouch.

'You men, come here and start clearing the flooring,' said Hacun, pointing towards the ground around a stone table which must have been some kind of altar to the deity.

There were some flagstones which had been untidily placed all over the area around the walls. The two men used the spade to prise up the first flagstones, revealing wooden boxes underneath.

'Help them, slaves!' commanded Hacun.

Soon, all the flagstones had been dragged to the centre of the building. The roughly-hewn wood of the box lids bore marks of a Christian cross. The boxes themselves were of different shapes.

'Gunnar, take an axe and break open this box,' Hacun said, pointing to a long, narrow container.

Gunnar swung the axe several times, splintering the lid. He peeled back the split timber to reveal several unstrung bows covered in grease. Hacun told Gunnar to give the axe back to the man who had brought it and indicated to him and his companion that they should break open the lids of the other boxes. After a while, the arsenal was uncovered.

'Torsten and Finn, we want seven bows. The bowstrings must be somewhere in the box, twenty arrows for each bow. Gunnar, take Vanja and to find seven good swords. Siward and Pasha, seven axes. I will get *seaxes*. Put them all over here.'

Hacun indicated the area at the back of the building where the flagstones had not been moved.

'You two men put the flooring back over the boxes when we have finished.' Soon all the greasy weapons were stacked as directed. 'You all wait here, you two men of Birka come with me.' Hacun walked off down the slope towards the town. After some time, he reappeared with several women and the two men carrying buckets of hot water and cleaning materials.

'This is my third request: clean these and when the cart has come back from taking our food to the boat, use it to transport these weapons to the jetty.' Turning to the crew, he said, 'Come on, let's go and stow the food on board.'

As they passed the headman's house, Aneka came out carrying a bundle of cloth.

'We need a cooking pot to have on the boat, for if we get the chance to make a fire on our journey,' she reminded Hacun.

174

'Well, we won't be having fire on board, but if we go ashore it would be good to have.' Hacun pushed the door of the house open and went inside. There were some sounds of protest and then he came out carrying a cooking pot with a handle.

When they got back to the boat, they set about packing the food. They found leather containers of paint and a wooden keg of tar which the men who had been working on the boat must have stored under the decking.

'Throw out that stuff to make space,' said Hacun.

'No, I think we should keep the tar, in case we have to repair the boat,' said Torsten. From his time in the ship-yard, he was well aware that the hulls were made watertight with tar and fibres such as horsehair.

'Well, we don't need the paint anyway,' said Hacun.

Gunnar looked across at the rowing boats. He went over and stole one of the fishing nets and stowed it by the mast of their boat.

'You keep your set of weapons beside where you sit to row, then we are ready if we need to defend ourselves,' said Hacun. 'Now, Gunnar, do you still need to tie my hands tonight?

Those that could understand the comment laughed, apart from Gunnar who did not like to be the butt of jokes.

'You hit me again like you did yesterday and it is your neck the rope goes around,' he said grumpily. 'Now I take over giving the orders.'

'Don't you want to hear my plan, Gunnar, or do you have one?'

'All right, you arrogant sod, what is your plan?'

'I have provided you with food and weapons and prob-ably saved your lives. Perhaps you are the arrogant one; what have you done apart from endangering your crew?'

This was too much for Gunnar. He started to get up from his seat, reaching for his sword. Torsten and Finn leapt across the deck and jumped on their brother, knocking him backwards to the deck and pinning him there.

'You have just saved your brother's life,' said Hacun. Addressing Gunnar, he said, 'Have you ever used a sword before, blacksmith? Don't play games with a warrior!'

The two brothers held Gunnar down until they felt certain that his temper had cooled and then let him resume his seat.

'I don't want to risk my throat being cut when I am asleep, so I will tell you all you need to know at the moment about my plan; the detail you will see later.' Hacun hesitated while the crew gathered round him.

'Well, go on then,' said Gunnar irritably.

'By this time, the king's ships will have gone back to Sigtuna, except, and I am sure of this, one ship, which will be waiting for us to make a run for the coast along the only access waterway. They know that we are like fish which sooner or later will swim into their net. But what I am certain about is that they will not remember that there is a way out of this lake for a boat that can crawl.'

'Crawl?'

'Yes, and that is what we are going to do. Tomorrow, we head south.' Hacun was bombarded with questions, but refused to answer any of them. 'Now, I will sleep. Gunnar, we should leave at dawn; it is always possible that one of the king's ships might visit Birka.'

Chapter 12
Subterfuge, Mutiny and a Battle

The crew were woken by the light of a bright dawn. Their ship was now heavily laden with their newly-acquired supplies and weaponry, so they were pleased that the wind was still in the north-west and they were able to raise the sail as soon as they had cleared the jetty. They passed the hill and the ruined fort where they could clearly discern figures watching them, probably to ensure that they really were rid of these robbing mercenaries. The boat headed due south, a direction which the crew could easily calculate from the current position of the sun. Siward was at the steering oar.

'Aneka, put on the gown you were given yesterday,' ordered Hacun.

The slave girl looked imploringly at Finn. There was no room for her to change into the dress behind her little screened off area in the bows.

'You can't expect her to get changed in front of all these men!' he said.

'By the gods, she is a slave girl,' answered Hacun irritably.

'But she is a chieftain's daughter in her own country!'

'All right, turn round everybody,' answered the irritated Hacun.

Aneka went to the stern where she had most privacy. Most of the crew were sitting in their normal rowing positions,

177

but had in any case turned to watch the progress of the craft towards a clearly visible landfall directly over the prow.

When she had changed, Hacun said, 'A real improvement!'

The crew turned to see Aneka's new outfit. The transformation was a surprise to all of them and there was an audible gasp from the men. She wore a white blouse of fine linen, and a brilliant crimson silk dress which was supported above her breasts by shoulder straps of white wool with an embroidered crimson pattern. At the bottom of the dress, white linen underskirts covered her feet.

'You have to do something about your hair,' said Hacun.

'I have no comb,' she replied.

Hacun opened his pouch and gave her his comb. Despite the rough and sometimes violent life led by a warrior, he took much pride in his appearance. Because of a belief that hair could dictate a man's strength, there was status in caring for hair and in owning a fine comb made of elk or red deer bone.

'Now remember, and this includes you, Gunnar, you are my armed slaves and we are on a king's mission. You say nothing and do exactly as I tell you. And Finn, keep your distance from Aneka, keep your hands off her, she is to be a fine lady and you are but a slave. Aneka, sit at the prow.'

Throughout the voyage so far, the two Rossijans, Vanja and Pasha, had been very quiet apart from when they talked to each other, which was not often. Gunnar knew from his time working with the men that the bigger of the two, Pasha, was the dominant character and Vanja tended to yield to him. It was unfortunate that the crew could not communicate with them what was happening, but they seemed satisfied just to allow decisions to be made for them and to accept the behaviour required of them. Hacun went forward and did his best to mime his orders. He pointed to the distant shore and then to his mouth indicating that they should be silent when they got there.

Well before the sun had reached the south, they entered a long channel. They were able to use the wind through the channel, even though there was high ground on both sides. The wooded slopes reached down to the water's edge. They passed an island on the starboard side and then the way ahead appeared to be blocked. They lowered the sail and manned the oars just as they passed a narrow opening on the starboard side.

'Keep rowing!' shouted Siward as he swung the boat round in a circle and returned to the narrow opening. They slid through and the channel widened again for a while. They negotiated some small islands where there were several rowing boats with fishermen tending to nets. Ahead of them they saw a small village where the waterway seemed to disappear into a small stream.

'Siward, sit down here and take my oar,' said Hacun, grabbing the steering oar. He steered them into a jetty where several men were waiting to take the boat's lines. One of the men on the ashore said, 'I thought we were going to see the king! Who are you?'

'None of your affair, who is in command here?'

'I am,' said an elderly man in a grey cloak. In the heat of the early summer, it seemed unnecessary to be wrapped in a cloak, but the frequency and volume of his coughing indicated that this man was not in good health. He shuffled over to their boat and peered at the crew and then his attention was caught by the sight of Aneka sitting in the bows, her blonde hair now in a neat pigtail. He turned to Hacun and in a wheezing voice asked, 'What manner of business brings you and this fine young lady to Telgia with heavily armed slaves and the king's boat?'

'We are charged with returning this lady to her family in Scania. She was captured and brought to Sigtuna by mistake.'

179

'Where is your royal warrant?'

'We have none. Without wishing to sound disrespectful about my master, the decision for us to make this journey was made during the festivities on Walpurgis Eve and much ale had flowed. I was told to leave at once.'

'Oh dear, this sounds very unconventional, I do not want to take responsibility for assisting you without a royal order. I am unwell and I must take to my bed, you do as you need, I want no part in it.'

'Do you have slaves who can help us?'

'Speak to the guards over there, they might assist.' He pointed to a guard post where the stream ran inland, and then shuffled away towards the village.

Hacun walked off in the direction of the guard post.

'Hacun, you old devil! What are you doing here?' shouted one of the guards.

Hacun was not surprised that he was recognised. He had fought in several campaigns as a warrior and had many comrades in arms before he was promoted to the royal bodyguard.

'Dagr! I should ask you the same. At your age you should be sitting at the hearth telling grandchildren of our adventures!'

'Well, this is an easy life, not like campaigning. Very few ships come through here now, the waters get lower and lower and Styrbjorn could never bring his fleet through, not like the golden days of my great grandfather when all the Birka trade flowed through the channel. But what brings you here?'

'I am nursemaid to a wealthy woman who is to be transported to the southlands. The king was in his cups at the festivities and had the idiotic idea of sending her home in his boat as he needed to keep all the warships to guard Sigtuna. He gave me a crew of slaves, armed them and promised them freedom and land when we return.'

'And so you decided to take the shortest route to the sea!'

'I want this done with as soon as possible. Have you got slaves who can help us roll her to the other side?'

'This is not like the good old days when Telgia was an important town, but I can probably arrange a few men to help.'

'Tomorrow morning?'

'First thing after sunrise. It will take all day. Will you have ale with us tonight?'

Hacun agreed and returned to the boat.

'We stay here and wait until tomorrow morning. You are to stay on board until then and speak to no one. Tomorrow, we take her up to the stream and then we get out of the boat and make her crawl across the dried channel to the sea. Let's eat.'

At dawn the next morning everyone was ready to move the boat in towards the stream.

'Have you done this before, Siward?' asked Hacun.

'Never, but I have heard stories about longships traversing long distances between rivers.'

'They have told me that it is about a thousand paces from these waters to the other side and the sea.'

'I think it would be best if most of the crew gets off the boat now and that they walk to where we pull her ashore. Just two of us can stay on board to attend to the lines,' said Siward.

'Fine, I have friends who will help with the logs. Aneka, you stay on board too and sit in the stern.'

Siward and Hacun rowed the boat slowly to the point where the water shallowed. Siward lifted up the steering oar, tied it so that it was clear of the water, and they ran the boat aground. They passed the ends of the mooring lines to the waiting crew, who had been joined by eight slaves from the village and two guards. The other ends of the lines were made off on the boat amidships, one on each side, which when pulled would keep the ship upright on the shallow keel. The guards ordered two of the slaves to take logs from a pile by the side of the stream, and to put them under the bow, across the stream. The two men jumped off the boat and Hacun ordered Siward to join those pulling the ropes.

'Pull!' ordered one of the guards.

The boat began to mount the first log.

'More logs!' shouted the guard.

The two slaves placed a series of logs in front of the boat and she was drawn clear out of the water running through the stream.

'Wait, I think we need another line from the bows,' said the guard.

Siward was pushed back on board to make fast a line which the guard passed to him. Meanwhile, the slaves continued laying out a series of logs ahead of the boat.

'Heave!' the guard shouted. The boat started to move slowly forward again, sometimes sliding on the logs and at other times running on them as they rolled. Several of the slaves were continuously collecting the logs which had been traversed and dragging them as quickly as they could to place ahead of the boat and be crossed again. After a while, they reached a point where the stream had developed into a deep pool.

'Throw the lines back on board. We can float her for almost a hundred paces here.'

Siward and Gunnar took an oar each. The current was swift and they were easily carried by the water which was draining out of the lake into the sea beyond them. The difference in height between the two waterways was more than that of a man.

And so they continued for most of the day, sometimes running on the logs, sometimes rowing. Well before they reached it, they saw a wide channel ahead of them heading almost due south.

They came to a point where the stream deepened permanently. Gunnar and Siward rowed towards a small quay, which was in front of several houses.

'We will pick you up over there,' said Gunnar to the others, pointing at the quay.

Hacun turned to Dagr. 'Many thanks, old fellow.'

'You'll not stay here for the night and sup with us?'

'No, I want to get on with this business. Let's hope I can get back before Styrbjorn tries anything!'

'Farewell, and be careful. When you get down to the end of this channel, there is a very narrow entrance to the next one on the starboard side at a place called Brandal. Keep well to the south of the headland. You will see fishermen there trying to catch the fish carried through the narrows.'

The crew in place, they set off rowing down the channel in the sunset. Within an hour they had reached the narrows. They passed through and then sought a place to stop for the night, as it was unwise for them to continue in the channel in the dark. They rowed past the northern tip of an island and then on their port side found a sheltered bay where they dropped their anchor.

At dawn the next morning the crew had some fish and ale before setting off down the channel. There was no wind, so they rowed, keeping the island on their starboard side, and continued south for an hour until they came to another very narrow opening. Once through this, the channel widened and they were able to use the north-easterly wind to sail through the waters which, apart from many islets and rocks, were easily navigable. An hour before sunset, after weaving carefully between the islands, the waters broadened into the open sea. There was much back-slapping and mutual congratulating as they ate their supper in a fine sunset while heading south-west along the coast.

The evening was mild and the breeze persisted, though backing to the north-west. Gunnar expressed the optimism of the crew when he suggested that instead of seeking an overnight berth ashore, they should continue through the night, using the favourable wind.

'Let's split the watch-keeping between us. Finn and I can take the evening watch until midnight, Pasha and Siward take the night watch and Hacun and Vanja take over at dawn. Then Torsten and Aneka the next one. It's time she started to earn her keep again!'

This was agreed and Gunnar took the steering oar.

'Remember to keep well out from the coast. The moon is rising and you should be able to see the land easily,' said Siward.

The off-duty crew settled down for the night, wrapped in their cloaks, sleeping on the deck in front of their rowing positions. At midnight, Gunnar shook Siward and Pasha and they took over the watch. The night was quiet apart from the soothing swish of the calm sea hitting the bow as the thoroughbred boat ploughed its way south-west. The crew were sleeping soundly when, just as dawn was breaking the boat lurched and there was a thud. It was clear that the helmsman had dropped the steering oar for the boat was trying to round up into the breeze.

'What the hell is going on?' shouted a sleepy Gunnar.

He threw off his cloak and started to make his way to the stern, but was stopped in his tracks when he saw in the early morning light that Vanja was standing over the limp body of Hacun with a *seax* against his throat. Pasha was indicating that Gunnar should not move.

'Where is Siward?' demanded Gunnar.

The big Rossijan recognised Siward's name and drew his hand across his throat. Vanja said something to Pasha and he beckoned Gunnar to come to the stern and take the steering oar. It was clear that the two men did not know how to control the vessel, which was rolling drunkenly in the light swell with the sail flapping.

184

As Gunnar took the oar, he noticed that Pasha also had an axe in his hand. They had clearly used something to knock out Hacun as he came on watch with Vanja, probably the blunt side of this axe.

Gunnar shouted to Finn and Torsten, 'Don't try anything, these bastards have killed Siward and it looks as if Hacun is next. I suppose they have dumped Siward in the sea. We have no speed, she won't steer round. Man the oars.'

As they rowed and Gunnar started to bring the bow round to head south, Pasha grabbed him and held the axe over his head. He pointed to the rising sun indicating that this was the way Gunnar should steer. Gunnar pushed the oar away from him and headed east. It was immediately apparent what the Rossijans were about; they were trying to return to the eastlands, but it was also very clear that they had planned badly. If one of them intended to force the crew to do their bidding by threatening to kill Hacun, and bearing in mind that neither of them was capable of steering the boat, only three would be available to row when the wind dropped. It could be a very long voyage during which they could not sleep.

Pasha indicated that they wanted food by pointing to his mouth. Finn looked across to Aneka. 'Get some fish and bread for our breakfast.'

After they had eaten, Hacun showed signs of regaining consciousness. Pasha bound his hands and Vanja continued to sit with the knife against the prisoner's throat. Pasha sat on the starboard gunnel at the stern behind the helmsman, his axe in his hand. At his feet there were bloodstains, presumably the marks where Siward had been slaughtered.

They continued their course east during the morning. By the time Finn had taken over the steering oar from Gunnar they had lost sight of the coast. The wind continued to blow from the same quarter but towards midday it freshened and it became clear that even on this point of sailing, they should soon reef the sail as the boat was rolling markedly.

Gunnar shouted to Finn, 'We had better shorten the sail.'

Finn glanced behind him: Pasha was still there. 'Wait a minute, Gunnar and hold tight,' he said.

Finn pushed the oar away from him and the speeding boat responded immediately by turning across the wind and heeling violently. It all happened at once. Pasha fell backwards over the lee side of the boat, Vanja and Hacun slid across the deck and crashed against the inside of the starboard gunnel. The rest of the crew were flung across to the same side as the boat threatened to capsize. Finn pulled the oar back towards him, but it was deep in the water and very heavy to move as he fought the will of the wind. As he did so, he stamped on Vanja's hand as he sought to pick up the knife he had dropped. The boat was still heeling violently as Gunnar scrambled his way along the sloping deck to the mast. There he quickly located the main halyard and released it. The heavy sail crashed down onto the deck, enveloping Torsten and Aneka. The effect was immediate. The boat righted itself and Finn dropped on top of Vanja who was almost at his feet, to stop him recovering his knife or the axe which Pasha had dropped.

Gunnar came leaping over the seats towards Vanja. 'You son of the devil!'

Finn stepped in between them. 'Wait, Gunnar! We will need him to help us row. We can avenge Siward when we reach our destination.'

Gunnar stopped. They heard a shout and looked behind the boat; Pasha's head could be seen fifty paces away. He was waving his arms and shouting for help. He sank out of sight, but then reappeared. They all stood watching him as first his head and finally the tips of his fingers disappeared beneath the waves.

'By the name of Odin, get this rope off me!'

186

They had all forgotten Hacun, who was lying, badly bruised, hard up against where he been flung by the heel of the boat.

Hacun had a bad head wound and was very shaken by the force of blow when he hit the gunnel. It was Hacun's weakened state which enabled Finn to persuade him not to skewer the terrified Vanja with his *seax*. The injured warrior sat on the deck recovering from shock, while the rest of the crew, including Vanja, who received a number of kicks and thumps from Gunnar and Torsten venting their anger, tidied the boat and prepared to raise a reefed mainsail. Torsten and Gunnar rowed the boat round to catch the wind across the port quarter and then they were on their way south-west.

Later in the afternoon, when Hacun was much recovered, Gunnar took him aside.

'What happened?'

'I suppose that Vanja must have joined Pasha during the night and they silenced Siward before disposing of him. Pasha woke me to go on watch, I was just standing up when both of them jumped me and smashed something heavy on my head.'

'That must have been the thud I heard. Now we have a challenge. I have only ever spent a week on a boat before and we have lost our only seaman. Have you navigated a ship before?'

'No, I have been to the land of the Danes with Erik's fleet, but then I was rowing and you don't notice much about where you're going or how you get there when you have your back towards the destination.'

'As long as the weather stays fine, we can navigate by the sun; at it's highest point it shows us where we should go. At night, we can use Polaris. But if the weather turns nasty we are really in trouble.'

'I think it best then that we head back to the coast and

follow the land. We can night sail on clear nights, otherwise we go ashore.'

'Agreed,' said Gunnar.

There seemed to be a new affinity between the two men now that Hacun had been shown to be a mere vulnerable mortal after all; first by being captured by the Rossijans and then rescued through Finn's ingenuity.

So it was that they found their way down the coast of the country, sometimes in summer sunshine, occasionally in unseasonal but short storms. At one point, they passed a large island on the port side and spotted the first boats they had seen, by their appearance cargo vessels. Further south, several times they found small fishing vessels and robbed them of their catch. Later, they sailed around a deep bay to the south of which was an island, which they also passed on their port side. Then the coast they had been following turned to the west and then appeared to run north.

As they rounded the flat landscape which seemed to be the southern tip of the country they had left, enjoying a run before a light south-easterly wind, Finn pointed out a ship with a large red and white sail going in the same direction as them. Although they had seen many other vessels over the last six days, this one was much bigger. At the prow, it had a dragon's head and its sides seemed higher than the warships they had seen at Sigtuna.

'A Jomsviking warship!' said Hacun. 'Well my friends; you can fight them; in which case as a warrior I go straight to Valhalla. We have no chance. Or, you can capitulate and become slaves again.'

'We have not come this far to go into slavery!' said Gunnar.

'Gunnar, I could try to set fire to their boat,' said Finn.

'How?' answered Hacun.

'I have put those special arrow heads I took from the fort in Birka on three of my arrows.'

'Come here quickly, Aneka,' said Gunnar.

Gunnar grabbed the girl's underskirt and cut a piece of linen which he tore into small pieces. Meanwhile Finn took the cooking bowl and started trimming small shavings from his oar into it.

'Get the keg of tar from under the stern deck,' Gunnar instructed Torsten.

When they opened the keg, they found that the heavy tar had sunk to the bottom and the inflammable tar oil was on the surface.

'Dip the linen in the oil and arm the arrowheads with it.'

Finn was trying desperately to get the tinder to light.

'Try some of the oil on the tinder,' said Gunnar.

The Jomsviking ship was less than a hundred paces behind them now and was clearly chasing them. They could see the warriors crowding at the bow to get a sight of their unusual quarry, brightly coloured as it was, though the raven emblem was on the front of the sail and out of their sight.

'Yes!' exclaimed Finn as the tinder started to burn. He hastily leant on the top of his bow to bend it enough to string it. He picked up the first arrow and dipped it into the flaming cooking pot. The linen caught fire immediately. He turned and aimed at the huge sail of the following warship.

'Damn it!' he said as the flaming arrow hit the sail, dropped to the deck and was cast overboard by one of the Jomsvikings. 'I'm firing against the wind and by the time the arrow hits the sail it's flying too slowly to penetrate it.'

'Then we have to let them get closer!' said Hacun.

The tension among the crew mounted as the faster Viking ship changed course slightly to come alongside their craft. It was getting very close now, but because of the angle, the apparent size of Finn's target was getting smaller.

'Now!' said Gunnar.

Finn fired the second arrow. It lodged high up on the

sail, well out of reach of the crew. The woollen sail which, just like theirs, was impregnated with fat to make it wind proof to give drive to the boat, immediately ignited. They heard orders being shouted to the crew of the ship.

'Another one, Finn!' said Gunnar.

Finn loosed off his last flaming arrow. It struck the middle of the sail and added to the conflagration. The Viking crew were trying desperately to lower the sail to stop the spread of the fire.

'Man the oars: let's get as far away as we can in case they put the fire out,' commanded Gunnar.

The burning Viking ship was now stationary in the water and very soon the smaller craft under the power of its sail and the straining of those on the oars put a good distance between them. Judging by the pall of smoke, the bigger ship was unlikely to follow.

The wind was steady and the rowers were tired. 'All right,' said Gunnar, 'I think we have won our fight with the Jomsvikings! That's enough rowing, let the wind do the work.' Gunnar took the steering oar and the others all sat in silence watching the distant fire to the south-east. When they looked around them they observed that they were entering a broad channel with a large land mass on each side, but an island ahead of them. They decided to steer to port and sail between the island and the mainland to find a place to stop for the night where they might be safe, in the unlikely event that the Jomsvikings were able to look for them.

As they entered the narrower channel, they stopped a fishing boat and stole the fisherman's catch. Before they cast him adrift Hacun held his *seax* against the fisherman's throat and asked him the best route to King Harald's fortress.

'The king has moved his court from Jelling to Roskilde, where he has built a church. The town is easier to defend against his enemies.'

'How do we sail to find this Roskilde?'

'It is but two days' sail from here, north and then west,' answered the man. 'But very difficult to find.'

'What do you mean?'

'You will see, damn you.'

Hacun let him go and climbed back on board their boat. The angry fisherman started rowing away and left them to find an anchorage for the night.

ᚼᛆᚱᛆᛚᛏᚱ:ᚴᚢᛏᚢᚠᛚ:ᛒᛆᚦ:ᚠᛆᚢᚱᚢᛏ
ᚠᚢᛒᚱ:ᚦᛆᚢᛋᛁ:ᛆᚠᛐ:ᚠᚢᚱᛘ ᚠᛆᚦᚢᚱ ᛋᛁᛐ
ᛐᚢᚠ ᛆᚠᛐ:ᚦᚠᚢᚱᛏᛁ:ᛘᚢᚦᚢᚱ:ᛋᛁᛐᛐ:ᛋᛐ
ᚼᛆᚱᛆᛚᛏᚱ:ᛁᛐᛋ:ᛋᚽᚤ.ᚢᛐᛐ.ᛐᛆᛐᚤᛐᚢᚱᚠ

The runic text on the Jelling Stone raised in 965 by King Harald. The stone is known as the 'Birth certificate of Denmark', as it signifies, for the first time, the unification of the provinces and fiefdoms of that country. It states: 'King Harald ordered this monument made in memory of Gorm, his father, and in memory of Thyra, his mother; that Harald who won for himself all of Denmark and Norway and made the Danes Christian.'

Chapter 13
Gifts for a King

There was excitement on the boat as they tacked up the channel between the Land of the Danes and Scania. The wind was not kind to them and forced them to work hard to cover the last part of their long journey. They tacked to and fro from one coast to the other against a strong north-westerly breeze. At the end of each leg of the tack, they had to lower the sail and row the boat around to face the next leg, the strength of the wind making it too dangerous even for their small craft to turn facing the wind. By late after-noon, it was clear that they would not reach Roskilde by nightfall, so they sought shelter behind a low headland that was to prove to be the closest point between the two coasts, to anchor for the night. They saw many different craft sail-ing through the straits between the two coasts, but no one bothered them.

The liaison between Finn and Aneka had grown in intensity and now, when not rowing, he sat with her most of the time. That evening, Finn found Aneka in a very emotional state with tears running down her sunburnt cheeks. She was staring at the far coast, not an hour's sail from where they were.

'There is my father's country, it must be, for when he travels to the court of King Harald he sails from a harbour which is closest to the Land of the Danes. And my home is but a day's horse ride east of the harbour.'

Finn put his arm around her and attempted to comfort her, but she continued sobbing. Her distress had been noticed by the rest of the crew, but was ignored by them. Finn went over to where Gunnar was sitting in the stern.

'Gunnar, can we not cross to the other side and leave Aneka there?'

'You mean that you will be saying goodbye to her forever?'

'Well, no. You could leave me there with her. I want to live with her as her husband.'

'You stupid fool. You don't even know that her father is alive. She was taken in a skirmish with King Erik's men, he might have been killed. And what will you find over there? You have come from a hostile country; there is little chance that you will be accepted. No, I promised your mother that I would look after you. You stay with us.' And, with that, the discussion was closed. Hacun, who overheard them, was pleased that he did not have to intervene to point out that they needed Aneka to help ingratiate themselves with King Harald.

Next morning, the weather was overcast and there was a sea mist, but the wind had turned to the north-east. As visibility was poor, they decided to hug the coast on their port side. After three hours, just as the sun broke through, the coast turned and they could deduce that they were sailing west. Later, the coast led them to the south-west. By mid-afternoon, in a strong breeze, they were still following the low coastline looking for a harbour which might be Roskilde, when they saw a small fishing boat. The fisherman saw them and quickly set his sail and headed south-west.

'Try to catch him!' shouted Gunnar, 'shake the reef out of the sail!' They pursued the small boat, but it suddenly disappeared around a low headland. They followed and found themselves entering a wide bay. The fishing boat headed for the shore on the left side where there were several small shacks.

'Where now?' said Torsten.

'How do I know?' answered Gunnar. 'The town must be somewhere in this bay.'

They spent the rest of the day sailing then rowing around the wide bay, but apart from some small fishing settlements, there was no sign of a town. Disappointed, they spent a night at anchor at the south of the bay.

Just after dawn, Torsten was fishing with their net when he noticed a movement at the entrance to the bay. He shouted, 'Look, two ships!'

Everyone looked to where he was pointing. At the head of the bay, two large ships were being rowed southwards. But they did not progress far before they swung sharply to their left and disappeared.

'That must be the entrance to a channel!' said Gunnar. 'Ships of that size need a large harbour.'

They pulled in their fishing net and made ready for sea. The wind, which was stopping the large ships from sailing, was right behind them and they made good speed to the supposed opening to a channel. Just before they got there, they took the sail down and manned the oars. They found an extremely narrow entrance which, after a little distance, opened out into a wider waterway turning into a south-going channel. But the channel was very long, and their progress was slow as they spent almost all day following it. They had to be continually on the lookout for shallows, twists and turns. Late in the afternoon the channel emerged into a wide lake. They stopped rowing and all the crew turned to look at the scene ahead of the boat. Due south of them, in the distance, they could see a settlement of some considerable size. Two more hours rowing brought them within shouting distance of a group of longships anchored in front of a harbour. The crews of the longships were watching them intently as they glided towards the shore. The town in front of them was built on a hill at the summit of which was a large wooden building with a cross on top. There were rows of wooden buildings, mainly of wattle and daub, and near to the harbour some large warehouses.

On the quayside, a crowd had gathered to watch the approach of the unusual craft. They included some soldiers with bows and swords. The crowd parted and two men on horseback joined the onlookers.

The wind had dropped and Gunnar gave the order, 'Let's put up the sail so that they can see who we are!'

The gasp from the crowd was audible even at the distance they were from the shore as the royal raven of King Erik was unfurled. One of the men on horseback shouted out to them, 'Who are you and what do you want?'

Hacun looked at Gunnar and said, 'Let me deal with this.'

Before Gunnar had a chance to react, Hacun shouted, 'We were subjects of King Erik, but we wish to serve King Harald!'

A third man on horseback joined the other two and called out, 'Stay where you are!' He beckoned to a soldier and pointed to a large rowing boat. Several soldiers embarked in the boat and were rowed out to the new arrival.

'Give my men your weapons,' shouted the man on horseback.

Gunnar and the others delved into the recesses under their seats and took out the bows, axes and swords. Two of the soldiers had boarded their boat and were searching to see that they had handed over all their weapons. When they were satisfied, one of the soldiers shouted to the man ashore who then called out, 'Come alongside the quay.'

The crew lowered the sail and manned the oars. A few strokes and they had made landfall at their destination. The crowd had grown in size and the soldiers had to push people out of the way so that the crew could go ashore. Hacun walked up to the man on horseback and said, 'Sir, we wish to serve King Harald.'

'And who are you, who wish to serve?'

'I am Hacun, a member of King Erik's personal body-guard.'

The third rider was helped off his horse by two servants. He walked slowly across to Hacun. The crowd was parted roughly by the soldiers. This man was tall and had long grey hair, but his eyebrows were black, betokening that this was the colour his hair had once been.

'And why do you wish to serve?'

'My master now serves pagan gods; I can no longer be faithful to him.'

'Well said master Hacun, but how do I know that I can trust you? You have deceived your king.'

'My lord, I bring you three gifts. I have a slave for you; a Rossijan, a strong man.'

'I have many slaves already. And the other gifts?'

'The boat, my lord, this is the personal ferry of King Erik. We have sailed it all the way from Sigtuna. It is a fine craft.'

King Harald threw his head back and laughed. His henchmen did likewise.

'You have indeed done well, for this is a small craft to make a hazardous journey. And what else?'

'Your servant, Jarl, of the land with two shores, was robbed of his daughter by King Erik's men and put into slavery. We have returned her to her homeland.'

Hacun had played his cleverest card. He had learned from Aneka her father's name and that his farm was on a peninsula in the north part of Scania, hence the estate had two shores. The king knew immediately who Hacun was referring to.

Aneka was pushed through the crowed and bowed before Harald.

'We have never met my lord, but my father serves you well and you will know him.'

Harald tested her, 'What is your mother's name?'

'Dagmar, my lord.'

The king seemed satisfied. He looked past Aneka at the three brothers.

'And who are these men, Hacun?'

'They are three brothers from the far north country, iron-workers, but valiant fighters too. One is the sweetheart of the girl.'

'Well, we need ironworkers here.'

Gunnar pushed his way forward, 'But my lord we wish to learn to be warriors and to serve you.'

The king had difficulty understanding Gunnar's dialect and asked Hacun to explain what he had said. Then he turned to the two riders. 'Well, what say you to this Hacun who has brought us gifts?'

'A strange story my lord, but it can be true.'

'Then, leave your vessel, which is to be mine, and tonight we will hear the whole story. Make arrangements for the lady to be comfortable and the men can be housed in the garrison. Which of you is the lady's sweetheart?'

Hacun pushed Finn forward. 'He is, my lord.'

'Come, hammer-head, I would speak with you and Hacun,' said the king, referring to Finn's tattoo.

The three of them walked to the back of the crowd. 'Hacun, I cannot understand this man's speech, but explain to him that Jarl of the two shores was killed by the men who took her. He was a good warrior and will have gone to Valhalla for he was not of the Christian faith. We know nothing of her mother, but I fear that she is not alive. This man must tell this news to his lady. Also, Jarl had a small house he used when he came to court. It is now hers. But it is too dangerous for her to try to reclaim her father's estate. Oh yes, and also tell him that the union of a man and a woman in marriage is subject to the payment of the *mundr*, the bride-price. In our country this is eight pieces of silver, and the price of the morning gift should be agreed with the wife.'

'But my lord, if the lady's father is dead, who should the bride-price be paid to?'

'To me.'

With that, the aged king ambled slowly back to his horse which was being held by a servant. He climbed on a mounting block, clambered back on his mount and rode off up the hill.

'Sirs, will you take the slave?' said Hacun, pointing at Vanja.

One of the riders spoke to a soldier who, together with another, pulled the unsuspecting Vanja through the crowd and into captivity.

'We have avenged Siward,' said Hacun to the brothers.

Hacun and the three northerners were taken to the garrison and given beds in the barracks. Later that evening, a king's messenger arrived to tell them that they were awaited at the royal mansion. They followed the messenger and arrived at the large wooden building next to the one they had seen from the sea with a cross on. The messenger spoke to the guards and they were allowed into the large hall where the king was dining with his *godes* – chieftains who owned estates in the area and who supplied armed men for the king's army. The four new arrivals were shown to a bench on a step below the *godes* and offered food and drink.

Later, much later, the four of them were shown the way back to their quarters. Three of them were in high spirits and well satisfied with the appreciation that had been shown for the tale they related of their voyage from Sigtuna. Finn, however, was much preoccupied about how he was going to break the news to Aneka that her father had been killed and his estate was valueless while the land was disputed between King Harald and King Erik. Just as awful was the prospect that he could not marry her until he could pay eight pieces of silver to the king.

Hacun was instructed to join the garrison in the town. The king kept a standing army of experienced warriors for fear that his son, Sweyne Forkbeard, would try to usurp him. The three brothers were permitted to begin training as warriors. They had asked if they could have their weapons back and the king agreed. Gunnar and Torsten were somewhat embarrassed to find that the other would-be warriors were much younger than them, some of them hardly in their teens. After a few days of general fitness training through sports activities they started to train with spears, the foremost weapon used by the Viking warrior in battle. The spear had an ash shaft which was longer than the height of the carrier. At first, they trained with poles which were untipped, to learn the basic skills of throwing and thrusting. They practised throwing two spears at a time, one in each hand, and also catching spears which were thrown at them to throw back at an enemy. Later, their spears had iron blades and they were able to have more realistic, though dangerous, practice. The only protection afforded them was their warrior skullcaps of hard leather with an iron rim and two metal bands running over the crown at right angles to each other.

Finn did not have a chance to see Aneka for several days, in fact he did not know where she was, but one evening a messenger came to guide him to the lodgings where she was staying. She met him at the door and suggested that they should go for a walk and enjoy the warm summer evening. They were soon on the edge of the town where the rows of wooden houses gave way to a newly-mown meadow on the slope running down to the lake. They walked hand in hand, almost in silence. Their joy to be together was tangible and they needed no words.

The cut grass was stacked up around poles to dry. They sat on the grass, facing the lake, watching the swallows diving to feed on mosquitoes. Away to their left, the setting sun was casting a red glow over the western side of the lake on which several fishermen were working. The tranquillity of the scene belied the feelings of Finn. He would have to overcome his shyness and speak with Aneka of serious matters.

'The king spoke to me and asked me to explain that things are not well at your father's home.'

Aneka abruptly turned her head from surveying the scene in front of them and looked at Finn intently. Finn dropped his head and stared at his hands in his lap. He glanced at Aneka. 'The raiding party which kidnapped you killed your father and perhaps your mother too.'

Aneka turned back to look across the lake. Finn saw that tears were welling up in her eyes. 'I know, I think that I have known this for many months, but I hoped that I was wrong.'

'There is more. The land of your father continues to be disputed between the two kings and it is too dangerous for you to return to claim your birthright.'

'What am I to do?'

'The king has said that your father had property in Roskilde where you can live. I am sure that you will be looked after.'

'But we are betrothed, you should look after me!'

'Yes, but we cannot marry until I have the *mundr* which must be paid to the king.'

Aneka turned to Finn and he saw the trails of tears running down her cheeks. He put his arm around her.

'I am training to be a warrior so that next season I can go with the Viking and earn my fortune.'

'But that will be many months!'

'Will you not wait for me?'

'Of course, but it will seem an eternity. And you will be in danger.'

'My bear claws will protect me from death at the hand of a stranger. And now, you take one of them so that you too might be protected.' Finn untied the leather cord around his neck and slid off one of the claws. He gave it to Aneka for her to make her own necklace. And with that they wandered back to the town.

The warrior training continued all autumn and through the winter. The brothers learnt the use of the battleaxe, the sword, and how to defend against attack with a shield. They were each given a round shield made of lime planks, butted together and covered in leather with a metal boss on the front in the centre to protect the hand gripping behind the shield. They practised tactics, such as where they lined up with a wall of shields and defended a row of spearmen standing behind them, thrusting with their long spears. Many hours were spent working with the *svinfylking*, or boar formation. This favourite Viking form of attack was where the warriors formed a wedge of twenty to thirty men. The pointed end of the wedge advanced against an enemy with the strongest men in the leading edge, and then suddenly they broke the formation and tried to overwhelm the adversary. Although the training was hard and dangerous, the brothers with their previous experience and physical strength easily outperformed the younger trainees.

The king arranged for Aneka's father's house to be made available for her. While it was very well positioned in the square in the centre of town, it was in a poor state of repair. Finn persuaded his two brothers to spend their free time helping to refurbish the building and before the onset of winter the roof and external woodwork were repaired and Aneka was able to move in. In a curious turn of fate, to celebrate the event, the king presented her with a female slave to serve her. But her memories of being a slave herself were too fresh and she treated the girl more as a friend.

As winter gave way to spring, the masters of the fleet of longships which had been assembling in the harbour started gathering crews for the season's expedition to the west. Word spread that forty ships would be leaving after Walpurgis, for the westlands. They would sail around the north of Britannia and raid the villages on the west coast to capture slaves to sell at Dubh Linn, the black pool, which was the main slave trading centre.

The ships' masters were on the quay each day signing warriors up to crew their ships. Some of the ships were crewed by clans of kinsfolk who had made many plundering journeys together in the past. They had one or two spaces to fill. But other ships were new and the masters were forming crews. Each boat needed a crew of fifty to sixty men, so the three brothers were confident that they would find berths. The size of ship was measured according to how many *sessar* or thwarts she had. The master of a ship called *Ulven*, the wolf, was on the quay recruiting a new crew.

Gunnar went up to him and asked what he was offering as payment for the voyage.

'Have you got weapons?' he asked.

'Yes, but not swords.'

'Show me the man who owns a good sword and he is probably the captain of a ship!'

While training, the brothers had become aware of the scarcity of swords. Apparently, reliable swords were extremely expensive and only carried by wealthy men. The swords they had used when training were the ones they had got from Birka. They had been made of very poor quality iron. They bent easily when struck and by the end of the training they were useless.

'Is your ship well-found?' asked Gunnar.

'None better. She is new, thirty *sessar*, and well prepared for ocean-going.'

'What do you pay the crew?' repeated Gunnar.

'For every hundred pieces of silver we earn I take forty and the crew get one each.'

'I need eight pieces, will I get them?' interjected Finn.

'Shut up Finn,' said Gunnar.

'Tell your red-haired friend that he'll get his eight pieces and more.'

'We will think about it and come here tomorrow at this time,' said Gunnar.

They borrowed a boat and rowed out to see *Ulven*. She was more than thirty-five paces long and five paces wide. On her prow there was a fearsome wolf carving. The highest plank running around the hull was painted black, the one underneath red, then another black one and finally a yellow one. The boat looked huge compared with the craft they had sailed in earlier.

'Surely, this boat must be able to sail anywhere!' said Torsten.

'A boat is only as good as the people sailing her,' answered Gunnar. 'We need to find out some more about the captain.'

'How do we do that?' said Torsten.

'We ask,' said Gunnar, pulling the rowing boat alongside the longship.

There was a team of men cutting hemp ropes for the standing rigging of the boat. Hemp rope was the only type of rope known to the riggers which would absorb tar used as a preservative to stop rot. Standing up in the rowing boat Gunnar could just look over the gunnels of the big ship.

'Any of you sailed with the captain before?'

'Who is asking?' answered one of the men gruffly.

'I am Gunnar, I may join the crew.'

'You hear that lads! I hope that he can swim.'

There was laughter among the other riggers.

'What's so funny?' said Gunnar.

'Well, let's put it this way. Captain Ottarr needed a new ship this year, because when he came home last year, his ship was falling to pieces. He pushes a vessel harder than any man; he sails through storms that keep other captains ashore. But he gets home before anyone else and makes more money than most. If you are a sailor with strong nerves and a good stomach, *Ulven* could be for you.'

Gunnar sat down in the boat. 'Well, what do you think?' It was unlike Gunnar to ask the opinions of the others, and betray the fact that he was uncertain.

'I don't mind taking risks, as long as we make money and get back quickly,' said Finn.

'Yes, money and lots of it,' mused Torsten. 'She is a beautiful boat, and very fast I am sure.'

'All right, let's see Captain Ottarr tomorrow,' said Gunnar.

The following evening they met up with the captain. He was wearing a leather tunic over a linen shirt. His trousers were baggy and tucked into the top of his boots. On one side of his belt he carried a *seax* and on the other hung a drinking horn next to his pouch.

'Captain, we are three who would like to sail with you. But your terms are hard and we will only agree to them if you give us two silver pieces in advance.'

'You cheeky devil. I make the terms, not you.'

'If you accept my terms, then I may find another very experienced warrior to sail with us.'

Ottarr paused for a minute. 'Has he sailed before?'

'From Sigtuna, to here, twice.'

'All right, it's a deal. You must supply a bow and twenty-four arrows, a shield, a broadaxe and a spear.'

The brothers went off to see Hacun.

'I am already tired of standing around here just guarding

fat noblemen. So, well yes, I'll join you. When does the boat sail?'

'The day after Laugardagur, after Walpurgis.'

'Then we shall all start the journey clean!' joked Hacun.

Laugardagur was the day of the week when it was traditional to bathe, for despite their savage image, the warriors were fastidious about cleanliness. And so it was that the brothers got their advance of pay. Gunnar and Torsten used their money to buy a tunic and trousers like the captain's, and Finn gave his to Aneka to save for when he returned.

Two days after Walpurgis, the fleet was ready to leave. At dawn, there was frantic activity on the quay with last minute provisions being loaded for each ship, crew members in various states of intoxication being ferried out to the waiting craft and families bidding farewell to fathers, brothers and husbands.

Aneka came to the quay to say farewell to Finn. She was wearing a bright blue apron dress over her smock and her hair tumbled over her shoulders. The apron dress was decorated with red and white embroidery over the bodice. Around her neck she wore a simple leather cord on which was the bear's claw.

Gunnar teased Finn about the fact that he now only had two bear's claws to protect him. But the younger man ignored him and also the taunts of his shipmates, and gave Aneka an embrace and a kiss.

'I just need six more pieces of silver; I will be back with them in the autumn.'

She gently ran a finger over the tattooed cheek and with tear-filled eyes looked up at him and said, 'Be careful, remember I am waiting for you.'

Finn loaded his weapons into the waiting ferry, climbed aboard, and waved to the slender blue-clad figure at the end of the quay as a rising red sun bathed her in light. His

sadness at leaving her was easily overcome by the excitement of the adventure to come. She, with nothing to
distract her from her sadness, turned and walked slowly
back to her home.

Part 3
The Westlands

Chapter 14
The Wolf in the Wind

The fleet comprised thirty-six ships, including six cargo vessels of the *knar* type in which the brothers had travelled from the northlands. They were all anchored in deeper water off Roskilde. As the crews assembled, they hung their shields on the outside of their rowing positions, put their weapons in the armoury and set about preparations for departure. The armoury weapon chests were kept under the deck at the stern of the boats, in front of the helmsman's position. This was also the place where the officers of the ship were stationed. Between this position and three-quarters of the way along the length of the ship the main crew sat, rowed, ate, slept and fought. Between them and the bow, there were several crew who were responsible for trimming the sails, and the prow, which was by far the highest place in the ship, was the position for the lookout and standard bearer.

Every ship had some specialist crew such as carpenters, blacksmiths and sailmakers. There were also several men who had responsibility for providing the crew with food. When the ships overnighted near the shore and the crew could sleep in tents on the beach, then they could cook hot food, usually in a large bronze cauldron supported on a collapsible iron tripod. The usual cooked food consisted mainly of porridge, cabbage, roasted or boiled meat and bread. At sea, the diet was mostly salted or smoked cold fish and bread. They drank either water or ale, as the latter could be preserved much longer than water. The ships carried provisions for five or six days which was the time it usually took to reach the westlands. These victuals were stored in wooden barrels and baskets with lids, on and under the deck amidships. Water was kept in leather sacks and there was usually a sack near to each crew seat so that the men could easily get a drink.

There was a hierarchy among the ships and although they had different owners, there was a commanding officer who had been elected by the captains, and there were several deputies, mainly *gode* chieftains. The commanding officer's ship was the flagship. Thus it was that the ships set off in a particular order, the flagship leading.

All the ships except the cargo vessels had lowered their masts towards the stern, as they would be rowing through the channel to the open sea and the speed of the ships was increased significantly without the wind resistance of the mast and furled sail. The *knars* had to be towed through the channel as they did not have the rowing speed to keep up with the others. These cargo vessels, for which the whole fleet shared the cost, were heavily laden with timber, iron, tools and tar and served on the outward journey as supply ships with the spares which might be needed for running repairs to the fleet. On the return journey the Vikings hoped that they would be laden with plunder and slaves.

The rising sun highlighted the impressive procession of the thirty-six ships bearing over 2,000 men. Anyone watching from the eastern shore would have seen the glint of the sun reflecting on the wet blades of the oars as they dipped in and out of the water. Only half the oars were used at one time as the rowing positions were so close together that had all the men tried to row at once they would not have had sufficient space. So every other oar port was in use. When the first group of rowers tired, the second group took over propelling the ship.

Many of the ships had a figurehead of some description. *Ulven* had a fearsome wolf carving, others had dragons' heads, and some sported the shapes of writhing snakes or mythological animals. Those which did not have figureheads had a carefully sculpted curl of wood at the point where the timbers of the hull terminated at the prow. Most of the ships' hulls were painted – some had a single colour following a plank around the upper part of the hull, others were multicoloured, with yellows, blues and reds. At the prow of each ship there was a polished copper weather vane, which, as well as helping to show the helmsman the direction of the apparent wind, served as a pennant. These vanes were shaped differently on each ship and had delicate patterns cut out of the metal which identified the ship.

The warriors on the ships were infected by the display of mighty power portrayed by the view of the longships in front and behind them. They felt confident; indeed, invincible and undaunted by the prospect of a long voyage in the open sea and the battles to come. But their first day was only to take them as far as the opening from the bay into the sea. By mid-afternoon, they had cleared the narrow entrance to the Roskilde channel. The commander steered to the east and as the light wind was from the south-west, he ordered the fleet to anchor for the night near to the bay entrance. Some ships already needed maintenance. Two because they were new and leaks were found on untried hulls on the trip up the channel and the others because some detail had been neglected in their winter refit. Six ships were hauled ashore for the carpenters and blacksmiths to work on.

The other crews took the opportunity of raising the heavy masts. They weighed as much as five men, and were slotted into what was called the 'mastfish' between beams amid-ships. The yardarms were mounted and sails prepared for the following day's journey.

The captains of the fleet had a meeting to discuss their strategy and then returned to their ships to inform the crews. The passage plan was to sail clear of the northern tip of the Land of the Danes and then around the southern part of Norvegia before steering north of west, to Orkneyjar – seal island. This island was populated mainly by people from Norvegia; here, they would plunder food stores to revictual their ships and start their campaign to capture slaves. They had little hope of finding silver or valuables there as the farmers were poor. They would then sail down the west coast of Skotland and raid the fishing villages to get slaves to sell in the big slave market in Dubh Linn. There they would decide where the next part of their voyage would take them.

On the fleet's journey northwards to the open sea, they stopped twice more at overnight anchorages. The final visit ashore was to replenish the water sacks and commandeer fish from a coastal village. Having rounded the southern cape of Norvegia, they set course for Orkneyjar. The ships were to make their own pace to the islands and to rendezvous in the sheltered bay south of Kirkjuvagar, the biggest settlement. There they would wait for the slower cargo ships to arrive before attacking the settlement. They would lose the element of surprise, but with such a large force against them there was little the people of the settle-ment could do to defend themselves.

With a southerly wind, the fleet made good progress on their course. By the second morning in the open sea, they had covered almost half the distance. The wind became even more favourable as it shifted to the south-east and then to the east. But there was some concern among the more experienced crew members on *Ulven*.

214

'The weather's up to no good when the wind changes against the way the sun goes,' grumbled the sailor sitting in front of Gunnar. He pointed up to the high cloud formation where there were many wisps with curled tails, just like the ones Captain Leif had shown Gunnar on the voyage from the northlands.

'What do you mean?' he asked.

'Wouldn't surprise me if it goes on round to blow on our faces soon,' said the man.

And the wind did continue to go round the compass, but the sun was shining and they were making good progress even when the north-easterly blew. But then, later in the day, the wind dropped. The sea, which was rolling the boat with a gentle swell had a smooth, almost oily surface. The sun was slowly being extinguished by high cloud and was surrounded by several halos of light.

The crew waited apprehensively to see what orders the captain would give. Were they to start rowing or would he wait to see if the wind returned, and, from which direction?

'Make fast all the barrels and your gear on deck!' ordered Ottarr.

The crew started lashing moveable equipment and food barrels to the hull beams and the sides of the hull where there was some space. Some of the men opened the chests under their seats to get out their heavy rain cloaks before lashing the chests to the seats. *Ulven* was in sight of several vessels and Captain Ottarr could see other crews busy making similar preparations.

A breeze started gusting from the north bringing with it heavy rain. But the wind direction was still favourable enough for them to sail on their course. Soon the breeze increased in strength. The benign swell began to deteriorate into waves which were hitting them on the beam of the ship and making things uncomfortable for the crew. Just before the first squall hit them the Captain ordered a reef to be put in the sail, but no sooner had this been done than a flash and a long rumble of thunder announced the arrival of the next squall. A second reef was ordered. The waves, which had been lapping against the side of the ship, were now finding their way further up the hull and occasionally water would slop over the gunnels and reach the crew on the starboard side.

The opacity of the cloud cover hastened the dusk and nightfall found the ship running on course with a minimum of sail. The crew were supremely confident in the ability of their ship to cope with this weather, but several of the crew, both new and experienced, were suffering from sea sickness. Ottarr shared the confidence of the crew, but he and his more experienced sailors feared that this was just the prelude to the main act of the storm. His dilemma was that if the wind continued to back, the storm would hit them on the prow and then they only had three choices. They could turn back and run with the wind, thus negating the progress that they had made in the last day, or perhaps two days, depending on how long the storm lasted. Or, they could continue to sail forward with a deeply reefed sail as close as they dared to the wind, northwards, or southwards. He felt certain that the rest of the captains would not choose the first alternative unless their ships were damaged. So, which of the second and third alternatives would they choose? Would they go north or south? He reckoned that sailing as close as possible to a north-west wind would eventually bring them to Hjaltland. He had been to Leir-vik, the muddy bay; the coast was treacherous, especially in the dark. Not a place to be in a storm.

If he steered his best course to windward on the starboard tack the ship would probably be wrecked on the north-east coast of Skotland where there were no good harbours that he knew of. He made his decision, but kept it to himself, waiting to see if a wind change would force him to announce it.

And, quite suddenly, the wind did change, and it did blow dead against them and it did get stronger, much stronger. The rain started and flew almost horizontally at *Ulven*. Spray flew over the bow and added to the discomfort of the crew. The wind screamed in the shrouds and rattled anything it found which was not tightly secured. The progress of the boat was halted and it could not be steered.

'Lower the sail, man the oars!' Ottarr bellowed to the officers in front of him, whom he could not see, but he knew would be there. They in turn passed the message down the boat, crew member to crew member, from stern to bow.

The sail-trimmers fought with the wild sail, which was flapping madly as the wind was forcing it back against the mast, making the rowers' job of attaining enough speed to steer the boat impossible. Several other crew members attempted to assist in handing in the sail and lashing it to the yard. Of the sailors who tried to help, three were never to sit at their oars again: their cries for help, as the sea carried them away from the ship, inaudible, in the demonic cacophony of the duet played by wind and ocean. It was the wind and the sea which were masters and they decided which way the boat should go, and, as it happened their command was totally in accord with the captain's un-announced strategy – the bow was turned southwards; though it would have been turned homewards if the helms-man had allowed it. Captain Ottarr gave orders to raise the reefed sail again and for the oars to be shipped. He had decided to keep the wind behind his right shoulder and to sail south along where he thought the coast of Skotland was, until the storm blew itself out.

On the new course, the ship leaned alarmingly as the windy blast pulsed against the small sail. On this course, the rowing positions of the three brothers and Hacun were almost at sea level, with the hull on their side being forced into foaming waves as the ship surged along, bucking and twisting at the mercy of the weather. They and the other crew on the port side hauled themselves up the slanting deck, holding onto anything firm they could find in the darkness and gripped tightly to the thwarts on the windward side of the ship, to prevent being thrown into the sea. More importantly, for the safety of the vessel, the extra weight of the port side crew shifting over helped to keep *Ulven* more upright. Nevertheless, the breaking waves sent sheets of water over the gunnels and continued to drench the sailors, while the unrelenting wind whipped a maelstrom of rain across the deck. It was as well that members of the crew could not see each other in the dark for there were many faces betraying abject terror which were hidden by the cloak of night.

Both fore and aft there were compartments called well-rooms where sailors detailed for the work spent the night filling wooden buckets with water from the bilges and passing the filled containers to others who precariously emptied the water over the lee side.

By dawn, the sailors were suffering from nervous and physical exhaustion as well as hunger. But now at least, they could see through the rain squalls that they were not nearing a dangerous coastline. The battered ship appeared to be low in the water – clearly the men in the well-rooms had not been able to keep up with the ingress of rain and sea water. The captain realised that the vessel was acting sluggishly with the weight of water on board and was in danger of foundering, so he decided to temporarily change course so that the wind was behind them and the crew could bail out the flooded holds and move around to relieve themselves and get food and water. He had been anxiously looking around the horizon, as far as the poor visibility would permit, to see if they were in company with any of the other ships, but no sail was to be seen.

Chapter 15
The Wolf in the West

By mid-morning, the storm began to abate, and Captain Ottarr decided that it was safe enough for them to steer further to the west to try to get sight of the coast. Soon, the rain stopped, the skies began to brighten and visibility improved markedly. There was some shouting at the bow of the ship and a message was passed back to one of the officers, who turned to the captain and said, 'The lookout can make out a coastline and can see two sails between it and us.'

Ottarr turned to the helmsman and told him to steer further to the west, so that they could close on the two ships which had been sighted.

'Shake out the reefs in the sail!' he ordered.

Three hours later, in the early afternoon, they were in company with two other longships keeping the coast within sight, but maintaining a respectful distance from it. The other two ships came closer and closer to *Ulven* so that eventually they were within hailing distance. Ottarr recognised one of the ships and knew that the captain, Axeln, was a *gode* and senior to him.

Axeln shouted to him, 'We follow the coast until to-morrow morning and then turn into the bay of Din Eidyn. Come with us.'

Ottarr was happy with this plan, as they needed to get provisions. He knew that there were some villages around the bay where there should be easy pickings.

'Don't go too close to Din Eidyn. Sweyne Forkbeard is in exile there under the protection of King Kenneth of Skotland. He has a fleet in the harbour!' shouted Axeln.

With the appearance of the sun in mid-afternoon, all three ships were proceeding along the coast with lines rigged along the decks, which were festooned with cloaks and other clothes as the crews tried to dry out their belongings. The bilges had been emptied and *Ulven* was once more responding easily to the helm. The wind, which was now no more than a stiff breeze, had continued to blow from the same direction and the crew could relax and doze until the officers barked new orders to them. They passed an easy night holding the same course, as Ottarr knew that there was no land ahead of them, only to the west.

They had not been sailing for long the next day when they saw a break in the coastline and a bay opened up on their starboard side. *Ulven* was turned to the west and followed the other two ships for over four hours until they came to a place where a shoreline was running north south, directly in front of them. They could see the smoke of cooking fires rising from a village in front of high ground behind a sandy beach.

The other two ships closed up to *Ulven* and the captains had a conference. Captain Axeln shouted across to Ottarr, 'Din Eidyn is an hour's sail to the south of us. So this is the closest we go. The village on the coast here is like a ripe plum ready to fall into our basket.'

There was a roar of enthusiasm from the crews who were listening in to the conversation between the officers. Ottarr encouraged his crew by shouting back to Axeln, 'We will eat hot meat on the shore tonight and make things hotter for the villagers!'

'We go into the beach abreast and attack the village together. Later, we can drag the ships above the tide line for the night,' ordered Axeln.

The officers on *Ulven* opened up the deck at the stern and several men were detailed to lift up the weapons chests and distribute the arms to their owners. The warriors donned their leather helmets which were similar to the ones the brothers had used when training. The same activity was taking place on the other two boats. The three ships headed for the shore under sail. At about a hundred paces from the sandy beach they lowered their sails and the rowers did their work in running the vessels up onto the soft shore. The big ships only needed water half the height of a man to float so they were very close to the land when they heard the crunch of the grounding. The anchor men let go the heavy weight to hold the ships temporarily and the fully armed men started climbing over the gunnels into the sea.

The invaders ran unsteadily up the beach. Five days at sea had affected the sailors' sense of balance and it took a while to get used to having their feet on dry land again. Their landing had been dramatic, too dramatic. There was no enemy in front of them, only a seemingly empty village. On the grassland where the beach ended there was a collection of twenty or thirty simple huts. The cooking fires were still burning, goats and sheep were tethered outside the buildings and here and there small children scampered out of the houses and away from the advancing warriors. An old man walking with the aid of a stick had left it too late to flee. As he emerged from one of the huts a warrior hurled a spear which pierced the old man's back.

The warriors walked through the village to the hill beyond. There they could see a large group of peasants – men, women and children. The men were lining up in a defensive row to allow the women and children more time to escape. They started hurling rocks at the advancing invaders. Some of the missiles found targets and the effect was for the Vikings to form up into a line with the shield men in front and the spears directly behind them, crouching for protection behind the shields.

The rain of rocks and stones continued unabated until some of the warriors behind the defensive line fired a volley of arrows. Several of the defenders screamed with pain but the majority did not flinch from their position. Suddenly the men on the hill started to run down towards the Vikings, shouting and waving all manner of implements which they were using as weapons. Some had wooden spades, other staves and a few simply carried a rock. Their momentum was checked by another volley of arrows, but then they were on the warriors, fighting with demented fury.

Finn and Torsten were in the front line with axes in one hand and their shields in the other. As the Skots attacked, the spearmen behind lunged forward between the shield men, stabbing at the human onslaught. Finn saw a large bearded man with long straggly hair charging directly towards him with a stake in his right hand. Before the man made contact Finn raised his axe to strike at him but the man crouched low, avoiding the spear and the axe. He swung the stake hard at Finn's leg. The man had recognised the weakness of the classic Viking defensive shield and spear wall: the defenders legs were unprotected. The stake connected with the inside of Finn's right knee. He crashed to the ground and the Skot was immediately on him with his hands round Finn's throat, screaming abuse at the injured warrior. It was over quickly as Torsten planted his axe deep in the man's skull.

And the battle was over quickly too. The wild Skots lay dead or dying in front of the invaders. A few were captured and Finn, unable to walk, sat on an upturned rowing boat where he had been carried by Gunnar and Hacun and watched as the Skots were executed.

He felt revulsion at the gratuitous brutality and eventually shouted to the executioners, 'Why kill them? We can take them as slaves. They are no good to us dead!' But his entreaty was ignored as the warriors wreaked revenge for their number who had been injured by the defenders. Ottarr had heard what Finn had said and came over to him. 'Shut up Finn, don't make enemies! We are here as an army. I am a merchant warrior; I am here to make money not kill people, unless we have to, but you have to realise that among all the crews there are many who are sadistic and think that they will win their way into Valhalla by slaughtering others in battle, no matter how uneven the contest.'

Finn was in pain, but he was also angry at what he had seen and was not to be fobbed off with Ottarr's justification of the violence.

'When we trained to be warriors, we were told that true valour guarantees entry to Valhalla. Where is the valour for us in this behaviour? It is the Skots who defended their families and homes with no real weapons who showed courage today.'

Ottarr was furious. 'You watch your tongue, hammer-head, or I'll leave you here when we sail and give the Skots a chance of revenge.'

With that, the conversation was ended, but Finn had damaged his relationship with the captain, a man not given to forgiving or forgetting.

Finn sat as a spectator and watched as the Viking warriors ransacked the small village. It was a scene of much activity. Some chased chickens and geese around the dusty yards, trying to ensure a good dinner. The tethered goats were being slaughtered to be prepared for roasting. Goods were being thrown out of doorways in a search of anything valuable or edible. He heard some loud banging and a crash followed by the unmistakable sound of women and children screaming. Some warriors had demolished the little wooden church door and found some villagers taking refuge inside. The church was obscured from Finn's view by other buildings but he could guess what was happening.

A few minutes later, Torsten appeared with blood streaming from scratches on his face. 'By the gods, these women are even more like savages than the men. I tried to take one and she tore my face open. I have left her for the others. One woman stabbed a warrior in the throat when he caught her; he is bleeding to death by the church.'

Torsten went off to join those ransacking the houses. Far away, high on the hill, Finn could see the women and children who had taken flight. He hoped that they would stay in safety on the hill and not return. He turned his back on the scene of ravaging behind him and looked at the view across the bay. It seemed extraordinary to him that the sea which had carried them safely to this shore had receded, leaving their ships high and dry on the sand. In all their travels by ship, the brothers had not encountered the effect of the tide before, apart from when they had landed for the overnight stops on the coast of the Land of the Danes. There the waters had changed in height by only the length of his hand, but here they had already gone down more than the height of a man and were continuing to recede.

Bizarrely, among the chaos and carnage, several small children were playing on the shore. He hoped that some of his fellow warriors' lust for blood would not extend to harming them. Sweeping his gaze from across the bay towards the seaward entrance, he saw, to his consternation, far in the distance, four vessels which had entered the bay and were heading in their direction.

Finn called across to Gunnar, who was carrying empty

leather water sacks from their ship to the shore. 'We have company!'

Gunnar looked in the direction Finn was pointing. 'I had better tell Ottarr!' He placed the water carriers by Finn and ran off in search of the captain.

Soon, a crowd of warriors had assembled on the shore and were looking down the valley to where the ships were battling against the ebb tide. They could now see that three vessels had sails up. Of those under sail, two appeared to be longships and the third a *knar*. As they got closer, they could see that the ship without a sail did not have a mast, but it too was a longship and was being rowed down the bay.

At first the fear was that this flotilla was an enemy force, but it soon became apparent that these were ships from their fleet. Their progress against the tide was laborious, but as night was falling the tide changed, and the newcomers anchored by the village, though some way away, as *Ulven* and the others had arrived at high tide.

The crews of the new arrivals waded ashore and were welcomed to the camp fires where goats and sheep were being roasted. Word went round that the newcomers had also been forced south by the storm and that one of the ships had been de-masted and had lost several crew overboard.

Later in the evening Ottarr called his crew together. 'We are going to stay here for another day to repair the damaged ship. Do any of you have shipwright experience?'

Gunnar spoke up for himself and Torsten and told the captain that they had both worked in a shipyard in Sigtuna. There were several others who had had similar experience.

'Right, you men will help the repair team tomorrow. The rest of you I want to come with me after sun-up. I'll tell you then what you are to do.'

Finn spent an uncomfortable night with a badly swollen right knee. He and his brothers, together with Hacun, slept in one of the villagers' huts.

'Hacun, is it always like this, that we attack poor people where there is no chance of finding gold, just to get food?'

'No, we were lucky. This village was undefended. You will see that sometimes we have to work a lot harder to get our dinner.'

'Why didn't we take prisoners we could sell as slaves?'

'There are only a few places where it is safe to do trade with these people and sell slaves, and they are far from here. If we take slaves now we must feed them until we get to Jorvik or Dubh Linn. The captains will decide tomorrow what we are to do; perhaps they will sail and try to meet up with the main fleet which must have gone north during the storm.'

Next morning, Gunnar and Torsten went off to work on the damaged ship, which had been pulled up onto the shore at high tide. With the aid of a stick, Finn hobbled out to the meeting with Captain Ottarr. The crew was gathered out of earshot of the other crews. Ottarr stood up and addressed them.

'We are on this voyage to make money, so we are not going to waste a day chasing women and children up a hill. This is a poor village and as you have seen there is nothing more than food for us here. However, there is a church here, and often these buildings have objects of silver. If there is any silver here, what do you think that the priest did when he saw us coming?'

'Hid the silver!' ventured several of the crew.

'And where would he do that?'

'Buried it?' said one of the crew.

'Exactly. What I want you to do is to search the area around the church to see if you can see where the soil has been dug recently. This is a matter for our crew only, don't tell anyone else what we are doing.'

There was an excited hubbub of conversation before the men went to get some breakfast which was being prepared for them by the ships' cooks.

It was not long before one of the crew sought out Ottarr and said, 'We have found a place where the soil is very disturbed.'

The captain hurried to the place and gave a wooden spade to a crew member to dig. Very soon they were unwrapping a package covered in tar-soaked cloth. The captain pulled out a silver communion cup and a large book. The only other contents of the package were some manuscripts. Ottarr discarded the manuscripts and examined the heavy book. He flicked through the hand-written illuminated pages, closed the book and took his *seax* to prise off the silver hinge. He threw the book back into the hole.

'Well men, we have started our silver collection!'

There was a loud roar from the assembled crew, many of whom followed Ottarr because of his reputation as a lucky captain. There was a spirit of competition between the crews, and they had stolen a march on the others.

The working party on the damaged boat took all day to shape a new mast from timbers which the *knar* had carried onboard from Roskilde. By supper time, the work was complete and the fleet could sail on the morrow. The question was, where would they sail?

As senior officer, Axeln brought the captains together for a conference to look at the alternatives. After the meeting Ottarr addressed his crew.

'We are now a fleet of six longships and a cargo vessel. There are over three hundred warriors to feed and so we have decided to spend several days going around this bay looking for other villages and building up our food supplies. The captains think that if the main fleet reached Orkneyjar, they will by now have left to sail towards Dubh Linn. We won't easily catch up with them. So, we are going south. Now we are stronger, we will raid some wealthy towns. Then, at the end of the summer, we will go west round Britannia, and sell our slaves in Dubh Linn before heading home.'

'Have you ever sailed round Britannia captain?' asked one of the crew.

'No, not many Vikings do. Two years ago we went as far as Hamwic on the south coast.'

Once more there was much conversation between crew members. Several of them had been with Ottarr two years before when the fleet had plundered Hamwic and they attested to the fact that there was great wealth along that coast.

Next morning at high tide, the fleet launched and left the site of their first conquest, but not before some of the more vindictive crew set fire to several of the huts in the village. Two or three of the crew of *Ulven* were involved in this fire-raising and Captain Ottarr gave them a severe reprimand. His cause for rebuking them was not on any humanitarian grounds, but that the pall of smoke would be a certain warning to other villages in the bay that the Viking were upon them. They spent four days plundering other undefended villages before heading for the sea and turning south. Finn had resumed his work as a crew member but his knee was still very painful and he could only walk with the aid of a stick.

After two days at sea, the fleet entered a wide river and spent some days raiding small towns. At Monkchester they had their first real battle when they encountered a force of soldiers defending an unoccupied residence of Waltheof, the Earl of Northumbria. But such was the strength of the Viking force that the soldiers were soon overcome and for the first time the invaders found valuable trophies when they sacked the residence. For Gunnar, Torsten and Hacun the bounty included a fine steel sword each. So for them, their personal armoury was complete.

And so they continued down the east coast of Britannia.

Each ship had a captain's chest which was chained to the mast and only the captain had a key. The chests on each ship began to fill with items of jewellery, silver and ivory. The fleet lost some men in various encounters with those who attempted to defend their property, but once more Ottarr was lucky and apart from the three men they had lost during the storm, the crew was complete as they rounded the south-eastern tip of Britannia. But they had spent too much time plundering on the east coast and it was late summer when they started cruising west against the pre-dominantly south-westerly winds along the south coast. The crew was restless; several expressed their reservations to their friends.

'We have good profit from this journey. It is time to turn and head for home,' said one.

'If we travel round Britannia it will be autumn before we sail around the north of Skotland on our way home, and the autumn storms will have started,' said another.

The crew decided that they should have a meeting with Ottarr to discuss these things. The first opportunity was when the fleet had attacked Winceleseia. They had raided the port and found good supplies of food and wine in cargo ships waiting to unload at the quay. There had been little violence as the ships' owners realised that it would cost them more to resist the Viking than to hand over the goods.

The crew of *Ulven* was eating together on the quayside when several of them went up to Ottarr and said that the crew wanted to discuss with him the plan to go to Dubh Linn. Ottarr agreed to address the crew about the plan. He surprised them by saying that he agreed with them that it would be better to turn back now before the weather became unstable. However, he pointed out that Axeln was in command.

'He is a powerful man at home. Powerful men make

good friends but fearful enemies. If we disobey him we could find ourselves in serious trouble.'

'But surely he realises the danger of an autumn voyage around the north of Skotland?'

'Yes, I think he does. But I suspect that when we get to Dubh Linn he will decide that we should over-winter there.'

There was some tumult among the crew. Most of them had wives or sweethearts at home. Those with wives and children needed to take home their earnings to support their families. Those with sweethearts could not depend on the fact that the girls would still be waiting for them next year, especially if they thought that the men had perished at sea.

The meeting broke up, but discussions continued in small groups. There were those who feared reprisals from Axeln if they tried to abandon the expedition, and so accepted the situation. There were some who thought that they should try to persuade Ottarr that they should turn for home, and there was a small group which, in their desperation, had decided to take the outcome into their own hands. Several from the latter group approached Gunnar, Torsten, Finn and Hacun and tried to persuade them to take part in a plot to take over the boat and sail home. But only Finn had reason to wish to return to the Land of the Danes as soon as possible. The others were quite happy to let the adventure continue. Finn considered joining the rebellious faction, but then remembered the consequences of the last mutiny he had been involved in and that it had led to slavery for them.

The plotters made the mistake of trying to solicit the help of one of the officers. He betrayed them to Ottarr. The captain, a generally reasonable man, exploded with demented fury. 'Damn them, damn them a thousand times. I have led them to their fortunes this summer and this is how they intend to repay me.'

He had the ringleaders brought to him and announced that they would be executed, but not by him. He would never have his crew's blood on his hands. No, the act would be done by others. And thus he carried out the treatment he had once threatened to Finn. As the ships left the beach at Winceleseia, four of the crew were left tied up sitting on the shore, watching the ships depart. The plot was quashed and the ringleaders awaited the retribution of the Anglo-Saxons.

In 982 came up in Dorsetshire three ships of the pirates, and plundered in Portland.

Anglo-Saxon Chronicle

Chapter 16
A Change of Plan

It was with reluctance that Finn began to accept that as a result of his first battle he had acquired a handicap which was likely to affect him for the rest of his life. His leg was very stiff, but three months after receiving the wound in Skotland he had learned to cope with the disability and although he had a limp he now walked without the aid of a stick. He had missed much of the action of the marauding crew as, in view of his lack of mobility, he had frequently been detailed to stay with the guard crew on the ship when the others went ashore to plunder. One of the things which the Vikings feared most was to lose their ships, and thus whenever an attacking party went ashore a number of warriors stayed on board to prevent the fleet being attacked, or worse, set on fire by the suffering local citizens. As the captain's chest got more and more full, there was also the issue of protecting their ill-gotten earnings. The guard crew were also responsible for adjusting ships' lines, as required by the tide and the wind.

Thus it was that apart from the few occasions when his archery skills had been required, Finn relied on his brothers to recount the activities of the day. From time to time he could see the fires of torched buildings, and hear the clash of steel on steel, the screams of women and the battle cries of men. Sometimes crew members came back injured, sometimes they returned leading men and boys who were destined to be sold as slaves. These were loaded on to the *knar* or taken onto the longships to take the seats of crew members who had been slain. In either case they were bound or chained.

After the sack of Winceleseia, Ottarr decided to meet Axeln to express the concerns of his crew. As they sailed slowly westwards with a light breeze he brought *Ulven* alongside the flagship and clambered across into the other vessel.

'My men are discontent with the prospect of an autumn northerly passage home,' stated Ottarr.

'Yes, I have heard the same from other crews. We have good booty and almost as many slaves as we can carry. We can sail immediately for Dubh Linn.'

'Why don't we sail home directly from here?'

'We will get better prices for our slaves at Dubh Linn. If we stop to get provisions at Hamwic and then again at Hlidaforda we can be round Penwithstert in three days.'

'Where is Hlidaforda?'

'It is a capital of the west country province and very wealthy.'

'And Penwithstert?'

'This is the end of Britannia; we turn this corner and sail north to Dubh Linn.'

'And then directly home?'

'Yes, if the weather permits.'

Ottarr returned to *Ulven* and informed the crew that they would be sailing to Dubh Linn without delay other than revictualling en route. The mood on board seemed to ease at this news. If they sold their slaves quickly they could be on their way before autumn set in. But in Ottarr's mind there was a nagging suspicion that Axeln intended to trick them into overwintering on Hibernia.

They found that Hamwic was still in a pitiful state after

the burning and looting of two years earlier and they only stayed there to plunder food and fill their water bags. Heavily laden, they left at dawn and then followed the tide west through the narrow waterway between Hamwic and an island before emerging once more into the open sea. *Ulven* and one other ship, *Ormen* (the 'snake'), had been given the task of escorting the *knar*, the slowest-moving vessel, but they kept in sight of the other four longships.

The fleet followed the coast, well out to sea. They had a slow passage across a bay after the tide had turned against them, but in the late afternoon it turned in their favour once more. Eventually they saw that ahead of them was a long spit of land. At the seaward end there was a high hump which eventually ran down to near sea level at the outermost point. It was unclear if the spit was joined to the mainland or if it was an island. If it was an island they might get through a channel to travel west. Axeln took no chances about this and had taken a course towards the mainland and then turned to clear the headland. They were sailing well, though the south-westerly wind was strong and gusty, and spray occasionally flew over their craft as *Ulven* dipped her bow into the waves. Evening was coming on, but because the full moon was already rising, visibility was still good.

The leading four boats were about 1,000 paces in front of *Ulven* when they neared the headland in the strong ebb tide and came out of the lee of the high hill. Suddenly, the crew on the trailing boats saw the leading four start dancing wildly, their masts waving madly from side to side and the hulls being tossed around by wild water. It was as if a giant's hand was shaking them violently. First one, then a second and finally the third and fourth longship tried to change tack to reverse their course and return the way they had come, but as they tried, broadside to the wind, in the same order the heavily laden ships were rolled over by the violent sea.

The crew of *Ulven* watched, horror-struck. At the distance they were from the disaster, they could not hear the cries of the drowning men, but they could see wreckage being tossed around in the angry sea. They had already turned for their approach to the headland, but it was clear that they should not stay long on this course, which would lead them to the same fate as the other ships. The tide was pushing them ever nearer. Soon they would be leaving the lee of the hill. Ottarr decided that the only course of action was to try to head for the spit and find an anchorage. They turned again and together with the other two ships headed for the landward side of the high hill. As they approached there was a world of difference in the weather and the sea. The breaking waves were now no more than ripples and the wind was effectively blocked by the hill. The three ships ran ashore onto the beach, which was a mixture of sand and shingle.

The crews were tough men, but there was a sense of shock which subdued them all. Many of them left their boats and stood around in groups talking about what they had seen. They realised that there was no chance that there would be survivors from the capsized ships.

'What manner of place is this?' said Gunnar to Ottarr, 'that the sea can swallow up ships when there is no storm?'

'I have seen places like this at the north of Skotland, but none of us have been here before. Over two hundred warriors will have to find Valhalla the hard way, as they did not die in battle.'

The captains of the two surviving longships and the *knar* walked up the beach together and sat on the grassy bank. The captain of *Ormen* was called Ingolf. It was unclear which of the captains was senior, so Ottarr had to consult them. It was getting dark and they had to decide on a course of action. They spoke for some time while the crews anxiously awaited news from their captains.

'We go no further. Tomorrow we will raid the villages on this island and then turn for home, the way we came,' Ottarr announced to his crew. There was a cheer from the men, much back-slapping and many smiling faces. They proceeded to set up camp and light fires for the cooks.

'It looks as if you have got your way, Finn,' said Torsten.

'The gods have granted me my will, but at great cost to others.'

'Every man's span of life has an end to it. It will be the same for you and me, who knows when.'

The full moon lit the landscape behind them, but from where they were, even in daylight, they would not have been able to see the villages on the high plateau. That was for tomorrow.

Soon after dawn, the warriors breakfasted and then started to get their weapons ready. This had become routine for them on their long passage along the coasts, but today was special because they knew it would be the last time before they left for home. Already they could see the tell-tale signs of habitation on top of the high hill in the form of curls of woodsmoke trailing off into the windless sky. The warriors knew that they had lost the element of surprise, but they were as ever supremely confident about over-coming any resistance. This, even though they were now an attacking force of only a little more than a hundred men, as twenty would stay behind to guard the slaves and the ships. Once more, Finn was left onboard the ship. He was really disappointed not to be involved in the final raid of their voyage and complained to Gunnar.

'You will have many tales to tell when you return, but for me all I can describe is the tedious wait on the ship for the warriors' return.'

'It is important work that you are doing. If we lose the ships then this whole voyage will have been in vain and then you won't get your six pieces of silver.'

237

'And Aneka will die an old maid!' joked Torsten.

They all laughed. While he was often in his elder brother's shadow, Torsten was always good company and often cheered them up during the boredom of the long passages.

The two brothers and Hacun put on their swords, checked their arrows and marched off to join the others, leaving Finn with the ship's guard. There were several other injured men who were allotted this duty and they knew each other well. As soon as the warriors had departed, several sets of dice appeared and they started playing.

The warriors tramped up the beach and over the grassy slope towards the high hill. The closer they came, the more formidable they saw the mound was. They found a narrow track and started walking up the steep slope. Suddenly, there was confusion ahead of Gunnar, who was halfway along the procession, and the climbers halted. The word quickly came back that they were being attacked by villagers rolling boulders down the slope at them and hurling rocks from their superior position. It was like Skotland again, only worse.

Two men pushed their way down hill past the procession with a badly injured warrior, and then another pair with a bloodied member of the *Ulven* crew. Ottarr followed this pair and when he reached Hacun he said, 'There is no easy way up on this path without many casualties. Take forty men from the end of this line and try to find a way around the hill. If you can, attack them from behind. We will keep them busy while you try.'

Hacun grabbed Gunnar's arm. 'Come on you two, let's go.'

The forty or so men retraced their steps to the bottom of the hill and surveyed the scene. The land to the west of the hill was very steep and did not look promising, but to the east there seemed to be a better chance. They started to move in this direction when they heard shouting from the boats. Pushing through the low bushes they found that there was a group of villagers firing arrows at the ships. The warriors rushed at the bowmen who now found themselves between the warriors on the ships and Hacun's men. The action was over quickly and bloodily. The warriors went across to the ships and found that although hulls were peppered with arrows there had been few casualties among the guards, as they had had the benefit of taking refuge behind the gunnels. On the *knar* the slaves had not been as lucky, as many of them were tied to beams amidships. A number of them hung limply from their bonds, arrows marking their wounds.

Finn grinned down at Gunnar who shouted up to him, 'You wanted some action and you got it!'

'Thanks for the help,' answered Finn.

'We've got to find another route to the summit,' said Gunnar.

With that, the troop of warriors left and at a slow trot started making their way around the east side of the island. Not far from the shoreline, they found a track through the low scrub and followed this for over an hour. It was hot work and the sun was still not at its peak for the day. Soon the track started to turn more towards the south-west and the incline to the hilltop became less steep. The warriors decided to try to cut inland.

They passed groups of women and children fleeing southwards, but paid them no heed and continued to work their way up the slope which was now to their north. An hour later, they found themselves at the back of a milling crowd of poorly-clad peasants who were near the edge of the steep incline, passing rocks forward to others who were precariously balanced on the cliff edge.

Aware that they might be detected at any moment, the warriors did not even stop to catch their breath after the long walk, but with whoops and battle cries they launched a savage attack on the peasants with swords and battleaxes. The element of surprise was complete. Some of the rock-throwers tumbled over the steep cliff towards their adversaries, others started to run along the edge to escape the armed warriors who were slashing wildly at the throng in front of them. One turned and hurled a white rock at Gunnar. It hit him on the forehead and he collapsed. Hacun's men were quickly reinforced by Ottarr's men who were now rushing up the path and extending the awful slaughtering ground.

The massacre of the hapless, innocent villagers would have gone on unabated had not Hacun called out to Ottarr, 'The ships have been attacked, we have lost some slaves. We should be taking prisoners.'

Ottarr's pecuniary sense quickly overcame his need to reap retribution and he bade his officers to go round telling the demonic warriors, who had not yet sated their bloodlust in revenge for their wounded comrades, to take prisoners. The slaughter stopped and a few wretched peasants were rounded up and guarded.

'Take twenty men and go back to the ships with them,' said Ottarr. Looking down at the bleeding forehead of the unconscious Gunnar he said, 'If he is still alive, take him with you.'

With the remainder of his men, they struck out southwards. The first village they found had a small wooden church but the valuable ceremonial objects had vanished. Two priests stood at the table at the dark end of the building.

'We don't have time to start digging holes,' Ottarr said, alluding to their first raid in Skotland. 'Make these two tell us where they've hidden the silver.'

One of the crew of the other vessel spoke some Anglo-Saxon and he was brought forward to question the priests.

'They won't help us,' he said to Ottarr.

'Behead one of them,' commanded Ottarr.

Two men took one of the priests and held him over the table while a third swung his sword down heavily on the man's neck. His aim was not accurate and he had to try again before the head bounced on the ground. But still the other priest would not tell them what they wanted to know. Ottarr ripped a wooden cross on a chain off the priest's neck and threw it against the wall.

'Torch the church!' ordered Ottarr. One of the warriors grabbed a candle which was the only light in the church, and tore some parchment from a book which was lying open on the table. Once the parchment was burning others added dried grass and twigs. The burning wood was placed against the church wall. When he was sure the building was alight, Ottarr withdrew with his men and slammed the church door closed with the priest inside.

'His obstinacy has cost us time and him his life. Let's see what else we can find.'

The invaders roamed round the empty village ransacking the hovels which had been the villagers' homes. They collected all the food they found to take back to the ships. Then they moved further south and came to a larger village.

Here too was a wooden church, but this one was larger. When they arrived some women were kneeling in front of a table surmounted by a silver cross with their hands together in front of them. They did not flinch as the warriors walked up behind them, despite the noise of their approach. Some of the intruders grabbed the women and dragged them outside. Ottarr paid no attention to them and cared not for their fate, but marched up to the table and picked up the cross. He looked around and saw a chest under the table. It was locked. He said to Torsten, 'Break it open!'

Torsten and Hacun swung their axes at the lock clasp.

After a few blows, it broke off. Ottarr stepped forward and opened the chest. Inside there were several manuscripts. He threw these aside and underneath found three silver cups of varying sizes.

Finding nothing else of value in the village, the warriors were called together to return to the ships with their booty. On the long walk back, they passed the burning church and signs of their earlier struggle to get up the hill, but there were no Viking bodies among the corpses littering the late summer grass. The warriors were in good heart: on their last raid they had got more silver.

On the shore the tide was ebbing and the ships were some way up from the receding water. The group of warriors which had returned with the prisoners had the cooking fires burning. They had put the bodies of the slain slaves in a heap fifty paces away down the beach with the dead peasants who had raided the ships.

'How many slaves did we lose?' asked Ottarr of Finn.

'Five, but there is one more who is badly wounded.'

'Throw him out on to the beach with the others.'

'But he is still alive.'

'Do as I say!' shouted Ottarr. 'Is your brother still alive?'

Finn pointed to Gunnar who was sitting on his seat with his head in his hands. A bloodied cloth covered the wound.

'He'll be all right, but at the moment he is confused and complains he has ringing in his ears, and that he sees double.'

'Then we will only need to give him half as much silver as he's entitled to,' quipped Torsten.

Ingolf walked over to *Ulven* and took Ottarr aside. 'My man Birgir, who speaks Anglo-Saxon, has heard the prisoners talking about buying favour from us by telling us how to attack their wealthy enemy.'

'Who is the enemy?'

'I will ask him to try to find out.'

Ingolf went back to *Ormen* and spoke to Birgir. Later Ottarr saw Birgir in conversation with the new slaves. After supper the three captains met, this time with Birgir.

'They say that their enemies live in a town called Dorncester. The town is inside the high walls of an ancient fort, but parts of the walls are broken and it's easy to get in. They say that there are wealthy farms and a big church.'

'How far is it?' asked Ingolf.

'They say that we can sail halfway there. If we go north from here there is a long sandy beach in front of marsh-lands. From there it is three hours' walk over a high hill.'

'Will they show us the way?'

'Yes, apparently it is difficult to find the trail through a marsh. They seem desperate to see their enemies slain.'

'But I have told my men that they will be leaving for home tomorrow,' said Ottarr.

'Do you wish to miss a chance fill your chest?' answered Ingolf.

'I don't like the sound of it. We are no longer a strong force, and the men want to go home,' argued Ottarr.

'Why don't we give them the choice? We need at least fifty men to attack a town. If that many want to take part then we go. Those that don't want to can stay and guard the ships.'

Ottarr considered this idea and then said, 'Fine, but I am not going, I am tired from today's work. We'll let the young men have the chance.'

All the crews were gathered after supper and Ottarr explained the situation to them. 'This could be easy, it could be dangerous, or indeed it could be a lie the peasants have told us. We can let half of you go if you want to. The rest of us will wait a maximum of two days in the ships. If you don't come back, we leave without you.'

'What happens to any silver or gold we bring back?' asked one of the crew.

Ottarr realised that this was a trick question. Any warrior

risking his life tomorrow would not be happy for Ottarr to take his usual forty per cent when he had not taken part in the raid. Nor would they want to share any spoils with crew members who stayed on the ships.

'I take twenty per cent and you share the rest equally between those taking part.'

There were murmurs and mumbles before another crew member shouted, 'If we don't come back, what happens to the silver we have won so far?'

'As usual, your family at home will get your share.'

There were more questions before Ottarr said, 'So, how many want to go?'

It was too dark to see a show of hands so Ingolf suggested that those who wanted to go on the raid should file past where the captains were sitting and be counted. As they came past the fire they would be recognised.

Hacun, Torsten and Finn joined the queue and shuffled past the captains to be counted.

'That is fifty-two then!' shouted Ingolf when the last of the file of men had passed him.

Ottarr bawled out, 'I nominate my man Hacun to take command, any objections?' There were none. 'Then we sail north at dawn.'

Chapter 17
The Parting

The next morning the usual south-westerly drove the three ships quickly north across the bay to a long sandy shore, just as the prisoner had described it. The vessels were run onto the beach at half tide and the warriors who were going on the expedition started to prepare. As well as arms, the fighters had to take some food with them. Two men were detailed as water-carriers and took leather water bottles.

Gunnar was feeling better but was clearly in no condition to join the war-band. He was becoming less confused, though he still had vision problems and the gash on his forehead was still bleeding. When he came to the realisation that his brothers were going off to seek plunder without him, he became very agitated and tried to persuade them against it.

'We have good earnings from this voyage, why embark on this risky venture? Especially when I cannot be with you.'

'Maybe that is why we are going, Gunnar. It is a chance for us to show what we can do without you nurse-maiding us,' said Torsten, taking a brave line against Gunnar which he would not have dared to have done had Gunnar not been frail.

'And Finn, I promised mother that I would look after you.'

'Don't worry Gunnar, we can look after ourselves,' said Finn.

'Here, Finn, take my sword.'

Finn was surprised and moved. The sword which Gunnar had captured at Monkchester was very dear to him.

'Hacun, I depend on you to look after these two!'

Hacun did not reply, he just grinned at Gunnar and nodded.

While they were waiting for everyone to be ready, Hacun and the two brothers surveyed the land in front of them. The sand led up to a low bank which was covered by grass. The land immediately beyond the bank was hidden from them, but in the distance they could see a long ridge of high hills running parallel to the shore. Some way down the shore to their left there was a small settlement, probably a fishing village, for there were several small craft pulled up on the shore. Smoke curled up from fires in the village which had clearly not yet been abandoned by the peasants, who must by now be well aware of the presence of the Vikings. They had after all been in the area for two nights. But the village was of no interest to them; their quarry lay over the high ridge.

The warriors assembled on the beach. The prisoner who was to show them the way was with Birgir. Hacun gathered the warriors around him. He noticed that most of them were younger members of the crews, clearly up for an adventure.

'The prisoner tells us that we have to cross a marsh to get inland. He knows the trails through the wetland. As we travel, look for landmarks so that if we have to return in a hurry, you can find your way. I am going to lead the column together with the prisoner and Birgir. If we meet resistance I will decide whether we fight or return to the ships. Is this clear?'

There were shouts of agreement. The men shouldered

their weapons and started walking up the beach and onto the grass. Once there they saw the marsh. Beds of tall reeds were waving and bending in the direction dictated by the prevailing wind. The prisoner led them off towards the settlement. They could see adults and children scurrying to be out of sight and some fishermen, who had been repairing a net, left their work and ran as fast as the sand would allow them. The warriors came to an area where there were some hawthorn bushes and several small trees. There, they turned off inland, following a trail on a broad ridge of slightly higher ground, with the marsh on both sides of the track. They were heading due north and soon they found themselves on the lower slope of the ridge. Their progress was slowed as the trail got steeper. The pathway, which was deeply rutted by cart wheels, was wide enough for them to march two by two.

As the going got steeper, Finn was having trouble keeping up with the column. His knee ached and he realised that not having spent as much time ashore as the others, he was not in good condition. The trail plunged into the heavily-wooded slopes and Finn lost sight of the column altogether. He continued, making the best speed he could, leaning heavily on his spear.

At the head of the column, Hacun strode along the tree-lined trail, spear in hand, confident that they would soon reach the summit of the ridge and then have a quick descent to Dorncester with the element of surprise.

The trees began to thin out, and they were replaced by dense bushes, all leaning in the same direction, pushed by the omnipresent south-westerlies. Apart from the grunts and puffing of the men behind him, it was strangely quiet. They marched on and as the ground began to level out they realised they were coming to the top of the hill. The bushes parted revealing an open space, farmland probably, though there were no crops, only several overgrown pits or quarries. They could still not see over the hill, but ahead of them they could see the brow. Soon the whole troop, except Finn, who was now some way behind, had emerged into the open space.

Hacun looked up. Ahead of him he could see some sticks moving on the other side of the brow. They quickly got longer and he realised they were spears. He held his hand up and stopped the column. The heads of the bearers of the spears appeared at the same time as Hacun became aware of the tramp of marching men. But before he saw the marchers, the carriers of the spears appeared over the brow on horseback.

'Form defensive order!' shouted Hacun to his men.

In the turmoil to get into position, no one noticed the prisoner racing off to one side. He had done his work well. Portland would be avenged.

The riders halted and the foot soldiers appeared over the brow. They spread for over a hundred paces and there were at least three rows of them.

Hacun heard shouting from behind them and glanced back to see what was happening. Saxon warriors were running out of the bushes where they had been hiding as the column passed. It was clear that their possibility of retreat was cut off. They had two choices: to fight or surrender.

The Saxons in front of them realised what was going through Hacun's mind. The riders sat motionless, the troops in front and behind waited in silence.

The raiders started to talk between themselves.

'We have no chance, we should surrender and become slaves,' said one.

'We might be able to do a deal with them and trade the silver on the ships for our lives,' said another.

Hacun was aware of the comments and knew that most of his men wanted to surrender. He walked out in front of the line of Viking warriors and turned towards them.

'You men do as you want: I am going to Valhalla!'

He turned, threw away his spear and drew his sword. Clearly, he had decided that dying in battle was the only honourable choice for a true warrior. His walk to the leading horsemen seemed to take an infinite time. To the surprise of the rest of crew, as he approached the riders a mounted Saxon in the centre of then line shouted something to the other horsemen and held up his hand to restrain the troops. The man spat in the direction of Hacun. He leapt down from his horse, unclipped his shield from the saddle and drew his sword.

The two adversaries were evenly matched in build and similarly armed, but the Saxon had a shirt of chain mail. There was complete silence until the first clash of steel. Then there came ring after ring as the swords clashed. Occasionally there were thuds as swords hit shields. The Saxon troops roared support but the Viking band watched in uneasy silence. Neither man gave ground as the well-balanced fight continued. Eventually, whether he was caught by the glare of the sun, made a misjudgement or was just tired, the Saxon took a swing at Hacun's sword and missed. The Viking's sword crashed down onto the Saxon's shoulder, and though he had the protection of the chain mail, the blow was so heavy that his shoulder was broken. He sank to the ground on his knees. Hacun dropped his shield, took his sword in both hands, and with a quick downward stroke split the Saxon's skull.

One of the riders beckoned to another and together, mounted on their horses, they started attacking Hacun. He tried to protect himself from the blows, but without his shield he had no chance. While the rider on one side occupied him, sword against sword, the rider behind him drove his spear into the back of Hacun's neck. As the wounded warrior sank to the ground, other horsemen crowded around, all trying to claim some part of the kill as they jabbed their spears into the jerking body.

The crew in the defensive line were shocked by the death of their leader and first one, and then the others, laid down their shields and swords in front of them as the horsemen rode forward. One of the Saxons shouted an order and some foot soldiers came forward and collected the Vikings' arms. He shouted again, this time at the Vikings.

'He says we should strip our clothes off,' said Birgir.

'Can't you ask him if we can do a deal?' one of the crew shouted.

Birgir shouted to the man who was obviously in command of the Saxons.

'We have silver on our ships; can we deal for our lives?'

'The deal is death,' responded the horseman.

Birgir, feeling remorse for the fact that he had instigated this whole venture, decided not to translate the reply, but told the crew to do as they had been commanded.

The Viking warriors undressed and were dragged, together with Hacun's corpse, a short distance to the side of the hill where, on a fairly flat piece of ground, there was a large rocky depression which could once have been a quarry. The Saxons made a mound of rocks and on top placed one of the Viking shields. Hacun's body was dragged across to the mound and his body was placed on it with his head on the shield. One of the Saxon horsemen dismounted, took out his sword and hacked the head from the lifeless body. Soldiers took the body and threw it in one corner of the quarry. The Saxon executioner held Hacun's head up high. There was a loud cheer from the soldiers. He threw the head into the opposite corner of the quarry. The distance between the body and the head emphasised the finality of the victim's death and symbolised what both the Saxons and the Vikings believed: that without a complete body, the warrior could not proceed into the afterlife.

Finn had finally reached the area where the dense wood-
land gave way to the bushes and scrub when he heard the
clang of steel against steel. He hurried on and was just
about to emerge into the open ground when he heard a
loud cheer. Surely the noise was made by more than fifty
men! He walked more cautiously as he approached the
opening at the end of the bushes. Just beyond the last bush
he saw a huge throng of armed men. Creeping low, he left
the trail, went through the bushes to his right, and in their
cover moved further up the steep escarpment to get a view
of what was happening. Well hidden, he peered through
the bushes at the scene below. There was a vast band of
Saxon soldiers, some on horseback, crowded around an
indentation in the ground. They had a group of naked
prisoners who were being held by the soldiers. One of them
was being dragged to a bloody mound. The soldiers forced
him to lie down and then, to his horror, Finn saw a Saxon
draw his sword and try to hack off the victim's head. It took
several blows before the head was held high and then cast
into the corner of the pit.

Finn was terrified. His comrades were being executed
one by one. Some were calm as they waited their turn,
others were struggling and shouting, but to no avail. It was
dreadful to watch. The soldiers took it in turn to humiliate
and then execute the Vikings, but few of them managed to
kill a warrior with one blow. Judging by the screams, some
of the crew suffered terribly before death brought them
relief. Finn was choking back tears and shaking from the
shock of what he was witnessing. But then his mind
suddenly focused when he recognised that Torsten was
being pulled to the killing ground. His brother must not be
allowed to suffer this incompetent butchering. Finn stood
up, took his bow off his shoulder and carefully aimed an
arrow at the dignified figure of Torsten as he walked to the
place of execution. The arrow found its mark and drilled

deep inside Torsten's chest. He fell to the ground instantly.

There was a stunned silence in the throng of Saxons, and then fury as hundreds of eyes swept the hillside to locate the assailant who had cheated them of their sport. Torsten's lifeless body was dragged away for posthumous execution while a group of Saxons started to fan out to search for the Viking they had missed.

Finn was in good cover and not to be easily discovered, but he realised that he could not stay where he was for long without being caught. He tried to think clearly, but was in shock from what he had just seen and the act of killing his own brother. Way below him to the south, he could see the sea, where the prospect of safety lay. The Saxons would expect him to retreat to the coast as quickly as possible and he could not outrun them. He judged that the main army would be busy with the executions for some time yet, but that eventually they would move south to try to capture the ships.

Instead of going in the obvious direction, he moved off eastwards along the escarpment and continued for some time until he was level with a small village about halfway down the hill. He then started to descend towards the sea, carefully avoiding the village until he found himself at the back of the marsh. If he skirted around the wetlands to find the trail they had used to travel inland, he might meet the search party, or worse still, the army, so he struck out eastwards and found that there was high ground which led all the way down to the beach. Exhausted, he started walking towards the three ships. The tide was out and Finn was surprised that although the tidal height variation was slight in the bay, the ships had been moved out into deeper water. Unbeknown to Finn, some archers had been firing on the ships from the shore and the captains had had to withdraw to safety.

Drawing level with the ships he saw movement further

along the grassy bank as horsemen emerged from the trail the Vikings had taken on their ill-fated mission. They started galloping along the bank towards him, followed by soldiers at a run. Finn wrenched off his bow and sword belt, dropped them to the ground and ran down the sand and into the sea. He waded as fast as he could through the shallow water as a rain of arrows started splashing around him. The archers too were wading as they were firing and Finn's progress was slowing as the water got deeper.

The wading bowmen were now within range of the ships, and Finn could see the crews raising the sails and pulling up the anchors.

'Wait, wait!' he pleaded. He was now not more than twenty paces from *Ulven*, and he saw Gunnar hanging over the side ready to pull him aboard. Behind Gunnar, Ottarr was grinning at Finn's futile attempt to be rescued. Then came the dreadful realisation that the distance between him and *Ulven* was increasing as the wind took hold of the sail.

Gunnar was desperately holding out one of the long oars for Finn to grab, but the possibility of doing so diminished by the second. The elder brother, his head still wrapped in a bloody cloth, threw the oar in Finn's direction. The younger man grasped it and lifted his feet which were now only occasionally touching the bottom of the sea as waves lifted him, using the oar as buoyancy. With his refuge fast leaving him behind, Finn struck out with his feet to increase the distance between him and the archers.

As he turned to see how close the Saxons were, he heard a swish and felt a stinging pain as an arrow grazed his face and cut across his right eye. The pain was intense and made worse by the sea water which was splashing onto his face. Yet he hung on and started to drift eastwards along the coast, almost parallel to the wake of the three fleeing ships. Soon the archers gave up firing and Finn started to recover from the abject terror caused by being hunted. His situation was desperate. He was beginning to feel very cold even though the water was reasonably warm; this was probably as a result of shock from the eye injury. He had to find a safe place ashore where he could recover from the trauma of the injury, before he passed out and drowned.

Chapter 18
Stranded!

It was late afternoon when Finn's feet touched the bottom. He had propelled himself eastwards across the bay, supported by the oar. He staggered up the stony beach and collapsed on the grassy bank behind. He was hungry, thirsty, exhausted and in pain. He touched the injury to his right cheek. It was still bleeding slightly but the most awful thing was that he was blind in his right eye. He gingerly touched the eye. It was still there but he saw no movement of his hand as he moved it across his face, the eye seemed to be without life. He had no dry dressing to put on it. He considered cutting off part of his shirt, but feared the painful effect of covering the wound with the salty cloth.

He rested for a while and then remembered that he still had his backpack on. In it he had some fish and apples which the warriors had brought back from their attack on Portland. He ate the food while watching the sun sink over the distant hill which had proved such an obstacle just a day ago. Just a day ago! Was that all it was? Everything had seemed so positive, they had silver and slaves and they were going home. But now, his brain was full of dreadful images of his friends being executed, he had killed his brother; he was stranded in a country full of enemies with an injured knee, one eye and only the clothes on his back. The only

255

weapon he possessed was his *seax*. What should he do? He could not stay where he was; his only chance was to try to catch up with the ships and that meant going east. If, and it was only a small chance, the ships stopped nearby to get provisions or to raid a coastal village, he might find them.

Feeling refreshed after the food and a short rest, he set off along the hilly coast. The route was steep in places and as it got dark he found it difficult to walk on the uneven ground, especially as he was trying to get used to judging distances with one eye. At least there was enough moon to keep him aware of where the cliff edge was. This was very important, as he could tell from the shimmering water below him that at times the cliffs were very high. After about three hours, he found himself walking down a steep slope, which seemed to go down to the sea. As he got almost to the bottom of the slope a dog started barking and he realised that there must be some form of habitation nearby. Then in the moonlight he saw three or four small houses close to the sea or, rather, an inlet from the sea, as the cliffs seemed to form a small u-shaped bay. He hurried past the houses and was thankful that no one was investigating the reason for the dog's excitement. Sure enough, the path took him to the water's edge and then the cliffs continued on the other side of the bay. Walking on the beach made a terrible noise. It did not help much to walk slowly, but he tried. Looking up at the hill in front of him, he did not notice the boat until he fell over the line tying it to the shore. It smelt strongly of fish and there was no doubting what it was used for. He felt around the boat. It was perhaps five paces long, it had a mast with a sail tied around it and there was a pair of oars and a fishing net in the bottom. He tried to lift the boat; it was heavy, but he thought he might be able to slide it down the shingle.

Finn pulled out his *seax* and made short work of the mooring line. He then started pushing the bow, to try to launch the boat. He strained with all his might, but the stern just stuck in the shingle. Finn stopped to think. How could he move this heavy craft into the water? He knew there was a way, and then it came to him. He remembered how they had transported the king's boat overland. He searched around to see if he could find some logs, but his search was fruitless. Then it occurred to him! He could use the oars.

As quietly as possible, he recovered the oars from inside the boat. He walked round to the stern and while lifting it up he kicked one of the oars underneath to act as a roller. Round at the bow again, he pushed as hard as he could: this time, the craft shifted. He went back and put the second oar in place and tried again. The boat slid down towards the sea, and once its stern was in just a little water, it slid the rest of the way easily.

Finn recovered the oars and, with the boat now afloat, he climbed over the stern. He quietly rowed seawards and through the opening to the bay. When he stopped rowing, he realised that the tide was moving him slowly back the way he had come. He stood up and with some difficulty managed to undo the lashing to the little square sail. He set the sail and the south-westerly breeze started to push the craft slowly eastwards. He wanted to get far from the bay as quickly as possible and so he rowed and sailed eastwards, but the tide was strong and in reality he was not moving far. The wind against tide caused the sea to be quite choppy and an occasional wave slopped into the boat. He really was not making much progress at all, but he was not going backwards. It was not until the early hours, just as it was getting light, that the tide changed and the small craft began to speed along with wind and tide, but with the wind came rain. It fell heavily for an hour and obscured the spectacular coast which Finn was passing. But it did give him the chance to wash his clothes in fresh water and importantly to get a drink. He cut round the bottom of his shirt and fashioned a bandage which he tied around his head and over the injured eye.

Looking along the coast Finn could just see through the rain a fat finger of land which appeared to point out to sea. At the end of the finger there was a steep slope plunging seawards. Had the weather been clearer Finn would have seen, even from this distance, the mighty vertical cliffs which led up to the point dedicated to St Aldhelm. Eventually, the small craft approached the headland. Suddenly, Finn was aware that his boat was being thrown around like a cork. He held on tightly to the gunnels to avoid being thrown out. It pitched and twisted; one moment he was looking straight down at the sea in front of him, the next directly up at the rain. It was a fearful experience which in truth did not last more than five minutes, but to the lone sailor unable to control his boat, the torment seemed to go on for hours. And then suddenly he was past the point and into calm water. The rain continued, but he was making good time travelling east and for the first time for hours he felt optimistic.

By midday, the rain had stopped and the sun shone weakly through high cloud. Ahead of his boat, Finn saw an extraordinary rock sculpture of two white pillars, after which the coast disappeared round a corner. As the little boat rounded the two tall chalk columns, the sail lost the wind. Finn wrapped it round the mast and started rowing along the base of the tall, white cliff. There were several caves and he considered going into a large one to hide and rest, but as he got nearer he heard the screeching of gulls inside and realised that he would not get much rest.

The tall cliff gave way to lower cliffs vertically streaked with brown. Bushes hung tumbling over the edges, and as the cliffs extended round the bay they lost their height and eventually the bushes gave way to small trees leaning over the water's edge. There appeared to be a gap behind the dangling branches and the low embankment from which they grew. Finn ran up to the shore, pulled the mast out of its post-hole, laid it down in the boat and then jumped onto the sand and dragged the boat stern-first as far as he could, under the canopy of the branches.

As he had come into the bay, he had heard a dog barking and had seen smoke rising beyond the heavily-wooded shore. He hoped that after dark he might find a village with some fruit trees where he could steal some apples or pears. As he was making himself comfortable in the boat, to await nightfall, he noticed that some of the bushes around him were laden with blackberries. They were not really ripe, but in each bunch there were one or two which were edible enough to taste good to a hungry man.

Finn stretched out on the folded fishing net to get some rest, but sleep did not come easily. His eye throbbed terribly. He cautiously peeled off the rough dressing, which was caked in blood. Fortunately, the bleeding appeared to have almost stopped. He cut a slice of cloth from the sail and replaced the bloodstained dressing. It got dark early as the bay faced east and the sun had set on the other side of the cliff. As the sun lost its influence, the moon increasingly lit up the bay. Apart from the gulls, there was no sign of life. If he had been seen from the beach there was no indication of anyone taking an interest in him. It was eerily quiet, disturbingly so.

When the moon was well up in the sky Finn left his hiding place and wandered along the sandy beach until he found a narrow track leading inland. He was delighted to find that a small brook tumbled down the hill beside the path. He crouched on the edge of the stream and scooped up water to drink with his cupped hands. The path was well-trodden and easy to follow, although it soon became fairly steep. After a while it reached an open space. Around the centre there were several small stone buildings which he approached cautiously. In the moonlight he saw that all of the houses were just shells, with no roofs or doors. A smell of recent burning pervading the air reminded him of the morning after the fire at Floga. In the centre of the open area was the base of a stone pillar. Lying on the ground beside it was stonework which Finn recognised as the broken remains of a Christian cross. He continued up the hill and saw a larger stone building which had also been burnt. He guessed that this had been the Christians' religious place. On the grass in front he could see a number of mounds of earth, the length of which betrayed them as graves. He went closer and saw that they had been dug very recently.

The ships must have come this way, he thought. *Damn Ottarr! He preferred to plunder this tiny village for whatever paltry wealth they had instead of turning back to look for me.* Then the reality struck him: this was no place for a lone Viking to be found by Anglo-Saxons looking for retribution. He forgot his hunger and the reason for his visit to the village and ran as fast as he could back down the track to the beach. When he had climbed up the hill, the moon had lit his path, but running back as fast as his knee would permit, with light shining against him, the features were less distinct and more so because he was finding his way with one eye. The blackberry bushes at the side of the path seemed to reach out to hinder his progress with their clawing spikes and he stumbled over tree roots. Eventually, he reached the beach and turned right along the sand. He stopped and listened carefully. He did not want to lead anyone following him to his hiding place. All was quiet apart from the lisping hiss of the gentle waves brushing the shore. Now certain that he was not being followed, he walked along the sand to his boat.

Once on board, he tried to think clearly about what to

do. The longships could not be far ahead of him, so he needed to continue to travel east, but he must sail faster. If he left now, the tide which brought him here having turned, and there being no wind to sail with, there was a danger that his boat might be swept back along the coast and to the dreadful wild water at the point, which had terrified him. He reasoned that if he waited until the tide seemed to be at its lowest and then set off, he would get a favourable current to carry him east for a quarter of the day. It was his only chance to catch up with the longships and rejoin the crews on their journey home.

Finn dozed for short periods and periodically, by the light of the diminishing moonlight, tried to judge the height of the water along the beach. Although well sheltered from the south-west, he noticed that there were more ripples on the sea each time he looked: the wind was increasing from that direction. Well before daylight, he judged that the level of the sea had stopped receding. He pulled the boat down the beach, rowed out a few yards and set what had been a square sail before he had cut parts from it. The boat accelerated as it left the protection of the land and Finn felt the pressure on the steering oar as he tried to guide the craft eastwards. Once clear of the bay the strong flood tide caught the vessel and this together with the increasing influence of the south-westerly breeze propelled the small boat quickly.

By sunrise he was well across the bay and the features of the land ahead of him had become more distinct. He had decided to sail between the island and the mainland in the hope that his friends might have stopped to raid one of the coastal villages along the island shore. Finn was desperately tired, but he had discovered that with the forces of nature in his favour he could lash the steering oar and the boat would keep its course eastwards. He lay down on the floor and fell asleep. His sleep was deep indeed, as he did not notice the violent pitching of the small craft as it crossed an area of serious turbulence approaching the channel between Vectis and the land of the Anglo-Saxons. But as the boat emerged from the turbulence he woke and suddenly found himself back in Lapland as he saw the huge snowscape in front of him. He squinted with his one eye at the awesome sight. It was seconds before he realised that the vision in front of him was not snow, but the dazzling effect of sun on the chalk face of the enormous cliffs above him.

Terror struck him as he realised that his boat was in imminent danger of colliding with one of three huge chalk pillars which reached out into the sea from the bright cliffs. He slashed the lashing on the oar with his *seax* and grabbed it, straining with all his might to turn the boat northwards and enter the channel. He could almost reach out and touch the chalk of the towering edifice as he dashed past and followed the cliffs on his starboard side.

Soon he felt that the boat was beginning to slow down despite the fresh wind carrying him forward. It was clear that the tide was spent and would soon turn the other way. Ahead of him there was a cliff which was much darker than those he had just passed. There appeared to be a beach at its base which he might be able to land on. By now the boat was just creeping forward against an ebb tide. He grabbed the oars, pulled as hard as he could towards the shore and ran his craft up on to the sand. It was still only about midday, but the beach was curiously dark as it faced northwest and was in shadow until early afternoon.

Finn's main preoccupation now, apart from the discomfort of his wounded eye, was to find food. He looked up at the massive cliff above him and wandered along the beach to see if there was any way to get to the top to look for autumn fruit. He saw that there was a long, winding gully which had been scored by water draining from the top of the cliff. He tried to climb it but the surface was muddy and very slippery. It was clear that an ascent would be very difficult. However, this did reassure him that he was very secure from capture by anyone ashore. Since there was no chance of finding food on the land it was the sea which would have to provide it.

Taking the fishing net from the boat Finn unrolled it on the beach to try to discover how it was used. The net was rectangular and on the two short sides there were cords attached to weights. It was similar to the nets he had used in Lapland. He put most of the net back in the boat, leaving one end just on the shoreline. Having tied a rock to a rope to use as an anchor, he pushed his craft out from the shore, paying out the net. Then he settled back in the boat, when he had anchored, to wait. It was getting towards late afternoon when he noticed some disturbance in the water near to the net. He stood up and from this position could see not one but three fish struggling to extricate themselves from the mesh.

He raised his anchor and gently pulled himself to the shore. He leant out and grabbed at the nearest fish, which he recognised as mackerel, but in trying to detach it from the net it slipped from his hands and escaped. He decided that rather than leaning over the gunnels to pick the fish out of the net he would pull the net aboard first and hope that as it wrapped and tangled it would hold the fish fast. Soon he had two mackerel aboard and had gutted them with his knife. He tried fruitlessly to light a fire to cook the fish, but quickly gave up. He scraped as many scales as he could from the fish before gulping them down raw.

He dozed uneasily through the night and at dawn, when the rain started, he pulled the boat into the sea and set off again.

Chapter 19
A New Life

With the wind gusting from the south-west driving drizzle from which he had no protection, Finn's boat rounded a wooded headland on the island, which was partly shrouded by the rain. In the protection of the headland, the sea was calm enough for him to pause to consider what to do. But hunger again soon overcame other considerations and he rowed for the beach. The shoreline was covered in shingle which ran like a thin orange band as far as he could see around the bay.

Enfeebled by the pain in his eye and hunger, Finn struggled as best he could to draw the boat up the beach and into the bushes which lined the shore. Here it would be protected from the sea and hopefully from detection by anyone living nearby. He broke off some leafy branches to cover himself and the boat, and crept as far as he could under the protection of the hull. Despite the pain and the rain he soon fell asleep.

It was a strange chorus which woke him. A cockerel was crowing, adding its call to the 'cheep cheep' of oyster catchers and the shriek of seagulls. The sun was shining through the branches which still covered him. He carefully moved them and looked out to sea. This was a very different scene from yesterday. The sea was smooth and apart from

265

the gentle swish of small waves hitting the shore all was quiet apart from the birds. Just off the beach he saw two small boats, a fishing net between them, circled by gulls looking for the discards of the fishermen.

To his right he saw that beyond the bushes the shingle beach ran round an arc of shoreline in the middle of which was an opening. A third boat was passing seawards through the channel. The beach itself formed an embankment on top of which was scrub and low bushes. These prevented him from seeing over the embankment but it was obvious that the cockerel's call was coming from the other side.

Driven by hunger, in the hope that where there was a cockerel there would be hens and the possibility of stealing eggs, he crept through the bushes parallel with the sea and then scrambled to the top of the embankment, as it was impossible to walk quietly on the shingle. On the landward side, on flat, low land, there was a small settlement with two or three shacks and some animal enclosures. In the waterway in front of the shacks there were some wooden fish traps. On the other side of this hamlet he could see that the waterway which entered from the sea formed a lagoon. On the far side, judging from the smoke rising from a number of buildings, was a small town or village. There were a number of trading vessels tied up to a quay by the village, which was itself surrounded by pastures with sheep grazing on them. Beyond the settlement there were long, low hills covered by forest.

Finn noticed that the hamlet near the embankment was isolated from the village by the waterway and that the low bushes in which he was hiding appeared to run right up to the animal enclosures. His best course of action would be to wait until dark and then creep up to the chicken pen to look for eggs. He decided to go back to the boat and hide there for the rest of the day.

He turned back to look seawards, but to his horror he saw

that the boat he had seen coming out of the lagoon was heading for the shore where he had left his. He heard some shouting and then a crunch as the boat hit the beach. Two men jumped out into the surf and pulled their craft up the beach before walking over to investigate his boat, which he had carelessly left uncovered. He quickly realised that since there was a trail on the shingle where he had dragged the boat up the shore the men would realise that it had not just drifted there. They would now be aware that there was an interloper in their territory. The loss of his boat meant that he had no chance now of catching up with the Viking ships.

Finn crawled under the scrub on top of the embankment in an attempt to hide, in case the fishermen decided to look for the owner of the abandoned boat. The sun was now high up above the low hills in the distance and the light was finding its way through the sparse foliage of the bushes, making Finn's hiding place very hot. He became aware of a crunching sound on the landward side of the embankment. It got louder as someone approached his hiding place. He grabbed his knife and tried to creep further into the bushes. But his efforts to do so were extremely painful as the thickest cover was spiky gorse. He heard a girl's voice and a bleating sound as first the head of a goat and then that of a girl appeared up the slope next to where he lay. The goat was so close that he could smell it as it munched the bushes nearby. He hoped that the animal would avoid the gorse and come no closer. With his attention on the goat, he did not immediately notice that the girl had come around the other side of the bushes and was standing looking at him. She was stooping, peering into the bush with one eye. Across her head was a band of cloth bound diagonally so that it covered the other eye. Her hands were swollen and blistered and she leant with the support of a roughly-hewn pole. He realised immediately that she was a leper. His instinct to silence the girl with his dagger was overcome partly by his fear of close contact with her and possible contagion, but also he felt some pity for the wretch.

He knew that leprosy first attacks the hands, feet and sometimes the eyes of the infected person. His crew had often joked that the only people who were safe from a Viking raid were those living in a leper colony.

The girl looked at him for some time and he realised the reason for her quizzical gaze: they both had diagonal cloths wrapped across their heads obscuring one eye. The girl called the goat and hobbled down the embankment towards the hamlet, guiding the animal with her pole. He heard her call out to someone. He had no doubt that she was announcing the presence of a red-haired stranger in the bushes. There was no point in hiding any longer; all but one of his options had evaporated. If he ran along the beach he would meet up with the fishermen who by now must have taken possession of his boat. In front of him was the hamlet and beyond it the lagoon, and behind him was the sea. His only chance was to run, in full view of anyone looking, along the embankment towards the trees where he had landed the boat. He was about to take this last option when he saw two men come out of one of the shacks. One was obviously blind; he was being led by another who walked with a crutch. It suddenly became clear to Finn that the little isolated hamlet was a leper colony. The fear of catching leprosy was overcome by the terrifying prospect of being slaughtered by the fishermen. What better place to hide! Even if a search party combed the area they would not think of searching the leper colony. He turned and ran down the embankment towards the hamlet. When he approached the two men he felt foolish standing in front of their pathetic figures, *seax* in hand. He dropped his hand to his side and the man with the crutch beckoned him to come into one of the shacks. The girl was in the doorway, watching, and as they approached her, Finn realised how stupid he had been. Because of his bandaged head, the girl had assumed that he too was a leper.

The stench inside the hut was appalling. When Finn got used to the half-light inside he saw a rack of dried fish. He went over and grabbed one. The sighted leper said something to the girl and she went outside and returned with a cup of goat's milk which she gave to Finn. An old woman and a teenager appeared at the door, peering in at the stranger. Both of them were showing signs of leprosy – she had both hands bound in rags and he had facial sores.

Their examination of the newcomer was interrupted by the sound of a barking dog and many feet crunching on the shingle on the other side of the embankment. A group of men, some carrying axes, mounted the mound and started walking along the top in the direction of the channel leading into the lagoon. Finn stayed inside the hut while, all apart from the blind man, the lepers shuffled outside and watched the group as they reached the end of the shore and then turned back. The dog was sniffing around the area where Finn had hidden and picked up a scent. Fortunately, the scent was that which led back to the boat. The smell of the goat and the girl had obviously obscured Finn's trail down to the hamlet. The sound of the hunters receded into the distance and the lepers came back into the hut. Finn had learnt a few words of Anglo-Saxon in the last four months and tried to thank them for the food and drink, but that was as far as communication went.

Finn spent several weeks with the lepers. As he gained in strength, he was able to help them more and more. He repaired the dilapidated hovels, helped prepare food, cleaned the animals' enclosures and generally did the sort of things which were normal for an able-bodied person but which challenged the weak lepers. He became used to his own handicaps, although his eye caused him pain for many days. He soon started to pick up a little more Anglo-Saxon.

He was careful not to be seen outside the buildings, but his presence was known to one person. The granddaughter of the blind man came to the colony regularly with food for him and the others. She was the only person who dared to come into the houses. Other supplies, such as firewood, were left outside by villagers who kept the colony supplied. They did this partly because they had an obligation to relatives who lived there, but mainly because they knew that if they kept the colony supplied, then the lepers would not come to the village in search of things they needed. At first, Finn tried to hide when their benefactor was seen rowing across the lagoon towards the buildings, but soon he realised that there was no point in doing so, as the residents could well have told her anyway that he was there with them. Her name was Hilda, and he thought that she was probably in her late teens. She always greeted him cheerily when she arrived and tried to speak slowly so that he would understand, but in truth he understood little. However, it was clear that she too thought that he was a leper, though as far as he knew she never tried to find out where he had come from.

As time went on, Finn became more and more daring about venturing out of the buildings. Winter was coming and fire logs needed to be cut from the timber left by the villagers. More and more, he felt the need for physical exercise. He dug the vegetable plots, worked the fish traps and repaired the fences, but always kept the now unnecessary dressing over his head. Inevitably, he was finally noticed by passers-by, and eventually questions were asked about who he was.

While tending the goats one day, Finn saw some rowing boats approaching the settlement. Several men armed with spears and bows leapt out of the leading boats. As they all disembarked he noticed that two men wearing long brown robes were among the passengers in one of the other craft. Finn made to rush into the buildings, but his path was blocked by the spearmen. One well-dressed individual started to shout at Finn and point at his clothes. It suddenly occurred to him that he must be clearly identifiable as a foreigner and probably as a Viking, from the style of his clothes. The fact that he could not understand much of what was being said to him confirmed to the visitors that he came from far away.

Very quickly, the attitude of the mob became very aggressive. Several men held Finn's arms while others kicked and punched him.

Is this the way it will all end for me? he thought as the blows rained down on him.

The two priests watched impassively as the heathen stranger was being beaten to death, awaiting their turn to win the spirit of the departing soul for the glory of their own church. Finn collapsed at the feet of one of the priests; his bandage had become dislodged and had fallen off. The priest looked down at him contemptuously, but suddenly his face changed and he shouted to the mob.

'Stop, stop, for here we have a miracle. He has the mark of the holy cross on his face, this man is a Christian!'

The crowd jostled to get a look at what the prelate was referring to. Those who could get sight of him saw that Finn had the mark of the cross tattooed on his right cheek. Not only that, but he had no sign of leprosy.

'This man has been delivered from the leprosy by God!' cried the priest.

Several men bent down to touch the sign of the cross on Finn's cheek to see if it was real. Finn understood none of what was being said. He just lay waiting for the abuse to start again. Instead, he was helped up and supported as they took him back to the boats. Finn was taken to the village on the other side of the water and given lodgings next to the priests' house. His wound was tended by one of the priests with poultices of St John's wort and herb Robert and other healing plants. His pain was eased by an infusion of willow leaves which he had daily. Eventually, the open wound healed but no herbs could save the sight in his eye.

It was some time before Finn was accepted as a normal member of the village community. At first, he was held in awe by the superstitious islanders. The priests had had an eye patch fashioned for him which hid the blind eye while leaving revealed the mark of the cross. They insisted that he should fulfil his perceived role as a blessed man by attending church and receiving religious teaching. This he accepted gladly, not from religious fervour, but from recognition that it provided the key to his survival. For the priests, it gave even more credence to their teaching to have a living miracle among them.

Initially, his mind was full of thoughts of how to escape and find his way home, but as time went on his knowledge of the language improved, he made friends and eventually found employment assisting the blacksmith. But there was another attraction. Hilda lived in the close-by village of Selceeflet, and from time to time he saw her about her errands. She always had a cheery smile for him and, increasingly, he was capable of exchanging greetings and conversation with her. Eventually, he offered to go with her when she visited the leper colony and while there he performed jobs such as those he had done when he had been resident with the lepers. There was of course a risk that one or both of them might catch the dreaded disease, but unbeknown to the pair, the illness is not easily transmitted.

Finn's emotions became increasingly turbulent. *Is it possible to be in love with two women?* he frequently asked himself, and for the convenience of his conscience he became increasingly convinced that it was. Hilda did not have Aneka's classic beauty but the Anglo-Saxon girl was lively and generous; she had a personality which mesmerised him.

One day the realisation suddenly dawned on Finn that Gunnar would, long ago, have returned home and would have told Aneka the circumstances of his being parted from his brother. With the prospect of the deep salt sea in front of him and an Anglo-Saxon army behind him it was most likely that Aneka would have assumed him dead. And in such a case, how long would it be before a Danish suitor would take his place? She was beautiful, she was wealthy and she had the ear of the king.

Finn began to reason that even if he could find his way home, by the time he got there, Aneka was unlikely to be available to him. And thus his conscience was salved and he allowed himself to actively court a very responsive Hilda. Within two years of arriving on the island, he had a wife and, despite his sight handicap, he was fully employed as a blacksmith in a workshop adjoining their simple house at Selceeflet.

Anno 1001 ... Then they returned eastward again, till they came to the Isle of Wight. The next morning they burned the manor of Waltham and many other small villages ... and there they roved about, even as they themselves would, and nothing withstood them ... Then was it in every wise a heavy time, because they never ceased from evil doings.

Anglo-Saxon Chronicle

Chapter 20
Finn's Fate

Five years after Gunnar had returned from his first voyage to Britannia, he had a new master. Sweyne Forkbeard, the illegitimate son of King Harald, had grown up in the household of a nobleman called Palnatoke. The old king had had varying fortunes in the shifting politics of his time and several wars, but as his power waned he made an enemy of Palnatoke and consequently his son. Sweyne started a rebellion in 987 which culminated in the death of his father and his being crowned king.

Sweyne Forkbeard was the instigator of many voyages of great Viking fleets to Britannia and such was the death, destruction and loss of property that in 991 the English King Aethelred paid him a huge amount of silver to leave his country in peace. This was the first *geld* but not the last, for Sweyne made ever-increasing demands on the English king, which culminated in the Dane seeking the English crown. Now, the Viking expeditions to Britannia were not just summer campaigns. They often over-wintered in their own settlements in Britannia or Normandia. This allowed their ruthless reign of terror to extend through the whole year.

Gunnar had fought in many campaigns and had won the king's favour. He had carried out several missions on behalf of Sweyne. At the age of forty-three he was an old man, but he had had remarkable luck: he had never been seriously wounded and was still a capable fighter. In the campaign of 1001, Gunnar had been given the task of plundering several towns in the west country and then to go to Vectis. On the island, he was to develop a permanent Viking harbour at a place called Werrar on the river which ran from north to south in the centre of the island. It was a year-round settlement where the Viking fleets could spend the winter. In the future it would also serve as a port for the settlement which the King was building on the site of the former summer residence of the Bishop of Winchester, at a place to be called Sweyne's Town.

The growing Viking community relied on plunder from the island farmers for their food supply and Gunnar frequently led raids on farms and small villages to ensure a plentiful supply of rations for his men and their families. For, by this time, some Vikings had brought their womenfolk and children to live at the settlement. Here, protected by Viking warriors, they were safe from the forces of King Aethelred who had already ordered pogroms of Danish settlers in an attempt to rid his kingdom of the Viking menace.

Watching a small fleet of ships coming into the harbour Gunnar shouted, 'Have you come back empty-handed?' He had sent the ships westwards around the coast to raid the village of the creek people who owned many sheep.

'It is impossible to get into the creeks; they have a heavy chain which they pull up across the entrance to stop enemies getting in.'

'Why didn't you land and attack them?'

'The sea bottom is rough and uneven and besides there was a strong northerly which would have caused us real trouble.'

'Then we have to find another way.'

There was thick forest between Werrar and the creeks which made it difficult to transport animals and goods. Sea transport was the only way. Gunnar called several of his captains together and drew up a plan. He would lead a group of warriors through the forest to attack the village from the south, and then some of his men would proceed to the spit of land on which the chain barrier was situated and destroy it so that the ships could come in.

And so it was, in the late autumn of 1001, the first dry day since Gunnar had devised his plan, that he set out through the forest with sixty warriors. At the same time, five long-ships and three *knars* left the harbour for their rendezvous at the creek. The foot soldiers, unfamiliar with such forest paths as existed, made slow progress through the brambles and the deep undergrowth. Eventually they found a trail which led west and followed it. What they did not realise was that the track was leading them further south than they would have wanted.

Although it was a cold day, Finn was comfortably warm as he worked in front of his forge. The workshop and his adjoining cottage were a little way outside Selceeflet for fear of the risk of fire spreading from his forge. And there was plenty of work. The village benefitted from the dual incomes of farming and fishing and there was wealth in the community which brought work for the blacksmith. He also got work from the creek village where he had first lived. There, as well as farming and fishing, they had income from the salt pans, shallow fields which were flooded with salt seawater in the winter and then allowed to dry out through the summer, leaving salt to be harvested. Life was good and he was content.

Gunnar began to catch sight of the sea through the trees as they thinned out where they had been cut for firewood. He became aware of a very familiar sound echoing through the forest – the *clang, clang* of a hammer on an anvil. Soon he could smell the woodsmoke from the forge. He signalled to his men to tread quietly and crept forward through the bushes. There in front of him was the smithy; the blacksmith was working his bellows, the noise of which made him oblivious of the warrior's footfall. The blacksmith was bent over the bellows and all Gunnar could see was his broad back. The warrior raised his spear and then hesitated as his target shifted slightly before settling again. He drew his arm back and then sent the shaft straight towards the crouching figure. There was a thud as the spear pierced the man's back and a simultaneous groan as the blacksmith fell forward across his bellows. Gunnar gave a war cry and the other warriors rushed past him to attack the village.

At his age, Gunnar did not rush into attacks with the young blades. He watched them go and then walked forward to the smithy to recover his spear. It had passed straight through the blacksmith's body. He put his foot on the dead man's back and pulled the spear out. The man fell backwards, his eye patch fell off and he lay with his sightless eyes gazing skywards.

Gunnar glanced down at his victim. 'No!' he screamed. 'No, no!' It was if there was an explosion in his mind as he tried to grapple with what must be a terrible nightmare. But he was awake. In severe shock, Gunnar looked at the face staring up at him. The ghastly truth was dawning on him that this was not a dream, this was reality. But it could not be! He stared down at the contorted face which was framed by red hair and beard. And there, on his right cheek, the sign of the hammer! It could not but be him!

Aghast at this monstrous quirk of fate, Gunnar knelt down and lifted the lifeless form in his arms. He hugged the body, willing that he could undo what he had done, willing life back into the corpse that had been his youngest brother. The one whom he had promised his mother he would look after. Finn's head fell back, and as his chin lifted, Gunnar saw a bear's claw on a leather necklace. There could be no doubt. This was Finn. Absurdly, though grappling with a chaos of his emotions, he found himself wondering where the other claw was.

There was a scream and a commotion from the cottage next to the smithy. He gently laid Finn on the ground and ran to the house. There he found two of his warriors holding a woman down on the table in the kitchen. A young teenager was bravely clinging onto the back of one of the warriors to try to stop him violating his mother.

'Kill that little bastard will you!' shouted one of the assailants to Gunnar.

Gunnar rushed over, axe in hand, directly towards the young boy, but instead of aiming his blow at the boy he buried the axe deep in the skull of the man.

The other man let go of the woman and turned to Gunnar. 'What the hell are you doing?'

Gunnar had drawn his *seax* from the scabbard and with a horizontal sweep he slashed a gaping hole in the man's throat. There was a crash as he went to the floor, sending pots and pans flying.

Gunnar looked at Hilda and despite his misery and grief, was happy that Finn had had the pleasure of this fine wife. The boy was perhaps fifteen or sixteen. He did not have Finn's red hair, but he did have the blue eyes and his face was redolent of his father. And there, on a leather cord around his throat, was the missing bear's claw.

The boy and the woman were shocked but relieved by this bloody intervention, and stood looking at the ageing warrior. They had no language in common, but kindness is a language of its own and they felt at one with this man. But the man was not at one with himself. How could he show these two what he had done? He did not have the courage to take them out to the smithy.

Gunnar stepped outside and called to one of his men.

279

'Come here. Guard this house with your life. Don't let these people come out and if anyone tries to hurt them then my vengeance will be terrible. For they are my kin.'

He sat on the bench in the smithy with Finn at his feet. Smoke was rising from the village and the air was filled with the distant screams of men and women, the war cries of warriors and the sounds of panicking animals. He suddenly felt very tired and alone. He had seen enough of this and heard enough too. He bent down, cut the leather necklace from the dead man's throat and put it in his pouch. He picked Finn up, carried him to the edge of the forest and went in search of a spade.

Chapter 21
Return to an Earlier Life

It had been a long journey for the lone traveller. At times he could ride on the pony he had bought at the harbour, but he was too heavy for the beast and she tired quickly. When he had to walk he used a pole to lean on, as his legs were no longer strong. Not only this, but his knee joints were stiff and began to swell and ache after a few miles trekking by the side of the pony. His appearance was a cause for concern to those who met him as one side of his face was paralysed. When he met other people he usually pulled a scarf around his face. His body was racked with pain and he felt feverish. These symptoms had developed in the last few months but over the last years the hand which grasped the pole had gradually lost its feeling and was becoming more like a claw.

It was autumn and the traveller was following an ancient track northwards. He was dressed in a tunic and baggy trousers, with legs stuffed into his boots. Although poor in health, his clothes betrayed him as a man of substance and his demeanour, despite his physical discomfort, was dignified. His pony carried a pack with food supplies for his journey and a bundle which contained his heavy cloak with a cowl that he used at night, when sleeping, or when the weather was inclement. The man had a *seax* hanging from his belt, but no other weapons, for in the area he was travelling there were unlikely to be dangers of the human kind.

The sun was going down on his left as he pushed his way through an overhanging bush which, during the short summer, had grown and hindered access along the track. He held the branches, now with their autumn leaves, back for the pony to get past. Turning forward again he saw his destination. The palisade was bigger than he remembered it. *Yes it is bigger,* he thought, *there seem to be more buildings inside it than before.*

He saw the charcoal burner and the iron foundry, which were placed well outside the high fence. No smoke was rising from the foundry but there seemed to be two fires alight inside the settlement. He led his pony up to the high fence, but the gate was shut. He wondered how he should announce himself, he could not be sure who was inside to call to.

'Halloo! A weary traveller stands at your gate!' he cried. The illness had affected his voice which was now hoarse and lacked volume.

There was no response. He took his pole, banged it on the gate and called again.

'Who is there?' called a woman's voice.

'Gunnar, son of Arvid.'

There was a long pause. 'What are the names of your brothers, son of Arvid?'

Gunnar hesitated, not because he could not remember the names, but because of the trepidation he felt about relating what had befallen them.

'Torsten and Finn.'

The gate slowly opened outwards. Gunnar stepped back to allow it to swing out. He covered his face.

'Gunnar?' queried the woman in Sami dress in front of him. She was in her forties and stood alongside a man of similar age. Behind them were several other adults and two children who, hiding behind their mother, were nervously peering at the stranger.

As Birna made to come forward, Gunnar stumbled.

'But, but what is wrong?'

'I have many things wrong with me, most to do with old age and injury, but what ails me most now started with an insect bite a few months ago.'

It became clear to Gunnar that of the small crowd of people in front of him, only Birna could understand his language. She turned around and said something to the others in Sami. They moved back as she had clearly bade them to do.

'You shall come in and I will make you as comfortable as I can. But where are Torsten and Finn?'

Gunnar took the scarf away from his face. He put his hand into his pouch and took out a broken leather necklace on which was a bear's claw. He stepped forward and gave it to Birna. She held it in her hand gazing at it, then looked up at her brother. The tears in her eyes confirmed that she had understood the meaning of the gesture. Gunnar looked down at her and slowly shook his head remorsefully.

'But how? Where?'

'Birna, I have much to tell you, but first, what of mother and father?'

'Come in, come in. I have no fear of your illness. You and I will eat and talk.'

Gunnar led the pony into the settlement. Birna called for a man to tend to the animal.

'This is my eldest son, Arvid,' she said.

Gunnar smiled at the man but kept his distance. 'A fine boy,' he said.

'Boy? He is a man and a father. You saw his children just now.'

Gunnar followed Birna into one of the houses in the compound and took a seat at the table.

'How many children do you have?'

'Two boys and a girl. They are all married and live here, they have a small house each. They have learnt the iron-worker's trade.'

'But what of mother and father?'

Birna sat down opposite him. 'After you three left father became very restless and spent a lot of time out hunting by himself or fishing on the river. He missed you a lot. Much more than we had expected. One day in springtime he went off to fish but never returned. We think that he misjudged the thickness of the ice and fell through. His body was never found.'

Gunnar was silent for a long time and then asked, 'What about mother?'

'After father disappeared, she was heartbroken but she was consoled by the fact that I had a man, Erke, who you saw just now. You must remember him; he helped you to train the reindeer!'

Gunnar smiled. 'Oh yes, so it was not only our reindeer which interested him?'

'No. We got married and together with his family and mother we rebuilt Floga, and he learnt the trade.'

'When did she die?'

'Just two winters ago. She is buried next to Agna. There is a grave marker stone at the head and feet of each grave. Erke tried to shape the stones like runes, but he is a much better blacksmith than stonemason.' Birna's tone became much more solemn. 'Now tell me about Torsten and Finn.'

'Birna, first I should tell you about my mission here. I have had a very full life, but I have little time left. This illness gets worse and may affect my mind. I have come to assure you and your kin that though Floga is my birthright,

I forgo this right in your favour. Your family are the rightful owners of this place.'

Birna reached across and took Gunnar's large, though now deformed, right hand.

'Thank you, I know that Erke and the boys were worried that someday you would come to claim what is rightfully yours.'

'Birna, I have a long story to tell you. We found everything we were looking for and more. We travelled to places you can only dream of and all three of us became wealthy; but tragically, only I had the chance to enjoy the wealth.'

Gunnar began his long tale. Birna stopped him for a while, so that she could prepare food and light the candle lamp. Later, Erke came in and Gunnar ate while Birna recounted in Sami what she had heard so far. When the flame in the lamp was flickering as the last of the tallow stump burnt, Gunnar sat back, his voice tremulous and hoarse. He had told his story. But the tale was not quite complete. He could not say what had happened to Torsten, because he had not witnessed that dreadful event. As for Finn, he could not bring himself to tell. Indeed he had never told anyone. His feeling of guilt was a heavy burden from which he could not escape, and with each passing year, instead of the memory fading, the burden got more difficult to bear. He had washed Finn's blood from his spear but could never cleanse it from his hands.

'Gunnar, happiness comes in many guises, just as misery does. You three brothers found what you called happiness in your roving. I stayed at home, but I don't feel the worse for it.'

'Perhaps you twins were the luckiest, for you and also Finn found a different kind of contentment. One which Torsten and I never did.'

Gunnar spent two months at the settlement. Autumn gave way to winter. He watched the comings and goings of the families, the doing of chores with which he was so familiar: splitting logs, feeding stock, drawing water, the myriad of duties to ensure their self-sufficiency. Each morning he woke to the sounds of swearing, laughter, orders being barked, goats calling and children playing. He would have liked to help with the work but his strength was ebbing fast and he spent more and more of his time sitting, watching and thinking. He soon realised that he was becoming a liability, an unproductive member of a family which was facing the annual uncertainty of survival through the cold winter to come.

*

The pack of wolves huddling together for protection from the snow were at first nervous about the figure slowly clambering up through the winter landscape towards them. He fell several times, seemed to rest in the snow, and then with difficulty regained his feet. They soon realised that the man was helpless, like a wounded animal, and no threat to them. The pack, a family of nine, was near its den which was on the steep rocky mountainside overlooking the frozen lake. There were three generations of the same family in the pack and as winter loomed the parents had been teaching the youngest pups to hunt. Their last hunt had not been successful and they were very hungry. As darkness began to fall, the pack left the safety of their den and started down the slope.

Epilogue I
In the North

The forest still holds its secrets, though now the trail from Floga to the coast is but a few hours' drive on a macadam highway which scars the landscape. Many things have changed since those times, the mightiest of which is beyond the control of man.

When, 8,000 years ago, the huge weight of ice was lifted from that country in the north, the land started to rise and it is still rising. Since the days of Arvid and Ingir, Floga has risen five times the height of a man. The coast has changed in shape and so too have the rivers, lakes and mountains. But the climate is the same, and the forests remain.

Somewhere, just north of the Polar Circle in the forest, near to the great river, there are four boulders formed in a square. They are coated in lichen now, but under the grey-green growth there are chiselled marks, betraying the fact that a long time ago they were important to someone. In winter they are covered in deep snow and remain so for many months. Wolves still roam past them on their constant hunt for food, leaving their footprints as they did at the time of the ironworkers. By the time the flocks of snow bunting arrive, the white cover is melting and soon gives way to spring and the appearance of white wood anemones and yellow colt's foot. Reindeer, roe deer and red deer all pass this way with their young, as does the mighty elk, and, from time to time, though less frequently, the father of the forest, the bear, who fears no one, comes looking for prey in his ancient hunting ground.

The short summer over, the birches turn yellow and then orange, and on sunny days look like fiery torches against the blue sky. But then they lose their leaves, which gently flutter down and form a mantle over the boulders. The four rock sentinels guard not only two women's bodies but the property of a blacksmith. The leather purse rotted away many winters ago, but the contents, the silver, are still there.

Epilogue II
In the South

There was a cluster of fine half-timbered houses around the market square. Here lived the wealthiest merchants and noblemen who had found favour with the king; but to keep a good relationship with the king was difficult. He was given to changes of mood and policy and expected his courtiers to support his ambitious and expensive projects. When he seized his father's throne in 987 many were caught with their loyalties on the wrong side and some lost their land and titles, while others fared worse.

The king's mansion was between the market square and the wooden church which his father had had built. Christianity was tolerated but no longer always embraced by the royal family, unless, periodically, it was politically expedient. The forty-year-old woman sitting in the window of one of the most opulent residences had been lucky. She wore a fine light grey dress neatly secured at the right shoulder by a round silver brooch with a pin of the same metal which crossed the silver circle and picked up the cloth in the centre. On her wrist was a silver bracelet with five plaited strands and on her left hand she wore a heavy, braided silver ring. As she sat and used the late afternoon sunlight streaming through the west-facing window to work on her embroidery, she reflected on how fortune had smiled on her in the midst of adversity. After the tragic death of her lover, who had drowned in Britannia, she had thought that she would be unhappy for the rest of her life, but she had been befriended and supported by the daughter of a neighbour. Eventually the friend had confided in her that she had a brother who was much older than her and who was secretly in the service of Palnatoke, the sworn enemy of King Harald. When the power struggle ended and Sweyne became king, the brother, Rolf, was able to protect the neighbour's family from retribution, and as a favour took Aneka under his wing also.

Eventually, despite the fact that she had a five-year-old child, Rolf became more than a friend. He was ten years older than her, a fine warrior and a kind man, and she loved him. It was the love borne out of familiarity, gratefulness, respect and interdependence. But although there was physical attraction between them, it was not the hot, heady infatuation and desire which shaped her first relationship. Could the passion between her and Finn have withstood the test of time? She would never know.

Rolf was dead now. She had not produced any children for him, but he was good, he had loved her young Olaf and ensured that he had a good education. And, much against her will, when the boy decided to become a warrior, Rolf arranged his training and smoothed his way to become a member of the king's inner circle of friends.

Aneka looked out of the window and saw her son walking across the square towards the house. He was clearly identifiable with his red hair and blue eyes, and around his neck hung the leather necklace with a bear's claw which once belonged to his father.

Epilogue III
In the West

The Roman road from Dorchester to Weymouth is as straight as Roman roads normally are, until it reaches the peak of the Ridgeway. There, because of the steepness of the south side of the hill, it snakes down the slope to the old Roman port. With the prospect of the Olympic sailing events being staged at Portland in 2012, it was decided that this very busy narrow road should be replaced by a wider highway.

In June 2009, during the construction of this new route, the builders discovered a burial pit at the top of the Ridgeway Hill. The grave contained 51 skeletons and some distance away the same number of skulls.

Samples of the remains were identified as Scandinavian by scientists at the Isotope Geosciences Laboratory, part of the British Geological Survey, based in Nottingham. Analysis of the men's teeth had revealed that they had grown up in countries with a colder climate than Britain's. One of the men was thought to have been born north of the Arctic Circle.

The bodies were mostly those of young men in their late teens to early thirties. There was no evidence of clothing fittings such as pins or toggles and it appeared that the men must have been stripped naked before execution. The executioners seem to have needed to strike the men several times before severing the victims' heads. The ragged nature of the wounds to the necks indicated that the men had been killed by hacking with a sharp weapon. Some of the skeletons had hand wounds where they had tried to protect themselves from the executioner's blade.

Archaeologists from Oxford Archaeology believe that the men were probably executed by local Anglo-Saxons sometime between AD 910 and AD 1030.

For more information see http://news.bbc.co.uk/1/hi/england/dorset/8563377.stm.

Author's Note

Who were the 51 men whose skeletons were discovered by road builders in Dorset? My story attempts to answer this question using the clues given to us by the archaeologists and the history of the violent times the men lived in.

This novel is interwoven with factual and historical information. I am aware from my research in Scandinavia that in some instances information which is stated categorically by some authorities is rejected by others. For the sake of the story I have had to make my own decisions about what to include. It is not my intention to be controversial.

It may be difficult for the reader to understand that men who came from a Christian country, albeit a fledgling one, could be so bestial and cruel to brother and sister Christians in other countries. To comprehend this we must remember two salient facts. Firstly, the pagan gods so recently worshipped by the Vikings existed to serve the people, not the other way round. Yes, they required sacrifices, and quite often substantial ones, but if a god did not perform then the people could change their allegiance to another god. Thus, for example, if a harvest was poor, a person might decide that Freja had failed them and therefore they would try a different god for next year. Secondly, the Christian faith has a code of morality which followers must embrace. This concept was totally foreign to the new believers, as their previous gods made no such demands. This code was to a large extent ignored as an inconvenience to them when other priorities, such as satisfying greed or hunger, took over. Even King Sweyn of Denmark, who built churches in his own country, including, it is claimed, founding the one in Roskilde where he is buried, had no qualms about plundering English religious establishments and killing monks when it was a matter of political expediency.

It will come as a surprise to many that Viking society was so dependent on slave labour. The distinguished Swedish historian Vilhelm Moberg estimated that 20 per cent of the Swedish population in Viking times were slaves, or bondsmen, as he called them. Thus, slavery was an integral part of life in Scandinavia in the tenth century. The land was underpopulated and there was a huge demand for cheap manual labour. This need was satisfied by slaves, mainly acquired as war booty. If this sounds impersonal, it was. For although slaves were generally treated well, because of their intrinsic monetary value, their lives were totally in the hands of their masters. Not infrequently, slaves were used as sacrifices to curry the favour of the pagan gods.

As regards England in the historical period of the book, I have found the *Anglo-Saxon Chronicle* particularly useful. This is a series of annals chronicling the history of the Anglo-Saxons. They were written by various authors, presumed to be monks, from the ninth to the twelfth centuries. They were copied and kept in monasteries. Nine manuscripts survive.

In the chapters about the Sami I was at a disadvantage as in my research in Lapland I found a paucity of written information about Sami life and culture a thousand years ago. The excellent Sami museum in Jokkmokk was my best source of material, but I have also drawn on accounts such as that of the Norwegian, Otheres, who lived in the north of Norway and described the way of life of the Sami to King Alfred of Wessex in the ninth century. I hope that this story does not offend those of Sami descent who still today embrace the traditions and culture of their resourceful, resilient and remarkable ancestors.

MW
Salisbury, April 2011

Glossary

Anglo-Saxon Chronicle   A series of annals chronicling the history of the Anglo Saxons. They were written by various authors from the ninth to the twelfth centuries, copied, and kept in monasteries. Nine manuscripts survive in whole or in part today.

apparent wind   The wind speed and direction taking into account the speed of the ship.

beam   The side of a boat or the width of a boat.

Din Eidyn   The tenth-century name for Edinburgh.

Dorncester   The Anglo-Saxon name for Dorchester.

geld   In the twelfth century known as *Danegeld.* Large payments of money made by the Anglo-Saxon kings to Viking leaders, to gain assurance that they would stop raiding Britain. These assurances were always broken. This first payment, in 991, was over 3,000 kilogrammes of silver.

gode   A Danish chieftain with a large farm defended by a troop of warriors (Old Danish).

Hamwic   Anglo-Saxon name for Southampton.

herb Robert   *Geranium robertianum.* The crushed seeds of this pink, flowering herb were used to treat wounds and ulcers. It was also believed to staunch bleeding.

Hibernia   Ireland.

Hlidaforda   Lydford, Devon. Once the largest parish in England and of equal importance to Exeter.

Hjaltland   The Shetland Islands (Old Norse).

Jomsviking   An order of warriors based on an island in the south of the Baltic. Members, who were both Scandinavian and Slavic, were selected for their physical strength and valour.

kawta   A Sami wooden dwelling house (Swedish: *kåta*).

Kirkjuvagar   Kirkwall, the present day capital of Orkney (Old Norse). The meaning is literally 'Church Bay'. The church referred to predates the cathedral which was built in 1137.

knar   A Norse trading ship up to 16 metres in length, designed to carry cargo.

laugardagur   Literally, 'washing day', the traditional bathing day. This is the derivation of the Swedish word for Saturday – *Lördag*.

lavaret   A European white fish found mainly in Sweden, Switzerland, Germany and the Baltic. Maximum weight 10 kilos.

Leir-vik   Lerwick. Literally, 'muddy bay' in Old Norse.

Monkchester   The site of present day Newcastle.

morning gift   A gift of money or valuables given by the bridegroom to the bride on the morning after the wedding.

mundr A payment made by the bridegroom to the bride's father. In Norway and Denmark in the tenth century the standard price was eight pieces of silver.

Penwithstert Land's End, Cornwall (on the Penwith Penninsula).

Raunrike Now a province in southern Sweden, Bohuslän.

Sami The inhabitants of northern Sweden, Norway, Finland and Russia. Sometimes called Lapps, a term which the Sami consider to be derogatory.

Selceeflet Anglo-Saxon name for Shalfleet, Isle of Wight. Literally, 'Shallow Creek'.

Scania Southernmost province of Sweden which in the tenth century was the most eastern part of the kingdom of the Danes.

seax A long knife carried by Viking and Anglo-Saxon warriors.

sessar The benches or thwarts on a longship (Old Danish).

slave Slaves had no rights and were bought and sold as chattels. They were mainly of three types: prisoners of war, voluntary slaves (often selling themselves to repay debt) and those who had been born into bondage by virtue of the fact that their parents were slaves.

St John's wort *Hypericum perforatum*. Used as a balm for wounds.

staket A water channel where access is limited, for defensive or other reasons, by the use of poles driven into the seabed (Swedish: *stäket*).

Sweyneston Originally from Old English *tun*, an estate. Here, the 'estate of Sweyne'.

Telgia   Swedish 'Tälje' – here a 'cut' through the hills (the town was renamed in 1622 as Södertälje).

Vectis   The Roman name for the Isle of Wight.

Werrar   From Old English *wer* and *ora*: 'the river bank by a weir'.

willow leaves   Salicylic acid, the main constituent of Asprin, is contained in willow leaves and bark. An infusion of the leaves or bark has pain relieving properties.

Winceleseia   Winchelsea, Sussex.

yoik   A traditional Sami form of music and cultural expression.